DARK AS NIGHT

MENU

MENU

. . . people this book is about . . .

Morris White—*Sous-chef* at Le Tour de Cochon

Vince Kammer—Morris's half-brother, a jewel thief

Billy Hope, Jr.—Small-time jewel thief, partner to Vince

Vicky Ward—Manager at Le Tour

Johnny Stacks—Bloated, hungry Philly mob bookmaker

Erasmo "Mo" Pacitti—Sleepy-eyed right-hand man to Johnny Stacks

Lenny Zielinski—Wanna-be gangster and lackey

Gina Romelo—Lenny's bitchy girlfriend

Nick Turner—Detective Sergeant, Philly P.D.

Dwight Wojcik—Officer, Philly P.D., a dinosaur

Dick Franks—Officer, Philly P.D., a vicious drug addict

Eva Beal—Tough, sexy waitress at a no-name diner

Jeanette Carpioli—Daughter of Eddie the Carp

DARK AS NIGHT

MARK T. CONARD

UGLYTOWN
LOS ANGELES

First Edition

Text copyright © 2004 by Mark T. Conard. All Rights Reserved.

UGLYTOWN AND THE UGLYTOWN COIN LOGO SERVICEMARK REG. U.S. PAT. OFF.

Library of Congress Cataloging-in-Publication Data

Conard, Mark T, 1965–
Dark as night/Mark T. Conard.—1st ed.
p. cm.
ISBN 0-9724412-3-9 (hardcover: alk. paper)
ISBN 0-9724412-6-3 (limited: alk. paper)
1. Philadelphia (Pa.)—Fiction. 2. Restaurants—Fiction.
3. Ex-convicts—Fiction. 4. Brothers—Fiction. 5. Cooks—Fiction. I. Title.

PS3603.O6223 D37	2003
813'.6—dc21	2003013926
	CIP

Find out more of the mystery: uglytown.com/darkasnight
Printed in the United States of America

10 9 8 7 6 5 4 3 2 1

To My Mother,
With endless gratitude for all her patience, love, and support.

"For I have sworn thee fair, and thought thee bright
who art as black as hell, as dark as night."
—*Shakespeare, Sonnet 147*

"Der Unterleib ist der Grund dafür, daß der Mensch
sich nicht so leicht für einen Gott hält."
—*Nietzsche**

* "The abdomen is the reason why man
does not easily take himself for a god."
(Friedrich Nietzsche, *Jenseits von Gut und Böse*, 141.)

CHAPTER I

Billy Hope Jr. was looking for the duct tape.

It was Wednesday, April 5th, and the rain hitting the roof sounded like bacon frying. Billy grabbed the bottle of Jim Beam, upended it, letting some run down his chin, onto his shirt. He checked the hall closet, dug through the boxes, all the coat pockets, ran his hand along the overhead shelf—no duct tape. Shit. Slammed the closet door, hard, breaking the latch.

Billy could feel the left side of his face doing gymnastics—the tic worse than ever. He took another pull on the Jim Beam, rubbing his big belly, then belched loudly.

Billy's father, William Hope Sr., prominent Philadelphia surgeon, at 62 the top cutter at Jefferson, walked into the O.R. one afternoon eight months ago, grabbed a scalpel and sliced his wrists and throat—dead before he hit the floor. Billy's mother, Catherine June Hope, always a little nutty, went off the deep end, had to be institutionalized. Billy's younger sister, Anita, *of course*, took over the estate, and now controlled the money. They weren't about to leave the house, the bank accounts, or the stocks in the hands of a 40-year-old drunken gambler, a career criminal like Billy, especially since everyone thought he took after his mother and was a little cracked in the head. He was ordered held for observation twice now, once when he found himself wandering down Broad Street naked, though that was just an alcohol blackout from mixing tequila and bourbon—but try telling that to a shrink on the city payroll; the other time when he exposed himself to the female Assistant D.A. And that was bullshit—did it on purpose, hoping to beat a B&E charge on a psycho. Didn't work, he still took the fall, though the judge reduced it to time served and probation. Thank God for prison overcrowding.

Now he was wandering around his parents' huge house in the Mount Airy section of the city, looking for the god-damned duct tape. Had to break in—Anita changed the locks and wouldn't give him a key, but what she didn't know was that he had the security codes to the alarm. She'd have them changed after today, but of course what the hell did he care what she did after today?

Billy walked over to the roll-top desk, the Jim Beam hanging at arm's length, bumping up against his leg, started searching the desk. Nothing there but papers—Mom's correspondence, sympathy cards for the old man's funeral. No duct tape, not even Scotch tape or masking tape, nothing. Shit.

It all started when he got the call earlier this afternoon. Sonny Jackson was the only person who knew where he was holed up, back of the Greek's TV repair shop, living on canned ravioli and sodas out of the machine, the Greek away for a month visiting the homeland. Billy was afraid to stay at his apartment, because he knew what was coming, he just didn't know when.

Sonny was a tall, skinny black dude, with a huge '70s 'fro. Pretty decent car thief. He wasn't any good with alarms, but without them Sonny could crack and hotwire most American-made cars in under 90 seconds. He was partial to Caddies and Lincolns, as Billy figured most sensible people were. Billy acted as a spotter a few times for Sonny. The order would come down from the Eye-tys, somebody wanted a Town Car or an Eldorado, late model of course. Billy'd find it, Sonny'd boost it. Three large, split any way they wanted.

So when the phone rang Billy knew who it was.

"Yo, man, Vince is gettin' out."

"When?"

"Today, man, he's fuckin' out now!"

"No shit?"

"Straight dope."

Billy dropped the phone, felt his face go into spastic convulsions, and went instinctively for the bourbon. He knew they'd be coming for him. They always said they would, once Vince got out. It would either be them or Vince himself. Well, fuck 'em, he wasn't going to give them the pleasure. Got into a cab, went straight to Mount Airy, his parents' home. Something just felt right about doing it there.

Billy thought of the utility drawer by the sink, stumbled through the dining room, knocking over a planter, went into the kitchen. Pulled open the drawer. Corkscrew, twist ties, cheese grater, menus from Chinese restaurants. No duct tape.

Billy and Vince must have pulled, what, a dozen jobs together? Liquor stores, check cashing agencies, one gas station. Maybe a baker's dozen. Of course! That was it, the last one, the one that went bad was number thirteen.

Shit!

Billy stopped in his tracks, standing in the middle of his parents' living room, thinking about it. He ran his hand over his bald head. He had a bad feeling about the whole thing when Johnny Stacks set it up. Didn't sound right, or, really, it sounded too right, too easy. Some old Jew's got a hundred grand worth of diamonds insured for a cool quarter million and *wants* them stolen. He's into Johnny for something like seventy-five grand, betting the ponies, and this is the only way he can pay him back. Whatever the diamonds sell for, Vince and Billy take half, Johnny Stacks gets the other half, and the Jew pays off his debt outta the insurance. Too easy, and he should have known better. You never pull 13 jobs with the same guy—it's bad luck. You just don't do it. End it at 12 and move on.

Billy upended the Jim Beam again, but found it empty. He let the bottle drop to the floor and stumbled into the den, opened up his father's liquor cabinet. No bourbon, no Jack. Lots of fancy single malt and a bottle of Cutty. He took the Cutty.

Well, it was a good ride. Made a lot of money from those jobs, even though he lost even more betting on football. Him and Vince and Sonny, they had a good time. Sonny was never actually in on the robberies, but he'd boost a car for them to use. Afterwards, they'd get together, the three of them, blow some of that dough on booze and broads, have a few laughs.

Until the jewelry store. Number thirteen. Goddamn, how could he have been so stupid?

Billy opened the Cutty, let the cap fall to the floor, took a long pull on the bottle, started gagging on it, nearly puked. He felt like spitting it out, but got it down, coughing, tears coming to his eyes. Goddamn his old man for not having any decent booze in the house.

Then it hit him: the garage. The goddamn duct tape's in the garage.

He went through the kitchen, into the laundry room, to the door leading to the garage, opened it. His old man's maroon Jag was still sitting there—Billy already had the keys to it in his pocket. He stumbled over to the workbench. There was a box sitting there—lying on top of a pile of nails inside the box was the duct tape. He grabbed the tape, walked around the Jag to where the garden supplies were kept. Took a long drink of Cutty, still wincing at the taste, set the bottle on top of the car. He reached down and grabbed the garden hose. Stretched it out, took an end, walked around to the back of the car. Started to bend down, but wobbled, grabbed the bumper and fell on his ass and grunted. Sitting there, he fitted the end of the hose into the exhaust pipe, and sealed it up with the duct tape.

Billy stood back up slowly, using the car as support. He grabbed the Cutty, walked around to the driver's side, pulling the hose along with him, opened the door and cracked the window. He fitted the other end of the hose through the open space at the top of the window, then sealed it up with the tape.

Got in the car and closed the door, then dug into his pocket for the keys. Took a long drink of Scotch, cursing his old man again, then thought it would be nice to have a tape to listen to, the Doors or the Stones, but he didn't bring one, and his parents sure as shit wouldn't have anything like that lying around.

Started up the car, took another long drink from the bottle and belched. Turned on the radio—it was set to the classical station, so he turned the knob until something else came on. It was a news conference. The mayor was saying there wasn't any money for city pay raises this year, the union leaders could bitch all they wanted to, there just wasn't any more money. Everybody was going to have to bite the bullet.

The exhaust fumes started coming into the car—Billy could smell them now. He took another long drink of Cutty. The bottle was half empty, and he was starting to get used to the taste, thinking it wasn't so shitty after all. Probably if you cut it with a little water, it ain't so bad.

Tears started coming to his eyes, and he wiped them away, noticing his facial spasms had stopped. He leaned back in the seat and closed his eyes.

Never, ever pull 13 jobs with the same guy.

Never.

Forty-five minutes earlier Lenny Zielinski was walking across the parking lot of Cat's Cradle, a strip club on Delaware Ave., thinking about how his life had turned completely around two days ago.

On Monday: Lenny got a call on his cell. He was told to come to the restaurant right away. As soon as he walked in the front door, Erasmo grabbed him by the arm, dragged him inside, saying, "C'mon we got a job to do."

Lenny pulled his arm away, smoothing out the sleeve of his jacket. He didn't care too goddamned much for being handled that way. "Jesus good God, Mo, fucking take it easy."

Mo said: "Johnny give us a job," his broken English dripping Italian.

Lenny couldn't tell if he was serious, could never read Mo, his dark face always a blank, and his eyes always sleepy, half closed. "What kinda job?"

"Johnny's niece—"

"Carmen?"

"No, the other one."

"The little one? Anne-Marie?"

"Yeah, her. Coupla niggers grabbed her after school, tore her dress, tried to rape her."

"No shit?"

"Yeah."

"Where's Johnny?"

"His sister's, takin' care of the girl."

"What's he want us to do?"

"We got a kid. Involved, or knows who done it, don' wanna say. Johnny says find out for sure."

"No shit?"

"Yeah."

"Where's the kid?"

"The basement."

"The basement *here*?" They were in Dominic's, Johnny

Stacks's restaurant and bar, a typical South Philadelphia dago place. Wood paneling covering the walls, the lights dim, pictures of famous guineas on the wall, Sinatra on the jukebox. Four-thirty in the afternoon, the place was closed. Lenny wondered why, driving up. Now he knew.

"Yeah. Here in the basement."

Mo grabbed Lenny by the arm, started dragging him down the stairs. Lenny was wondering why Johnny wanted him in on the job. This was the kind of thing Mo usually took care of by himself, the rough stuff. They hadn't ever used him on a job like this before.

The basement was dark and cool, the place lit by a single uncovered bulb hanging from the ceiling. There were boxes of booze stacked against the walls, and mouse turds all over the place. Then Lenny saw the kid. He was tied to a chair, hands behind his back. Seventeen, eighteen years old, he was wearing big, oversized jeans, a T-shirt and sneakers. Looked like Mo had already started on the poor fucker. His lip was busted, there was blood on his shirt, and his eye was almost swollen shut. He'd been wearing a blindfold, but it had slipped down around his neck.

Mo stepped up to the kid, leaned over slightly, and in his deadpan voice: "Hey, Sambo, playtime's over. Lenny's here now. He gonna ask you some questions. You better answer good, or else," and he backhanded the kid, blood splattering against the wall. The kid didn't make a sound, just kept staring straight ahead.

Mo wiped his hand on the kid's shirt, then stepped away from the chair and looked over at Lenny with his sleepy eyes. Then Lenny knew what was going on: Mo was busting his balls. That's what this was about. Johnny never said Lenny should handle this job. This was Mo's way of proving what he'd been saying all along: Lenny was pussy, couldn't handle the business, Johnny shouldn't have ever taken him on in the first place. Fucking Mo resented him 'cause his last name's Zielinski. The hell of it was, Mo wasn't even all Italian. His grandfather on his mother's side was from South America, Brazil or some fucking place. That made him one-quarter Brazilian, so he'd never be a made guy. New York would never have him. You'd think he'd be more sympathetic, cut Lenny some slack, but not this fucking wop. He busted Lenny's balls every chance he got.

Lenny thought, Fuck him, and he stepped up to the chair, took a deep breath. "Well, how 'bout it, Sambo?" and he smacked the kid hard, feeling his ring catch skin, blood splattered the wall again. The kid still didn't say anything.

Lenny looked down at his hand, there was blood on it, he felt a little queasy. He was hoping he wasn't going to get blood all over himself—he'd just bought the shirt he was wearing. He took another breath and said, "You know why you're here, don't you, Sambo? You're gonna tell us who fucked with the little girl, Anne-Marie Decongelio. 'Cause that wasn't just any little girl. That was Johnny Staccardo's niece," and he hit him again, openhanded, harder, the sound echoing in the little room.

Lenny braced himself and made his voice sound as hard as he could: "So who done it, homeboy? I heard *all* you niggers like white pussy. Maybe it was you. You don't give us a name, we're gonna tell Johnny it was you. You fuckers all look alike to me anyway. But lemme tell you somethin', you sure as shit wouldn't like what he'd do to you if he thought you raped his niece," and he slapped him again, feeling the blood spray over his shirt and pants. The kid still didn't say anything, but now his nose was bleeding fast, and he was sniffling back the blood.

Mo said, "This ain't going nowhere," and he turned to the workbench beside him and grabbed something. "Here, use this," and he handed Lenny a drill. A fucking Black & Decker drill with a big wood bit on it.

Lenny looked at the drill in his hand, knowing it was a test, a goddamned test. Mo didn't think he'd hit the kid, and he hit him, so now he's taking the next step, see if he'd use the drill on the stupid kid, see if he'd back down. Lenny knew what'd happen if he backed down: Fucking Mo'd tell everybody about it, especially Johnny. Lenny'd never hear the end of it. Mo'd ride him from now on, telling him he ought to find new work, if he ain't got the stomach for this kinda shit, tell him he wasn't cut out for the big time, he oughtta go back to pool hustling and shaking down junkies.

Lenny knew there wasn't any backing down. He grabbed the drill.

Mo reached over and plugged it in. Lenny pulled the trigger, the thing whirred, then died. He pulled it again, once, twice; the thing whirred and died, whirred and died.

He looked at the kid. "So how 'bout it, boy?" his voice cracked a little—he hoped Mo didn't notice. The nigger still sat there quiet, but Lenny thought he saw him shaking. He glanced over at Mo. The fat fucker still just stood there, emotionless, looked like he was half asleep, like nothing ever fucking bothered him. Lenny pulled the trigger, the drill whirred, and he lowered it. The kid flinched in his seat. He put the bit against his thigh, the thing started digging in, blood spewing, flesh tearing, the kid was still silent, his face clenched, gritting his teeth. Lenny pushed, feeling sweat pour down his face. The thing hit bone, finally the kid screamed, Lenny lifted the drill.

"All right!" the kid yelled out, bawling, crying. "All right, I'll tell who done it! I'll tell!" rocking back and forth in the chair, moaning.

Still holding the drill, blood and flesh hanging off the bit, Lenny looked over at Mo and smiled. Mo didn't say a word, just turned around and walked back up the stairs.

Now, walking up to Cat's Cradle, Lenny was thinking about nicknames. Since Monday, he was thinking about calling himself "Lenny the Drill." That sounded cool, but he didn't really like using the drill and didn't know if he ever would again. Too goddamned messy. Ruined a new shirt and a good pair of pants. He was also thinking about "Lenny Chompers," on account of his dental work— Lenny had a mouth full of silver teeth. That wasn't quite right, though. He was trying to come up with something about his black clothes—he always wore black, head to toe.

He'd waited until the rain let up and was heading into Cat's Cradle to find Sammy Foster, who was late on his payments. Sammy dropped four grand during March Madness. The stupid shit always bet the home teams, even *against* Duke and North Carolina. Now he was a week and a half late, and Johnny said to lean on him. This was the first serious muscle job Johnny'd given him. Johnny heard all about how Lenny made the nigger spill, of course—Lenny made sure he heard—and he was impressed. He told Lenny he'd give him muscle work from now on. He wouldn't have to answer no more goddamned phones, or do the fucking paperwork.

Lenny slipped a C-note to Frankie Lee, half-Italian, half-chink bartender at the Cradle, to keep an eye out for bad-luck Sammy, known to make the rounds of the strip clubs up and down Delaware Ave. Frankie called his cell this afternoon and tipped him that Sammy was there.

Lenny stepped into a puddle and cursed, pulling up his pant leg to get a look at his shoe, see if the shine was ruined. He squinted hard at his sock and swore again. They were navy blue. They weren't black. Goddamn it! He told the old bitch specifically, emphatically: Always black, *only* black. And what did she do? Went and bought him navy blue socks. It seriously ruined his look, no doubt about it. Well, he'd just have to go home and change, soon as he could, before anybody noticed. He wasn't going to have people laughing at him because of a pair of goddamned socks.

Still pissed, Lenny looked up to see Sammy Foster walking out the door of the Cradle. He called out: "Hey, Sammy!"

Sammy took one look at him and started running like a rabbit with the dogs hot on his heels. Lenny chased him between cars. Sammy tripped and fell face first into the bumper of an old Benz. Lenny caught up with him, turned him over, and grabbed him by the lapels. Sammy's lip was cut, and his nose was bleeding. "Jesus good God,

Sammy, look what you did to yourself. I'm supposed to be spillin' the blood around here. Now, let's have it."

Sammy was sniffling blood. "I swear, Lenny, I swear to God I ain't got it. . . . You think I'd try to stiff Little Johnny?"

"You asking me? Yeah, I think you're just stupid enough to try it."

"I swear to God."

"Then why you been hidin'?"

"I been trying to get the money together. I swear, Lenny. Johnny knows I wouldn't stiff him. Sometimes I'm late, sure, but I always pay! Johnny knows that."

"Yeah," said Lenny, "that's why Johnny sent me to lean on you, 'cause he trusts you so completely."

"I swear," said Sammy, blubbering, "I'll have the money next week, the whole thing!"

Just then a horn started honking. Lenny looked up. His girlfriend Gina stuck her head out of his copper-colored DeVille. "Goddamn it, Lenny," she shouted. "I'm gonna be late!"

Lenny sighed and looked back at Sammy. "Next week then. And don't disappear again, or Johnny's gonna get suspicious. *Capisce?*"

"Yeah, sure, Lenny, sure! Whatever you say."

Lenny let go of him, letting him fall back onto the wet pavement, and walked over to his car, straightening his clothes. He was still pissed about those navy blue socks. Couldn't believe his mother couldn't tell the goddamned difference between black and navy blue. Have to get her eyes checked or something.

Lenny got in the Cadillac, looked over at Gina, sitting

there completely pissed, of course. "Now I'm gonna be late for my class," she said, snapping her gum loudly.

Gina Romelo attended Gordon Philips Beauty School. Lenny encouraged her to go, thinking it might class her up a little. She dressed okay, but she was 26 now, four years younger than Lenny, and no hot young piece of ass anymore. More than anything, Lenny hoped she'd put on some weight—she was too damned skinny—and get surgery to fix her crooked nose. Whenever he brought it up, though, she told him to go screw himself. Her friends told her she looked like a model, even with the crook in her nose. Look at Lauren Hutton, she'd say, and that big gap between her teeth—it was kind of a trademark, and it was sexy. Lenny always let it drop there. He didn't know who Lauren Hutton was, but he thought any broad he'd ever seen with a gap in her teeth was butt-ugly.

"You ain't gonna be late."

"The fuck I ain't," she said, lighting a cigarette.

"Hey," Lenny gave her a serious look, "what did I tell you about using profanity?"

She frowned at him. "You curse all the time."

"Yeah, but it ain't nice for a *lady* to use them words."

"Ha!" she snorted. "Then I guess I ain't no lady."

"Well, try to be one, for God's sake."

She took a long drag on the cigarette and blew smoke at him. "Why?"

"So you're presentable, so we can go places, and I ain't ashamed to be seen with you."

"Go fuck yourself, Lenny."

"Just listen to the way you talk, goddamn it."

"Can we just go?"

Lenny shook his head, started up the car and pulled out of the lot. "We're gonna talk more about this later," he said. "And for Christ's sake use the ashtray!" Lenny's Cadillac was ten years old, but mint condition. The paint job was perfect—he waxed and polished it every week, and the interior was spotless.

Along Delaware they were quiet for a few minutes. Then Lenny spoke up. "You ain't gonna believe this."

Gina was looking out the window at the overcast skies. "Yeah, what?" She snapped her gum again.

"Ma bought me navy blue socks."

"So what?"

"So what?" he said, looking over at her, not believing he had to explain it. "I only wear black, that's so what! That's my look—all black."

Gina laughed at him. "You're so stupid, Lenny. You and your fucking black. I got news for you. You're not even a real gangster."

Lenny's face went red, and he clenched his teeth, staring out at the road.

"Johnny Staccardo's a two-bit hood. *He's* not even real mob, and you're just his errand boy."

"Oh, *Dios mio*," Lenny said quietly.

"See!" she screamed, laughing. "That ain't even Italian! That's *Spanish*, you stupid shit!"

"I swear to God, Gina."

"You ain't Italian. Your last name's Zielinski!"

"I *know* what my name is," he growled.

"You're probably thinking about changing it to sound Italian, ain't you?" She kept laughing, and Lenny's face went deeper red. Actually, he had been thinking about shortening it to "Zielini." He sure as hell wasn't going to tell her that.

"I swear to God, Gina, you keep it up, one of these days you're gonna get it."

"You wouldn't dare," she said, narrowing her eyes.

Emphatically: "Jesus Christ, I'll fucking kill you if I have to!"

"You wouldn't dare," she repeated. "My cousin's good friends with Joey Spinoza—Joey even came to his wedding, and if you ever lay a hand on me, Joey's crew'll chop you up and dump you in the Delaware. He's a *real* goddamned gangster—and a real *man*." She put out her cigarette in the ashtray.

That last shot stung, and Lenny was fuming. Silently, he turned off Delaware onto Washington Ave. He'd remember this conversation. Lenny didn't forget shit like this.

Gina lit another cigarette, took a drag, blew out the smoke, then picked gum off the filter. Tight-lipped, through his teeth, Lenny said: "So, d'you think about it?"

"Think about what?" Her voice still had an edge to it. Her voice *always* had that edge, far as he could tell.

"What we talked about?"

"Jesus, Lenny, you're gonna have to be just a little more specific!"

Lenny cracked the window to let a little air in. He was feeling warm. "You know . . . about Christina."

"What about her?" Christina was Gina's best friend. They went to beauty school together.

"You know, about the three-way?"

"Three-way? What are you talking about?"

"We talked about us having a three-way with Christina—you were gonna ask her about it."

"What the fuck are you talkin' about?"

"We talked about it the other day."

"You wanna do my best friend?"

"No, I don't wanna *do* your best friend. I want we should have a three-way with her. What are we talkin' about here?"

"Are you outta your mind, Lenny? I'm not gonna sit there and watch you fuck my best friend." She drew hard on the cigarette, shaking her head, blew out the smoke.

"You wouldn't be sitting there. You'd be, you know, *participating.*"

"Jesus, Lenny," she said, disgusted, "you're lucky you're gettin' any at all. I don't know where you come up with these crazy fucking ideas."

Just then a guy in a beat-up Escort cut in front of Lenny, flipping him off. Lenny had to swerve to avoid hitting the guy. Gina screamed.

That was it. That was fucking it. Lenny hit the accelerator, lead-footing it down Washington, Gina grabbing the dash, yelling at Lenny, asking him what the fuck he was doing. Lenny crossed the yellow, into the other lane, got ahead of the guy, pulled in front of him, slammed on the brakes. The guy went into a skid on the wet road, tires squealing, stopped just short of the Caddy.

Lenny jumped out of the car, pulled out his Smith & Wesson automatic, marched back to the guy. He was desperately trying to get his car started, staring at the gun, his eyes like saucers. A jig driving an Escort. A Ford fucking Escort, and he cut Lenny off. Lenny couldn't believe it, the guy dissing him like that.

Lenny stepped up to the car, grabbed the handle. It was locked. Gina was screaming out the window, people looking on from other cars. Lenny tapped the glass with the gun, telling the guy to open the goddamned door, or he was going to shoot him through the glass, right then and there. The guy, pissing in his pants, couldn't get the car started. Lenny yelled at him again: "Open the goddamned door, or I'll shoot you right now, you cock sucker!" then he cocked the pistol, pointed it right at his face.

The guy, with his hands up, terrified, unlocked the door. Lenny opened the door, grabbed the stupid nigger, dragged him out of the car, throwing him down on the pavement. Kneeling over him, Lenny put the gun barrel up against his cheek. "Look at me!" he screamed. "Goddamn you, look at me!" The guy opened his eyes. "You see me, motherfucker?! You see me?!" The guy nodded quickly, his hands still in the air. "My name's Lenny. You show me a little bit of fucking respect! You hear me?" he shouted at him. "I said, do you hear me, mother-fucker?!" The guy whimpered, nodding his head fast. "You pull that shit on me again, I'll kill you deader than . . . than fucking dead!" The guy kept nodding and whimpering. Lenny let go of him, leaving him right there in the street.

He walked back to the Caddy, putting away the pistol, thinking how much better that woulda sounded with a nickname: "You see me? My name's Lenny *Chompers*. You show me some respect!" Or: "My name's Lenny *the drill*. You show me some fucking respect!" Got to come up with a nickname.

He got back into the car, put it into gear, squealed the tires getting out of there. Gina sat there all quiet, *seriously* pissed off. She took a hard drag on her cigarette, and out of the corner of his eye Lenny could see her hand shaking. He smiled, turning his head away so she wouldn't see.

She said: "I hope you don't think that kind of shit impresses—"

He cut her off: "Don't even. . . . Just be quiet, don't even fucking talk to me right now, Gina."

Lenny's cell phone rang. He pulled it out of his pocket, pushed the button. "Yo."

The voice on the other end of the line said: "It's Mo. Johnny says to pick him up."

Lenny said: "Pick who up?"

The voice said: "Who the fuck you think? Who were we talking about this morning?"

Lenny said: "Oh. . . . Now?"

There was a sigh on the other end of the line. "Yeah, *right* now. At his parents' house." Then he hung up.

Lenny pushed the button and put the phone back in his pocket. He pulled the Caddy over to the curb, 11th and Washington, reached into his pocket, pulled out his roll and peeled off a ten dollar bill. "I got business," he said to Gina, handing her the ten, "take a cab."

She took the money, looking at him like she couldn't believe what she was hearing. "You're joking?"

"It's *business*," he said.

"I'm already late!" she screamed at him, "and it's fucking raining out, in case you haven't noticed!"

Lenny reached across her and opened the door, then pushed her out of the car. She slowly got out, swearing the whole time. She slammed the car door, and Lenny pulled away, grinning to himself.

He made it to Mount Airy in 17 minutes, drove down Sedgwick, just off Clearview, found the house, pulled into the drive. He got out of the car, walked up to the front porch, peeked in through a window. The place looked empty. He rang the bell two, three times, stood there, nothing.

He could break in through the back, but he thought he'd check the garage first. Walking up to the garage door he could hear a car running inside. He pulled on the door, and it came open. There was a Jaguar XJ-S sitting there, and what the hell? There was a garden hose taped to the exhaust pipe.

He walked around to the driver's side door, following the garden hose. It ran into the car, taped in place, and there was someone in the driver's seat. Lenny opened the door and choked on a wave of exhaust fumes. Billy Hope Jr. was sitting there, unconscious. Lenny grabbed him, pulled him out of the car, then dragged him out of the garage, out onto the driveway. Billy started coughing. Lenny slapped him across the face a few times. Finally, Billy opened his eyes, saw Lenny standing over him, and the left side of his face went into spasms.

Lenny grinned. "This must be your lucky day, Billy. Johnny Stacks wants to see you."

CHAPTER 2

Last night Morris and Vicky had their first date. They went to Dmitri's, Greek seafood, 3rd and Catherine, deep South Philadelphia. The place was little, a dozen tables, maybe fewer, and packed—on a weeknight—people standing outside, drinking in the bar across the street, a 45-minute wait, but it was the best scampi and grilled octopus in the city, he told her. Weird thing was, you couldn't find a Greek in the place. All the cooking was done by three Chinese guys right there in front, out in the open. But all of them trained by Dmitri how to cook Greek, and how to do it perfect every time.

She told him she'd never even had octopus before, that the very idea of it was a little weird, kind of freaked her out, you know, the tentacles—you can see the tentacles, right? This was when they were having a beer across the street, waiting for a table. He arched an eyebrow, giving her a look. Never had grilled octopus?

She shook her head. He broke into a subtle grin. She asked him what he was smiling about. He told her: God, are you in for a treat.

Morris White was a *sous-chef* at Le Tour de Cochon, a small but upscale French restaurant in Philadelphia, owned and operated by Chef Enin Neves, a petulant little Belgian with a flare for the melodramatic and exquisite taste. The two of them had cooked together at the revered Le Bec Fin, a Philly institution. Enin knew Morris's palate was brilliant, knew he was an artist. So, three years ago, when Enin left Le Bec Fin and opened Le Tour, he took Morris with him as his number two.

Six months ago Victoria Ward, Vicky, came on as manager. From the beginning, that very first afternoon, Morris saw her watching him, following him around the restaurant with her eyes. He was checking her out, too, wasn't like he didn't notice—you couldn't help but notice her. She was beautiful, early 30s, shoulder length chestnut hair, an aquiline nose, angular features softened on the ends, classically beautiful, *Main Line* beautiful. And those eyes, almond-shaped hazel eyes. He noticed her all right. But they'd both been playing it cool, since they met, like they were letting things simmer for a while before they jumped into anything.

At Dmitri's, almost as soon as they were seated, she asked: "So, what made you change your mind?"

"About what?"

She grinned. "About asking me out on a *date*."

He grinned back at her. "What makes you think I had to change my mind about anything?"

"Well, over the last few months you had lots of oppor-tunities, and now all of a sudden. . . ."

"Oh, not all of a sudden—we've talked, we've had coffee, what—"

"Half a dozen times."

"More than that," he said.

"No, trust me. I can name all six times."

"The exact days?"

"No, not the exact days—I didn't mark them on my calendar," she said, "but I could give you the circumstances. And, come on, coffee's not a *real* date."

"Well, why did it have to be *me* who asked *you* out? Why didn't you make the first move?" She smiled, almost blushing, and he said: "Never had to before, huh?"

"Shame on you," she said, with modesty he wasn't sure was real.

The waitress walked up, a girl in her early 20s in a tight flowered dress, with a ring through her nose, bringing them their bottle of wine in an ice bucket. The restaurant was a BYO, and Morris brought along a French Chardonnay. She asked if they'd heard the specials, Morris said yes, asked Vicky if it was all right if he ordered for them. She nodded. He told the waitress: Scampi, octopus, hummus, pan-fried flounder, they'll split all of them.

The waitress disappeared, and Vicky said: "I'm trusting you, you know."

"What, the octopus?" She nodded. "Don't worry, you'll love it."

"Tentacles and all?"

"Tentacles and all," he said, then added: "Sometimes appearances can be deceiving."

He watched her brush her hair back behind her left ear. The move seemed a little self-conscious, studied. But, damn, she *was* beautiful. And she looked fantastic—a form-fitting white top with a collar, like a man's shirt, and a tight navy skirt, pearl earrings. Casual, but with style. He was glad he hadn't put on a tie. Would have been too much. He looked around quickly—some guys were wearing ties, but they looked like they'd just come from work, in suits. No, the sport jacket over a green button-down and khakis was enough.

There was a pause, and she said, making conversation: "You and Enin seem to get along well."

"I understand him," he said, "and he respects me, respects my abilities."

"So you like Le Tour? You like working with Enin?"

He looked over at her. "I liked the way you said that."

"Said what?"

"You asked me if I liked working *with* Enin, instead of working *for* him."

"Well, you two run the kitchen together, like you're partners."

"Yeah, it's a good setup for me, the kind of control I have, but we're not partners, not really—it's his place." He paused, then added: "I'd like to have my own restaurant some day."

"You know," she said, "I think you're the only person I've never seen him yell at."

"He knows I won't put up with it. I did when I was younger, but I won't now."

"Why?"

"Why what?"

"Why did you put up with it when you were younger? You mean when you were a kid younger?"

"No, I meant since I've been a chef. Why did I put up with it then?"

"Yeah."

"I guess I thought I had to, you know, to get ahead, further my career." He looked over at her. "What are you smiling about?"

"You told me about your background, about how poor you were growing up." She already knew he was from a working class neighborhood in the northeast section of Philly, but he hadn't yet told her about the crime, the arrests.

"Yeah?"

"Well, I can't quite reconcile that kind of life—"

"With being a chef?"

"Yeah," she said, "and just your whole . . . character. Your tastes are so refined, you don't even talk like you're from the city."

"You don't either," he said.

"Yeah, but I'm from the Main Line." She'd already told him about growing up rich in the suburbs, her father a *very* successful lawyer. "You don't grow up in Ardmore talking like a Philadelphian exactly, at least the way people think of a Philadelphian."

"Like Rocky."

"Sure, like Rocky. How did you. . . ." The waitress set the scampi and hummus down on the table. Vicky said: "How did you decide you wanted to cook in the first place?" She took a bite of hummus. "Wow, that's good."

Eating, he said: "My mother's a terrible cook. I love her, but she could never make a chicken without drying the shit out of it. . . ." She looked up at him, he felt self-conscious, thought about apologizing for his language, but let it pass. "Her roasts were always tough, and her idea of a vegetable was creamed corn out of a can. So one day I came home—I swear to God, this is true—she was trying to *boil* frozen french fries." Vicky started laughing. "I thought to myself: I can do better than this. So I started doing the cooking for the four of us."

"You, your mother and father, and a sibling?"

"My brother. I have a half brother."

She said: "I can't believe how good this scampi is."

"Yeah, it's great, isn't it? Listen, I'm sitting here doing all the talking, talking about myself. Tell me something."

"What?"

He wiped his mouth with the napkin. "I don't know. Anything. Something about you." There was a pause, and he said: "Tell me a secret."

"A secret?"

"Yeah, something that you've never told anyone before."

She took a drink of wine. "Okay. But if I tell you a secret, you have to tell me one."

He grinned at her. "Okay."

She took another drink of wine. "Okay, once, when I was at Bryn Mawr. . . ."

"Yeah?"

She lowered her voice: "I slept with another girl."

He raised an eyebrow. "You had sex with a girl?"

"Shhhh. . . ." looking at the people sitting next to them, practically on top of them, they had to have heard. "Yeah," she said, blushing, "I *had sex* with another girl."

Morris leaned back in his seat. "Wow." He paused, then: "How was it?"

"How *was* it?"

"Yeah," he said. "How was it. Did you *like* it?"

She looked up, past him, like she was thinking about it. "It was . . . an experiment." She looked back at him. "I was a virgin when I got to college, and I was afraid, you know, of men, so it was a kind of . . . a kind of introduction, you might say."

"Yeah," he said, "but did you like it?"

She blushed. "Well, it was pleasurable, I mean the physical contact was nice, but. . . ."

"But what?"

"But there was something missing."

"I'll say. . . ."

She rolled her eyes. "There's that male ego."

Then the waitress appeared from out of nowhere and set the octopus on the table. Morris forked a couple of pieces, stuffed them in his mouth, nodded approvingly.

Vicky said: "So?"

"Yeah?"

"So it's your turn."

"My turn?"

"Don't be coy," she said. "Your turn to tell a secret."

"Oh, that. . . ." he said, and took a drink of wine, then refilled their glasses. He noticed she was avoiding the octopus, eyeing it curiously. "One time. . . ."

"Yeah?" She leaned forward this time.

"I shot a guy."

Her eyes got wide. "You. . . ."

"I shot a guy."

"Did you . . . did you mean to?"

"Oh, yeah. . . . Yes, I meant to. It was self-defense. When I went to Temple I lived on campus."

"Jesus, North Philadelphia?"

"Yeah, it's a bad neighborhood. I'd been carrying a piece since I was fifteen—"

She started choking, took a drink of water. "You carried a *gun*?!"

"Yeah. My neighborhood . . . sure, I carried a gun. One night, I'm walking across campus," the accent coming back to his voice, the city rhythm, "some dude comes up to me, tries to rob me, pulls a piece, sticks it right in my face."

"God. . . ."

"Yeah."

Still listening carefully, Vicky speared a piece of the octopus. "So what'd you do?" Put it in her mouth.

"He asked for my money. I told him I didn't have any, which was the truth, he started freakin' out on me, saying he was gonna waste me, all this sh— all this crap. He was stoned, and if I'd had the money, I would have just given it to him, no problem. But I didn't. Didn't have a dime on me. So I didn't think I had any choice. I drew on him, shot him."

She speared another piece. "Where?"

"Where? In the stomach. Then I just split, got out of there."

"Did he die?"

"No, he didn't die, at least I didn't hear anything—"

"Holy Christ!"

"What?"

Eyes wide. "God*damn* that octopus is good!"

Morris smiled at her.

★　　　★　　　★

Today, Wednesday, Morris was running late, pulled up in front of the restaurant, Passyunk Ave., just off of South Street, had to check on the deliveries, make sure the vegetables and the meat were okay, before he ran off to pick up his brother. The whole morning he'd been thinking about Vicky, thinking about last night. Dinner was great, then afterwards she invited him in—he knew she would. Coffee, sitting on the sofa, and then Jesus she just about tore his clothes off, pretty aggressive for a girl who used to be afraid of men. But he put the brakes on, told her they'd better take it slow. Which was weird. Here was a girl, a woman, beautiful, great body, he wanted her—no doubt about it, and ordinarily, meaning when he was younger, he wouldn't have thought twice about it. He would have done her, no problem. So why didn't he last night? Goddamn, it was like he was becoming mature or something. Like he was thinking in long-range terms, thinking of a relationship, not wanting to screw anything up by sleeping with her too soon. Now he was starting to wonder if maybe she'd be pissed at him because he *didn't* do her, wondering how she'd act today.

He found a parking spot, walked in the front door. A couple of the kitchen helpers, Andrew and Terence, were cutting the flowers, making the evening's table arrangements on top of the bar, stems and leaves all over the floor, and he could hear Enin back in the kitchen having one of his tantrums, yelling about something or other. He said hi to the two kids, couple of high school dropouts, asked if Vicky'd come in yet. Yeah, they told him, she was there, back in the office. He hesitated, standing there, looking at the irises, thought about asking them what kind of mood she was in, how she acted when she came in—did she seem pissed off?—but skipped it, decided he'd go check out the deliveries before he looked in on Vicky, see where she was at today.

Morris went through the swinging kitchen door, Enin was in form, a bunch of asparagus in his hand, waving it around, yelling, half-English, half-French, about how asparagus should look, how you have to cut it to make it look right. He didn't even seem to notice Morris. Morris slipped by, went back to the walk-in refrigerator, quickly went through the deliveries, made sure they had everything they needed for tonight's menu. The *poussins*, filets, wild boar, venison, and sea bass. It was all there.

Then he stood there a moment in the refrigerator, leaning up against a shelf, thinking about *her*, remembering how she felt last night, her body pressed up against his, running his hands over her, noticing his heart beat fast every time he thought about her. Jesus Christ, one date and this girl's got him all twisted up. But, really, what did he care? What was there to lose? Right? If she was pissed, then so be it. Look, if she didn't want to have anything to do with him after last night, then fuck it—you know, maybe that story about him shooting that guy freaked her out too much. Maybe their backgrounds were just too different. Jesus, maybe he shoulda just fucked her. If last night was the only shot he was going to get, then he definitely shoulda just done her. Screw it. Just go and see her, see where she's at, get it over with. She doesn't want to have anything to do with you anymore, then forget her. Just get it over with. No sense standing here, *worrying* about it. Christ, he never worried about a chick his whole life.

He pushed open the refrigerator door, slammed it behind him, Enin saw him this time, started to say something, Morris pushed right by him, didn't say a word, through the swinging kitchen door, down the hallway, to the office. Had to get it over with, get the shit settled. He started to knock, thought screw it, opened the door, went right in. She was sitting there behind the desk, looking through some invoices, looked up at him, soon as he came in. He said: "Hey there."

"Hey yourself."

He stared at her, feeling his heart pounding, a second passed. He said: "Well?"

A wide grin crept onto her face. She jumped up from behind the desk, threw her arms around him, and they kissed, deeply.

Graterford Prison is the largest maximum-security prison in Pennsylvania, 30 some miles to the northwest of Philadelphia, near Collegeville, PA, right off of Germantown Pike. It was built in 1929, revamped in 1989. At the time Vincent Kammer was released, it was running at 130% capacity, housing over 3,000 inmates.

The trip to Graterford took 40 minutes. The whole way there, Morris was thinking about Vicky, feeling good about the situation, how he was handling it, wanting to tell someone about her, about what was happening, reminding himself not to go overboard, get too excited. Don't want to mess this thing up. Then he laughed at himself, taking the whole thing so seriously like that. Just be cool.

He pulled up outside the prison gates, across the street, a little after two o'clock. The letter from the Board of

Paroles said Vince would be released at two. Morris didn't know if that meant he'd be walking out the gates at two, or if there were things he had to do, paperwork or collect his stuff, at two, and then he'd be walking out.

He got out of his old blue Chevy Nova, stretched, looking up at the overcast skies, leaned against the car. It was damp and cool out, but at least it had quit raining for now.

At a quarter past two the prison gate opened, and a guy, looked like Vince, walked out. Morris wasn't sure if it was him, so he crossed the street. The guy just standing there, blue jeans, black T-shirt, denim jacket, looking up at the sky. Up closer, Morris realized it *was* him, only he looked different—older, hair shorter, he was thinner. Vince was 40, five years older than Morris, but now, after three years in prison, he looked 60. Vince didn't know he was coming to pick him up, this was a surprise, so Morris was thinking what to say, walking up to him. "Good to see you" didn't exactly sound right, so a few feet away, he said: "Hey, welcome back," but he knew that sounded dumb as soon as he said it.

Vince looked at him. "What're you doin' here?" his voice hard.

"Came to get you, give you a ride—what brothers are for, right?"

"Half brother," said Vince.

They stood there, looking at each other a moment. Morris felt himself getting warm, said: "Well, you want a ride or not?"

Vince looked past him. "Still drive that piece of shit Nova, huh?"

Morris clenched his jaw. "I was gonna rent a limo, but I thought it might embarrass you."

Vince didn't say anything, walked past him, toward the car. Morris stood there a moment, then followed.

In the car, Vince said: "Gimme a cigarette."

Morris started the car, pulled away from the curb. "Don't have any—I quit."

Vince looked over at him. "You quit?"

"I'm *trying* to quit."

They were quiet a few minutes, Morris stealing glances at Vince, couldn't believe how much he'd aged, lines on his forehead, rings under his eyes. He didn't want to bring it up, though. What was he going to say? What happened— You look like shit? He said: "You hungry?"

"I ain't now," said Vince, "I will be, we get back to the city." There was a pause, and he added: "You still a cook?"

Morris wanted to tell him: Look, you stupid shit, for the thousandth time, I'm a goddamned *chef*, trained at a couple of the finest restaurants in New York and Philadelphia. But he didn't. He let it ride. "Yeah," he said, "only not at the same restaurant. A new one. Except for the head chef, I run the place."

Like he wasn't listening, Vince said: "Let's stop, get some cigarettes."

Morris sighed. "We get back to the city, you can get some."

Vince said, looking out the window: "Shitty fuckin' weather."

Morris didn't get it, why the guy was so hard. He ought to be happy, just got out of prison, for Christ's sake, be grateful he's out. He never did understand Vince, why he was so goddamned mean sometimes. Morris said: "I talked to Chester." Chester Reed, Reed's Automotive.

Vince looked over at him, his eyes narrowing. "What about?"

"About getting you your old job back. He says you can come back whenever you want."

"Yeah? And what the fuck business is it of yours?"

"Okay, so don't. Jesus, Vince, I thought you'd be happy, a job waiting for you. Least you could do is show some appreciation."

"For stickin' your nose in my business?"

Morris looked over at him. "What the hell's wrong with you, anyway? You've always been a mean son-of-a-bitch, since we were kids, now you're even worse. I thought you'd be feeling good, just getting out."

Vince forced a laugh. "Feeling good? Feeling *good*? You got no fuckin' idea what goes on in the joint. No idea at all—"

"Yeah? So enlighten me. Tell me about your hardships."

"Forget about it. My problem, I'll deal with it my own way."

"Deal with what? What's there to deal with, Vince? You're out. You had problems in the joint, they're over."

"No," Vince said, almost shouting, "some shit's never over, it stays with you. This's somethin' I'm gonna deal with my own way."

"Jesus, Vince, don't do anything's gonna land you back in the place."

There was a long pause. Morris was thinking it was probably a stupid thing to do, coming to pick him up like this. Seemed like a nice gesture, but if the guy didn't appreciate it—screw him. He *was* going to tell him about Vicky, but now, forget it. He said: "We get back home, you want me to take you to Ma's?" Vince snorted. Morris looked at him. "What's that mean?"

"It means Ma don't want nothin' to do with me."

Morris was thinking: Can't blame her, you're as big a jerk to her as you are to me. He said: "Where're you gonna stay?"

"Beats me."

Morris thought about it a minute. He knew it was a mistake. Knew it, but he said it anyway: "Well . . . you can stay with me a while, you want to."

"Yeah? That's cool."

Not, "Thanks, I really appreciate it." Or: "I wouldn't be putting you out, would I?" No, he got: "That's cool." Morris knew that was as good as he could expect from Vince.

They were silent a few minutes longer, then Morris said: "You're not gonna go back to work for those hoods?"

Vince laughed. "The Italians?"

"Yeah."

He looked over, their eyes met. "Not if I can help it."

CHAPTER 3

Dick Franks opened his eyes, rolled over in bed to see some broad he didn't recognize. Looked like a whore, a cheap one, in her 40s, heavy eye makeup smeared. She was still sleeping. He sat up, looked around, couldn't remember where he was. His mouth tasted like shit, and his head was pounding. No idea whose house he was in or how he got there. Damn, 46 years old. He was definitely gettin' too old for this kinda shit. Put his feet on the floor, saw the bathroom, got up, went in, ran the sink, splashed water on his face. No cups, he bent down, drank straight out of the faucet. Walked back into the bedroom, stretching, scratched his balls through his white cotton undies. Picked his clothes up off the floor, slipped on his pants, his shoes, pulled on his shirt. He checked his watch. 12:45. Shit—had to be afternoon. Whatever day it was, he musta been late for *some*thing.

Buttoning his shirt he saw a purse laying on an armchair in the corner. Glanced over: The woman hadn't moved. He picked up the purse, opened it. Some money, coupla joints, some pills—had some luck, they were bennies. He popped a few in his mouth, pocketed the cash and the reefer. His jacket was hanging from the back of the chair, he put it on. Noticed his piece was lying on the nightstand, walked over, grabbed it, clipped it to his belt.

Franks walked out of the bedroom, through a living room, down some stairs, out the front door, looked around. It was cloudy, drizzling rain. He didn't recognize the neighborhood at first, standing there on the porch, the house an old brownstone, run down, like all the other houses on the block. Then thought: Christ, this is Camden. He was in fucking Camden, his car nowhere in sight.

Down the porch steps, to the corner. Street signs said Woodland and 8th. Wasn't far from a dealer he knew on Fairview, Derek Ash, street name Bam, Bad-Ass Mother-fucker, a real hard case, an old school jig. Franks knew he could hit him up for cash, dope, maybe even a ride back to Philly. Ash had connections to all the illegal shit going on in Camden, so the fucker might even know what happened to his car, if it got boosted.

He turned up the collar on his jacket, walked down 8th to Fairview, not too goddamned conspicuous: a six-foot three-inch, two-hundred-pound white guy with blonde hair walking through the 'hood.

He made a right on Fairview, found the house, went up the front steps, walked right in without knocking. Inside the living room, coupla black guys jumped up from the sofa, pistols drawn. One was just a kid, had his hair in cornrows, wearing black sunglasses. The other guy was older, had short, tight hair with gray in it, wearing a Bob Marley T-shirt. Franks put his hands up, looking at the older guy. "Hey, Derek, how you doin'?"

The kid in the sunglasses kept his gun on Franks. Bob Marley lowered his, saying, "Shit, Franks, what the fuck you want?"

The kid in the sunglasses said: "You know this white-ass motherfucker, Bam?"

Derek said: "Unfortunately."

Franks put his hands down, grinning at the two of them. Derek turned down the TV—they were watching cartoons—and the two black guys sat back down on the sofa, laying their guns on the coffee table, next to a scale and a Nike shoe box with a big wad of cash in it and a Ziploc bag full of white powder. Just what the doctor fucking ordered. Franks said: "Well, well, looks like I got here just in time."

Derek said: "Like to share in the bounty, huh?"

Franks said: "That'd be a start." He sat down on an easy chair next to the shoe box. "You ain't seen my car, have you, Derek? '91 LeBaron? I mighta left it over on Woodland last night—"

Derek, sarcastically: "Then again you might not?"

"All I know is it ain't there now."

Derek said: "What the fuck I look like, Triple-A?"

Sunglasses said: "Who the fuck *is* this?"

Derek, looking over, said: "S'all right, just chill." Turning to Franks: "Look, we in the middle of a business transaction, expectin' comp'ny any minute now. This ain't the best time for a house call."

Franks ran his finger along the coffee table, picking up dust, stuck his finger in his mouth, massaged his gums. "I was kinda hoping," he said, "you might gimme a ride back to Philly."

Derek shook his head. "First I'm fuckin' Triple-A, now I'm the fuckin' nigga cab comp'ny?"

Sunglasses said: "They gonna be here any minute, Bam."

Derek said: "Just chill, Stones. Listen, Franks, can't help you. Got business. Walk over to Broadway, hail your ass a cab, else take the fuckin' train."

Franks picked up the Ziploc bag, and Sunglasses sat up quickly. Derek grabbed his arm, holding him back. Franks grinned, said: "My, but that's quite a load. Mind if I have a taste?"

Derek said: "Yeah, I mind. Look, you want a little somethin', a eye-opener, I give you some outta my private stash. You just leave that be."

Franks looked right at Sunglasses, the kid straining, like he wanted to jump out of his seat, Derek still holding him back. "Tell Cornrow here he oughtta relax. Bein' so uptight's bad for the digestion." He put the bag back into the shoe box. "I gotta take a piss."

Derek hooked his thumb, said: "Down the hall, second door on the left."

Franks stood up, turned the corner, walked down the hall, found the bathroom. The toilet was disgusting, looked like it hadn't been cleaned in months, but he used it anyway. He had to stand there a couple of minutes before the piss would come, and when it did it was still bloody, but it didn't burn as badly today. He flushed the toilet, then ran some water into the rust-stained sink, splashed it on his face, trying to get his head to stop pounding. He straightened up, looking at himself in the mirror over the sink. Man, he looked like shit: unshaven, bags under his bloodshot eyes, pupils dilated, lines on his face getting deeper, showing his age.

He opened the medicine cabinet, started looking through it. Razors, Pepto-Bismol, pack of Rolaids, toothpaste. Nothing interesting, nothing worth taking. Shut the cabinet. Opened the bathroom door, shut off the light. Soon as he did, he heard from the living room: "What the fuck is this?!" loud and angry. He stopped right there in the hallway. Derek's voice said: "Fuckin' take it easy, will ya?"

The other voice said: "You think this a fuckin' joke, nigga?" Franks took two steps down the hallway, toward the living room.

Derek's voice, panicked, said: "Jus' chill, we all cool here!"

The voice said: "No, we far from cool!" Three, four, five shots exploded.

Franks drew his 9mm, dropped to one knee.

Four, five, six more shots rang out.

He figured three shooters, maybe two. Better play it safe: Call it three.

Up off his knee, around the corner. Three big black dudes standing around the coffee table, all dressed in black, Derek and Sunglasses dead on the sofa, a bloody mess. Franks opened up, three shots, hitting the two on the left, both of them blown back against the wall. The third guy raised a gun, fired wildly, missed. Franks ducked back around the corner.

He heard the front door opening, looked back around, Number Three was halfway out the door. Franks shot, missed. One dude slumped against the wall was trying to get back up, still had a gun in his hand. Franks shot him in the neck, the guy went down.

Across the living room, out the front door, onto the front porch. Number Three was headed for a yellow Benz with mag wheels and tinted windows. Franks aimed, fired, one of the car windows exploded. Number Three made it to the car, ducked down on the other side, fired back, two, three shots. Franks jumped down off the porch, ducked behind a blue Olds, this side of the street.

Number Three was trying to get in the car, passenger side. Franks aimed, shot out a tire.

There was a pause, a few seconds, then Number Three stuck his head up, let loose three shots, took off running down the street. Franks was up, chased him.

Now two police cruisers, sirens screaming, lights flashing, turned the corner, down the end of the block, coming this way.

Franks took aim, fired, hit the black dude, he went down.

Police cars half a block away.

The black dude rolling over now, aiming back at Franks.

Franks squeezed off another shot, hit the guy in the chest, he fell back in the street, not moving.

The cops were out of their cars, four of them, three black, one white, guns drawn, shielded behind the car doors, their faces lit up by flashing lights. More police cruisers turning the corner now.

One black cop shouted: "Drop it! Drop the piece or you're dead!"

Franks put his hands up, the 9mm still in his hand.

The white cop yelled: "Drop it, asshole!"

Franks tossed the piece, it clattered against the wet pavement. He looked over. The black dude, Number Three, wasn't moving.

The cops were coming this way, guns pointed at him.

He looked back at them. "It's all right," he said, calmly. "I'm a cop. Philly P.D."

The white cop said: "Where's the I.D.?"

Franks said: "Right hip pocket," and he slowly turned his back to them, hands still in the air.

The cop pulled out his wallet, said to his partner: "Detective Richard Franks, Philadelphia P.D." Then to Franks: "Sorry, Detective, we didn't know you was one a the good guys."

Franks turned around, putting down his hands, grinned. "Yeah, I get that a lot," he said, and noticed his head didn't hurt anymore.

CHAPTER 4

Lenny said: "See, Angelo Bruno was the one built up the Philly mob, really put it on the map. He was one of the guys got Atlantic City started, like in *The Godfather*—you remember that part, they say it was Moe Greene started Las Vegas? Same thing with Bruno and Atlantic City. Only this wasn't no movie. This was real."

Billy's head was still swimming from the booze and exhaust fumes, sitting there sipping coffee, listening to Lenny drone on about the fucking mob. That going on in one ear, Sinatra in the other. "Summer Winds." Billy hated fucking Sinatra.

They were in Dominic's, Johnny Stacks's restaurant. Lenny'd dragged him here to see Johnny, and Johnny was in the crapper, been in there 45 minutes. They were sitting at the bar, Lenny talking to some Asian girl, looked barely pubescent, wearing a black leather mini and a white tube top that showed off her little titties.

She sat there with a bored look on her face, smoking a cigarette, drinking a wine cooler. Johnny didn't run girls. Billy figured she must have been from one of the escort places. They had places specialized in Asian girls, girls just come over, just got off the boat, looking for a better life in America, only to be turned into whores. Billy wondered if she even spoke English, hadn't heard her say a word since she got here half an hour ago.

Sitting at the bar, Lenny was turned in his seat toward the girl, said: "In them days Philly was second only to New York and Chicago, terms of mob, and Bruno had close connections with the New York families, especially the Genovese. Only he got whacked. You know who done it?" The girl didn't say anything, didn't even seem to be looking at Lenny or listening to him. "His own goddamned *consigliere*, Antonio Caponigro. They called him Tony Bananas. I don't know why they called him that, maybe he liked bananas. That was in 1980. Bruno was riding along in a car, and *bam!*, they whacked him. Know who was driving the car? Take a guess." The girl stubbed out her cigarette, took another out of the pack of Kools, lit it. Lenny said: "John Stanfa. You musta heard a him. He ended up becoming boss later on. Anyway, the Genoveses loved Bruno, see, so they put a contract out on Tony Bananas, had him killed—Vincent Gigante done it, and that's when Phil Testa became Philly boss."

Billy took another sip of coffee—cold and tasted like shit—and looked around the restaurant. Four-thirty, going on five o'clock in the afternoon, place was empty except for the three of them at the bar, and Mo sitting at one of the tables, smoking cigarettes, drinking espresso. A little

Italian guy, must have been in his 50s, thin, kind of grizzled looking, with a bony dark face like a shrunken head, was setting up the tables for dinner, laying out the silverware, lighting the candles.

Lenny took a break from talking—Billy thought he sounded like some kinda goddamned PBS special, "History of the Mob"—and the Asian girl said: "Where's Johnny?"

Lenny took a drink of soda. "In the can."

The girl said: "He's been in there a long time."

Billy looked over at the girl, her heavy makeup. It was weird, she didn't have a trace of an accent. Not an Asian accent, not even a Philadelphia accent really. He started wondering: If she's American, you know, didn't just get off the boat, then why's she do this, why's she hustle?

Lenny said: "Yeah, he don't feel good, something he ate or something."

Billy sighed. It was weird, now that he was here, facing Johnny, now that his worst fears were coming true, he didn't want to die anymore. In fact, he couldn't quite remember why he wanted to kill himself in the first place—outside of being afraid. He was still afraid, of course, of what they were going to do to him, but he didn't have any desire to off himself now, and he sure as hell didn't want them to kill him. It was almost like, when *he* was doing it, it was okay, but if they were going to whack him, then it wasn't okay—he wanted to get away and live.

He took another sip of cold coffee and belched. The Asian girl looked over at him. He mumbled: "Sorry." He felt like a slob, hadn't showered or shaved in two days, and had booze spilled down the front of his shirt from drink-ing earlier.

Lenny said: "Phil Testa was boss only about a year. He got whacked, too. Somebody planted a bomb under the porch of his house, blew him up. Can you imagine? That's when Nicky Scarfo became the head, and then things got *really* messy."

Billy heard a toilet flushing down the hall and a door open. He noticed Lenny turned his attention away from the girl, looked over toward the hallway, where the restrooms were. Then Johnny Stacks appeared around the corner. He was fat as ever, Billy noticed. Johnny was late 50s, about five-eight, must have gone 275 easy. He wore an expensive-look-ing dark blue suit, with a white shirt open at the collar, a gold chain around his neck. His black hair, gray at the temples, was slicked back, always looked kind of greasy. Lenny got off his stool, walked over to meet him. He said in a mild, concerned voice: "How you doin', Johnny?"

Johnny Stacks said: "Feel like shit. Somethin' I ate, I guess," his voice cigarette-raspy.

Lenny said: "Candy's here," pointing over his shoulder at the Asian girl.

Johnny glanced over at her. She turned in her stool to look at him, still with the bored look on her face. "Oh," he said. "Come here, Candy."

She put her cigarette out in the ashtray, got off the stool and walked over to him. Billy couldn't help but notice how little she looked compared to Johnny, like a little kid or some kinda doll next to the fat guinea. He wondered how they did it, you know, how he kept from crushing her in bed, she was so little. She was probably always on top.

Then he started thinking Johnny probably had some little dick, you know, compared to his big fat body. Like all those rolls of fat would make it look small, even if it was normal sized.

Billy shook his head, trying to clear it, wondering why he was thinking stupid shit like that.

Johnny reached in his pocket, pulled out his money clip, took a hundred off the top, handed it to her. "Look, sweetheart, I'm gonna have to take a rain check. I don't feel so good, and I got business. All right?"

The girl took the hundred, looked up at Johnny's fat face, shrugged, and walked away, disappearing out the door, without saying anything.

Johnny went over to the table where Mo was sitting, rubbing his belly, took a seat. "Tommy," he called over to the grizzled guy setting up the tables, "bring me some more Alka-Seltzer." The guy nodded and headed back toward the kitchen.

Ever since Johnny'd come in the room, Billy noticed that he was feeling nervous. He put his hand up to his face and could feel his tic, the muscles going into spasms. Sitting there at the bar, waiting for Johnny to deal with him, made it even worse. Finally Johnny looked over at him and waved to him to come over to the table.

Billy got off the stool, walked past Lenny standing there, all in black, hands on his hips, went over to the table. His head was still kind of foggy, and his stomach was queasy. He didn't know if he should sit down—thought he'd better wait for Johnny to tell him he could. He noticed the jukebox had stopped, the song was over, the place seemed really quiet now, like a church or a library.

Johnny said: "I ain't feelin' good, so let's skip the bull-shit, get right to it. You musta heard, Vince's gettin' out, if he ain't out already. You know the situation: Time's come to pay the piper. We had an arrangement. I set up the job, you guys pulled it off. Hundred grand worth of diamonds. Don't mean shit to me, Vince got caught. That's his own bad luck. All I want's my half a them diamonds."

The grizzled Italian guy came out of the kitchen with the glass of bicarbonate, set it down in front of Johnny. He drank half of it, grimaced. Billy wanted to speak up, but thought he ought to wait until Johnny said he could, kind of mood he was in.

Johnny said: "Do we understand each other?"

Billy took a step forward, eagerly, saying: "But Johnny, you know I was only the driver. That's all he wanted me to do. Man, can you believe the cops showing up like that? I couldn't believe it, they just *happened* to drive by? And, c'mon, nobody could expect me to hang around, the cops showing up—could they?" He looked around at the others. Mo just sat there, staring with his sleepy eyes. Lenny had his arms folded across his chest now. Billy said: "I had to take off, Johnny, I *had* to!"

Johnny put up a hand. "That's between you and Vince."

Billy said: "Johnny, you know Vince's been sayin' all along he ain't got them diamonds. I never saw 'em! I had to get the fuck outta there. He says he ain't got 'em."

Johnny drank the rest of the bicarbonate, belched loudly, mouth open. "Yeah, and Marty Cohen went to his grave insisting them diamonds *was* stolen." He belched again. "Hey, that's a little better," he said. Then to Billy: "So, whether or not Vince's willing to cough up them diamonds, I want my half. We figured a seventy-five percent fence on a hundred grand, so you two owe me thirty-seven five, or eighteen grand, seven hundred fifty apiece, you wanna look at it that way. So you better figure some way a collectin' that dough. You don't, you know what'll happen."

Billy looked over at Mo. His eyes were focused on Billy now, still no trace of emotion on his dark face. Johnny went on: "And don't go tryin' to off yourself again. Lenny told me 'bout that little trick a yours. You can kill yourself after I collect, but you go takin' the easy way out before I get my money, your sister could have a little accident." Johnny stared at him. "Or Sonny Jackson," and Billy felt his face jump, the spasms even worse. Johnny grinned, said: "Okay, Sonny it is."

Johnny waved his hand, and Billy knew the interview was over.

Lenny watched Billy Hope Jr. stand there for a second, all quiet, like he was in shock, the fucker's face doing some kind of dance. Then Billy turned and shuffled out the front door.

Johnny belched again and said: "Hey, Tommy, I'm feelin' a little better. Tell Donna to make me some spaghetti clams, will ya?"

Tommy said: "Sure, Johnny. You want it red or white?"

Johnny said: "Surprise me." Tommy nodded and went through the kitchen door. Johnny waved Lenny over to the table.

Lenny took a chair, sat down across from Mo, Johnny to his right. "So, you feelin' better, Johnny?"

"Yeah, little bit. Maybe I eat something, I'll be okay. So, we know where these little fucks live—the kids who tried to rape Anne-Marie?"

Lenny said: "Yeah, Johnny, Todd Ohal and Tyrone Bucknor—"

Johnny said, angrily: "I don't give a fuck their names! We know where they *live*?"

Conciliatory, Lenny said: "Yeah, sure we found 'em. We know where they live." He looked across the table. Mo was staring at him. Lenny knew this was his baby. He drilled the kid, he got the names. Johnny respected him for it. It was eating Mo up, even if he didn't show it, fucking wop.

Johnny said: "Good. They're dead. We understand one another?" looking back and forth from Lenny to Mo.

Mo nodded sleepily. Lenny said: "Yeah, 'course, Johnny, it's what we figured. We knew you wouldn't let the little fucks get away with somethin' like that." He was nervous, getting chatty. "Right, Mo?" The fucker still just stared at him. Didn't say a word.

Johnny said: "Just as long as we understand each other." Then turning to Lenny, laying a hand on his forearm, resting on the table. "You should know, this ain't somethin' we'd ordinarily do. We ain't in that kinda business," like Johnny was giving him trade secrets, you know, really bringing him into the club. "If this was the old days, you'd have to get permission to whack a guy, but now the rules ain't so clear. Besides, these are niggers. Niggers don't count, never did. You never had to have permission to do a nigger, 'less he was somebody special—a friend a some made guy or somethin'. But there ain't no way these little fucks gonna live after what they did to Anne-Marie."

Lenny said: "She all right, Johnny?"

Johnny said, angry again: "That ain't the point! Ain't the point, she's all right or not. They fucked with her, now they pay!"

"Yeah, sorry, Johnny. I was just, you know, concerned."

Calmer, Johnny said: "Yeah, she'll be all right." He grinned. "Fifteen years old, tough little broad. You should see her."

Lenny grinned back. He was excited, being initiated like this. "Any special way you want it done?"

Johnny shook his head. "Mo knows what to do."

Lenny's heart sank a little, lost some of his enthusiasm. It was like Mo was in charge now—by saying that, Johnny'd put *him* in charge. Lenny thought this was his job, his gig, and now Mo was going to take over. Probably because Mo had some experience. Lenny figured Mo'd already done a few guys, there was one for sure he knew about, but he never talked about any of them.

Johnny said: "Well, fuck."

Lenny looked over at him. "What is it, Johnny?"

"I gotta use the head again," and pushed back from the table, stood up and went down the hallway to the bathroom.

Lenny looked over at Mo, his sleepy eyes, waited for him to say something. Mo had a cigarette burning in the ashtray. He picked it up, took a drag, blew out the smoke, like nothing was going on, like Lenny wasn't even fucking there. Lenny sat back in his seat, feeling warm, getting a little pissed off.

Then he started thinking: After this, after he'd gotten one under his belt, Johnny'd put him in charge, next time something like this came up. Then he'd fucking tell Mo what to do, fucking ignore him, see how he liked it. Hell, maybe he could talk Mo into letting him do both the kids. Jesus, he'd have two under his belt.

Two? *Due* was Italian for "two." He could be Lenny *Due*. No, that was it: *Lenny Deuces*. Jesus, his new nickname. God*damn*, Lenny Deuces—that was perfect. Wait 'til he told Gina.

Tommy came back into the dining room, went back to setting up the tables for dinner.

Lenny cleared his throat. Mo still didn't say anything. Fucking wop. Lenny said: "Well, when do we do it?"

Mo said: "What?"

Like he didn't hear. "When do we do it?"

"Tomorrow, maybe the next day," Mo said, with his thick accent. "I got to see when we can get the guns."

Lenny was going to say: Look, you stupid guinea fuck, I already got a gun. But he hesitated. "Guns?"

"Yeah, we get 'em from a guy. I'll call him, see what he got." Mo stubbed out his cigarette, looked over at Lenny. "You don't wanna use your own gun, do you? Have the cops trace it back to you?"

Lenny forced a laugh. "Fuck no—I was only askin', 'cause I didn't know where you got 'em, that's all. What the fuck? Use my own? Shit."

"Tha's good," Mo said, "'Cause if you some kinda *testa di cazzo*, so stupid you use your own gun, I think maybe you too stupid to do this right, fuck up, get us caught."

Lenny felt his face go red. "I know what I'm doin'," he said. "Don't you fuckin' worry 'bout me."

Just then the front door opened, and Gina walked in.

Christina was with her. They were both laughing about something. Christina was two years younger than Gina, and she was a South Philly girl all the way, big dyed blond hair, big through the hips, big chest, and she always wore tight jeans and tight shirts to show off her body. Lenny liked the way she was built. Compared to her, Gina was a fucking skeleton. It was like doing a pile of bones, sleeping with her. He liked girls with a little something to them, especially ones with big tits. He'd had his eye on Christina ever since he'd been going out with Gina, but Christina had a little crush on Mo, and that drove Lenny fucking crazy. Why any girl looked like that would go for some dickhead like Mo, was some kinda fucking mystery. It was 'cause he was Italian, of course.

Still laughing, Gina said: "There he is!" Then exaggerating, so he couldn't tell if she was being sarcastic, she said: "C'mon, *loverboy*!" Christina laughed.

Lenny said: "C'mon where?"

Still sugary, in a sing-song voice, she said: "You're driving us to the mall, re*mem*ber?"

Lenny said: "Can't right now, I'm doin' business."

Not saying a word, Mo took another cigarette out of his pack of Camels, lit it. There was still no expression on his face.

The shrillness coming back to her voice, Gina said sharply: "C'mon, Lenny, goddamn it. We ain't got all day."

He couldn't believe she'd come here, bust his balls like this. Embarrass him in front of people he worked with. Fucking bitch. He said: "I'll be with you in a minute." Glanced over at Mo. The fucker was looking right at him, took a long drag on his Camel, blew out the smoke.

Still standing in the doorway, hands on her hips now, she said: "Goddamn it, Lenny, we got shit to do."

Tommy was even looking at him now, shaking his head. Grabbing the arms of his chair, Lenny said through clenched teeth: "When I'm through here."

Then Christina walked over, kind of swinging her hips. "Hi, Erasmo," she said. "You never called me like you said you was." She leaned up against his shoulder, rubbing her ass against him. He was still staring at Lenny. She said playfully: "You bad, bad boy!"

Then Gina came over to the table, eyeing Lenny, the other side of Mo, leaned up against him too, her bony hips. The girls looked at one another and giggled. Each put an arm around Mo, rubbing his back, touching his hair. Gina looking back at Lenny, teasing him. Lenny could not fucking believe it, Gina embarrassing him like this. He oughtta fucking kill her. Right now. Pull out his gun and fucking shoot her dead for doing this to him.

Mo was still staring at Lenny. He took another drag on his cigarette, laid it in the ashtray, then put an arm around each girl, started caressing their asses. He looked up at Christina: "*Mia Poppona*," he said in his quiet monotone voice. Then to Gina: "*Che fica di fiamme.*" Both girls giggled. Mo glanced at Lenny, then looked back at Gina and said: "*Te lo ficcherò nella potta per fartelo uscire dalla bocca.*"

The girls laughed, neither one of them understanding what he said. Christina said: "That sounds *so* romantic!" Tommy laughed out loud, dropped a salt shaker.

Lenny was going out of his mind. "What's that mean?" He looked at Mo, then over at Tommy. "Goddamn it, Tommy, what the fuck's that mean?!"

Tommy said: "He say he want to ram his thing so far in her *potta*, her pussy, that it come out her mouth," and he laughed again, shaking his head.

Gina crinkled her nose and stepped away from Mo, his hand still on her ass. Christina covered her mouth, laughing, and started turning red.

Lenny could not fucking believe the asshole would say that shit to his girlfriend, right in front of him.

He looked back at Mo.

There was a hint of a smile on his dark face now.

CHAPTER 5

Morris lived on Hoffman Street, between Front and 2nd, in the Pennsport section of the city, not far from Le Tour, also not far from the Italian Market. He rented the place—a typical red brick row home on a narrow treeless street—for the location, and for the kitchen, which had been modified by the previous owners. Six burner gas range with a convection oven, lots of counter space, and storage for his pots, pans, and utensils. He hadn't done much with the rest of the house. The upstairs had two small bedrooms and the bathroom. The ground floor was one long continuous space, running from the front door, through the living and dining area, back to the kitchen, which was partially separated by a wall, but no door. There was also an unfinished basement. A lot of his things were still in boxes he'd just never gotten around to unpacking. The furniture was old and worn, collected from garage sales and secondhand stores—except for the dining table and chairs, which he bought new when he moved in a year ago. He hadn't bothered to sign up for cable TV. He was never home in the evenings to watch it anyway.

When he and Vince got back to the city this afternoon, they stopped for cigarettes, and then Vince wanted a cheesesteak, so they went to Geno's. Vince said that was one of the things he missed most in the joint—a Geno's steak, with fried onions and Whiz, of course. The last cheesesteak Morris had was a couple of years ago. He thought the things were nasty now that his tastes had changed, you know, since he'd been to cooking school. Sat there and watched him wolf the thing down. Vince's demeanor hadn't changed the ride over, he was still acting pissed off, but after he'd eaten he seemed a little more content, maybe.

Geno's sits right there at the foot of the Italian Market, a row of shops and stores running along 9th Street in South Philly from around Federal up to Catherine or Fitzwater. The place is crammed with beautiful fresh produce, meats, poultry, game, live seafood, spices, bread, fresh pasta, everything. Vendors under canopies yell out the day's specials, and the sidewalks are jammed with shoppers. Since they were right there, Morris told Vince he wanted to pick up a few things for dinner. Earlier, talking to Vicky at Le Tour, they made plans to see each other tonight. He wanted to see her, wanted to be with her, and, besides, his next evening off wasn't until Sunday, so he decided they ought to take advantage. Told her he'd cook for her, and he'd been planning in his mind what to make all afternoon. Whatever it was couldn't be too time consuming, since most of the afternoon was being taken up with Vince. Besides, he didn't want to have to be spending the whole time in the kitchen when she was there. So he decided for the first course smoked salmon and capers, served cold, with chilled vodka. For the second course a scallop soup Enin had told him about, but which he'd never made himself, with a crisp French Chenin Blanc. Then for the third course roasted lamb chops in cognac mustard, roasted potatoes, and green beans, with an '89 Grand-Puy-Lacoste Pauillac, a nice full-bodied red. He wouldn't tell her how much it cost, if she asked, maybe make something up, or tell her not to worry about it. She insisted on bringing the dessert, so he didn't have to worry about that. Everything he needed for dinner he found fresh at the Market. It was all beautiful, high-quality stuff: The scallops, the lamb, beans, everything.

After they got home, Vince went upstairs and fell asleep. Morris cleaned up the place a little, and got his cooking preparations done. Vicky was due at 6:30. Morris hadn't told her about Vince, that he'd just gotten out of jail, or that he was staying there. He was wondering if maybe he should have told her, you know, not have it be a surprise—by the way here's my ex-con brother—*half* brother—he's going to be staying with me a while. Yeah, how long? That's the question, isn't it? If he didn't go back to the garage, he was going to have to find something to do with himself, some way of supporting himself. Jesus, just as long as he stayed out of trouble—and stayed away from those goddamned bookmakers and loan sharks.

At 6:25 the doorbell rang. Morris turned on Billie Holiday and opened the door. Vicky was standing there on the stoop with a pastry box in her hand. Their eyes locked, and he told her to come inside. As soon as the door was closed, she put her free arm around his neck and they kissed, first lightly, then passionately. In their embrace, he got a good whiff of her perfume—it was vanilla scented, and the smell sent him rushing back to his grandmother's kitchen, when she used to bake cookies for him. It made him smile, kissing her. After a few minutes, their mouths separated. She sighed. He said: "Have any trouble parking?"

She offered up the pastry box. "No, found a spot right out front."

"What's this?"

"Dessert—apple cake from the Pink Rose. Ever had it?" She took off her jacket and laid it across the chair. She had on a coffee-colored slim turtleneck dress, ribbed, with a matching cardigan, that accentuated her curves. She looked great.

"No," he said, checking her out. "But I'm sure it's good."

"Let's hope so." She was looking around at the bare living area.

"I know—it's not much to look at. But it's reasonably clean."

"*Reasonably?*"

He laughed. "Come in here, let me get you a drink."

She followed him through the living and dining area. She saw the elaborate table settings, three forks, two knives, three glasses—one for water, two for wine, dinner plate, bread plate, dessert spoon—all of it beautiful, in a classical style, with gold inlay. "Jesus—that's as nice as at the restaurant. Nicer."

"I've got beer, wine, something stronger. . . ."

"Something stronger," she said.

He took out the Beefeater's and vermouth, made a couple of martinis. While he was measuring the gin, the toilet flushed upstairs. He looked over at her, she'd heard it. "There's something I have to tell you," he said.

Her eyes got wide. "You're not married, or something like that?"

He laughed out loud. "No, nothing like that."

"Thank God," she said with exaggerated relief. "You don't know how many times. . . ."

He waited a second for her to finish the sentence, but she didn't. He said: "Taste this, tell me if it's too strong," handing her the glass. Then: "My brother's here—half brother."

She sipped the martini. "No, this is fine. . . . Your brother? Yeah, you mentioned him last night."

"He's staying with me for a few . . . for a while," he said, motioning her to the sofa. They sat down, knees touching.

Billie Holiday was singing "You're My Thrill."

"Yeah? That's nice. Is he here from out of town?"

"Not exactly," he said.

"Oh, God," she said, excited, setting down her drink. "You won't believe what Enin did today."

"Uh-oh," he said. "What was it this time?" Then added: "Are you hungry?"

She smiled, eager. "Famished. I didn't eat a thing all day, anticipating the feast you're preparing."

"Well, just keep in mind, I didn't have the whole day to work on it. Just so you know, it's something simple." He wasn't any good at false modesty, and he knew it.

She laid a hand on his thigh. "I'm sure it'll be great."

"Well, we can have the first course anytime now. Tell me about Enin, and I'll put it on."

"Okay. This was about an hour after you left. You know the guy who delivers the tablecloths and napkins, the laundry guy, that private service, he does it all himself?"

"Yeah, George somebody."

Her hand was still on his thigh, felt like it was starting to burn him through his pants. He was getting excited, very aroused.

"Right," she said, acting like she didn't know what she was doing to him. "George Stevens. I should know the name—I send him the check every month."

"He and Enin get into it?" Looking at her lips. Moist, full. Wanting to bite her.

"God, did they!" she said. "Remember that Enin was so mad last month that those tablecloths came back with stains on them?"

"Yeah."

"Well, he kept reminding people to tell him when George showed up, over and over again, 'Tell me when the laundry man gets here'—you know how he talks—because he wanted to yell at him in person. So the guy shows up, and Enin comes out and starts in on him. What's that word he uses, the name he calls people when he's really mad, the French word?"

"*Salaud?*"

"No, not that one."

"*Con? Un con?*"

"Yeah—that's it. What's it mean again?"

"Like 'idiot' or 'jerk.' What it literally means is. . . ." He looked at her. "Never mind."

"Bad, huh?"

"Bad enough," he said.

"What's the other one mean?"

"*Salaud?* Means 'bastard.'"

"Bastard," she repeated, like she wanted to remember it this time. "Yeah, so he starts calling him a *Con, un con*," giving it her best French accent.

He smiled at her, and she smiled back, leaning toward him a little, her hand shifting, so she was touching him now, touching *it*, the end of it, lightly, through his pants.

Her voice lowered, Vicky said: "So the guy gets really mad, right? And tells Enin he can't talk to him like that, and so he says, 'You don't like my work, you little Frog, you can go to some other F–ing laundry.'" She looked up at him for effect.

Her hand hadn't moved. The pressure, the sensation was driving him crazy. He was feeling a little lightheaded.

"God," he said, his voice a little hoarse, "he called Enin a *Frog*?" She nodded slowly, staring into his eyes, grinning. He said: "What'd he do?"

Softly, she said: "He ran into the kitchen . . ."

"Yeah?" Leaning toward her, their lips almost touching.

". . . and got a meat cleaver . . ."

"Yeah?"

He could feel her breath on his mouth, warm and heavy and moist.

". . . and chased the guy . . . out of the restaurant."

They fell into one another, kissing deeply, her hand caressing him. His arms went around her. Mouths open, their tongues exploring. She moaned.

Then: Footsteps on the stairs, they pulled apart, sat up

straight. Morris wiped his mouth on his sleeve, leaving a brownish-red lipstick stain on his white shirt. He glanced over at Vicky—her eyes were glassy.

Vince appeared.

Morris stood up, felt a little wobbly. "Vince—this is Vicky. Vicky, Vince—my half brother."

She stood, they shook hands.

Morris said: "I better get the salmon on."

Smirking, Vince said: "Don't let me interrupt nothin'."

Walking toward the kitchen, Morris said: "No, it's all right. You want a drink?"

"No, I'm goin' out."

Thank God. Morris breathed a sigh of relief. He noticed the lipstick stain on the cuff of his shirt, and rolled his sleeve further up to hide it. "You could eat with us," he said, "but when I asked you this afternoon, you said you didn't want to, so I've only got enough for two."

"S'all right," Vince said. "I ain't hungry anyway. Still full from the Geno's."

"Get some sleep?"

"Little bit."

Morris opened the refrigerator, took out the salmon and capers, put them on the plates. He glanced over, noticed Vicky and Vince were avoiding one another, Vicky sitting on the sofa, Vince just standing there, staring at the table settings, like he was wondering what they were going to do with all those forks and glasses. Morris felt like he ought to say something. "Vicky works at the restaurant."

Vince turned to look at her, said: "Yeah? You a waitress?"

Vicky laughed, then caught herself. "No, I'm the manager."

"That's cool," he said. Then to Morris: "Listen, I'm gonna get the fuck outta here, leave you two alone."

Morris said: "Okay. You need some money?"

Vince looked over with a scowl, then said, angrily: "What? Take money from my *little* brother, has to cook in a restaurant? No, I *got* money."

See? You try'n do something nice for the guy. "Thought I'd ask."

Walking toward the door, Vince said, acidly: "You kids have fun now."

Morris called over to him: "Hey, when you comin' back?"

Vince said: "Late," and left, shutting the door hard behind him.

Vicky got up from the sofa, walked over to the kitchen.

Morris said: "That was Vince."

"Yeah," she said, quietly, like she was embarrassed. "I guess I shouldn't have laughed."

He took a drink of his martini. "He was in prison, just got out."

"Really?" her eyes wide.

"Yeah. Sit down, please, we can start eatin' . . . uh, eating." He took the food out to the table, then got the chilled glasses and vodka from the freezer. He sat down with her. "He was arrested for burglary. This was about four years ago now, three and a half. A jewelry store on jeweler's row. The cops were never able to prove that he took anything, so he was charged with breaking and entering. He just got out today. That's where I went this afternoon—to Graterford to pick him up."

"He seems kind of . . . angry."

"Yeah, he was always hard to get along with, and now, at least today, he's being a real bastard."

She took a sip of ice cold vodka, said: "Can I tell you something?"

"Sure."

"You two don't seem alike at all. It's hard to believe you're related. Your hair's much lighter than his, your faces are so different. And he looks a lot older."

"Yeah, I know. He aged a lot in jail. He's only five years older than me."

"No kidding?" She took a bite of the salmon.

"Yeah, only five years."

"God, this is good," she said.

"You like it?"

"Love it," she said. Then added: "You know what, though? I noticed that you seem a little . . . different around him. When he walked in the room, you changed a little, your mannerisms and the way you spoke—it was different."

He looked at her, thinking about it. "Really?"

"Yeah," she said. "I mean, it was only a few minutes, but it seemed different than when you talk to me, or at the restaurant."

He shrugged. "I hadn't ever really noticed, I guess."

"It's not anything bad. It's kind of cute, shows me a different side of you."

He smiled thinly at her, but now he felt kind of self-conscious, and he hated that feeling. It was too early to show her everything, for her to know how bad it was, how poor he'd been. She'd grown up with everything, wouldn't be able to understand it, understand why he'd done some of the things he'd done. He shouldn't have told her last night about the shooting. That was stupid.

Billie Holiday was singing "Solitude" now.

She said: "I love this music even though it's so melancholy."

"Me too."

Their eyes met, a moment passed, just staring at one another.

She said: "So . . . is dinner ready?"

He said: "Well, the potatoes are about done. The rest of it doesn't take any time at all. But I *could* keep the potatoes warm, hold up dinner for a while. . . ."

She understood and smiled broadly. "Why don't you do that?"

He reached over, took her hand, kissed it. They both stood up. He led her upstairs, to the bedroom.

Vince called Sonny Jackson earlier, made plans to meet at Dirty Franks, 13th and Pine. It was a dive, didn't even have a sign outside telling you it was there, but Sonny liked it because of the art school chicks. The kids from University of the Arts, over on Broad Street, hung out at Dirty Franks, with their black clothes, dyed black hair, the tattoos, piercings in every part of their bodies you could imagine. Sonny liked those kinds of girls, though he didn't score with them very often. He'd hang out with them, have a few drinks, get high sometimes, but in the end most of them were just pretend cool, not really hip enough to do a skinny, 36-year-old black professional car thief with a huge Superfly afro, least that's the way he explained it.

The way over, Vince was thinking about how Morris embarrassed him in front of that girl, asking him if he needed any fucking money. Couldn't believe it—the fucker asking him right in front of her. But what the fuck did Morris know, right? He wasn't in the life, didn't know what kind of an insult that was. Good thing was, he'd only have to put up with that shit a few days. Soon as he got something together, he'd get his own place again.

He walked into Dirty Franks a little after seven. The place was mostly empty. Sonny was already there, sitting at a booth, chatting up some little white chick with neon orange hair. Soon as he saw Vince, he nudged the girl, told her he had business, but not to go away, he'd talk to her later, winked at her.

Vince sat down across from him in the booth, took out his pack of Marlboros, lit a cigarette. Sonny, wearing black jeans and a faded yellow T-shirt, grinned at him, showing his big white teeth, said: "How you doin', Vince? Good to see ya, man. Been awhile."

Vince nodded.

A girl came to the table, asked Vince if he wanted anything. Draft Bud. Did Sonny want another 7&7? Not yet, he was still working on the first one.

Vince looked at Sonny. "So what's happenin'?"

"Same ol', same ol'. You know how it is. You got out today, right?"

"S'afternoon."

"Shit," Sonny grinned at him. "Bet you got a lot a catchin' up to do, huh?"

Vince took a drag on the cigarette. "Where's Billy?"

"Oh, he around."

"Where?"

"He holin' up, back a the Greek's."

"Greek's away?"

"Yeah, like he do ev'ry year."

Vince nodded, thinking about it.

Sonny said: "You ain't talked to him?"

"No."

Sonny frowned. "Jesus, Vince, he sorry, man, you can't imagine how sorry he is."

"Fucker oughtta be grateful, what he oughtta be."

"Oh, shit yeah, he that too."

The waitress came back, set a glass of beer in front of Vince. He drank half of it straight off.

Sonny said: "You see my little *chiquita* over there?" nodding at the girl with the orange hair, "she got a girlfriend, gonna be here any minute. You want, we can party with 'em, maybe get laid. I got some fine weed, get 'em in the mood. What you say?"

Vince looked over at the girl. She was wearing faded bell-bottom jeans, a silver glittery top that showed her midriff and black thick-framed glasses like some accountant from the '50s would wear. Vince thought she looked stupid, like she was going to a Halloween party or something. He didn't know why Sonny went for those kinda girls, outside of them being young. Looked back at Sonny. "Nah, 'less her friend looks half normal," he said. "That fuckin' hair—she could be in the goddamned circus."

"Suit yourself." He took a sip of 7&7 through the little cocktail straw.

Vince said: "Look, Sonny, reason I called you—"

"Need a car?"

"Yeah, I need a car, but I got somethin' special goin' on I need help with."

Sonny said: "Shit, Vince, you know I don't do robb'ries."

"Ain't a robbery. Like I said, somethin' special." He lowered his voice. "I wanna snatch somebody, a broad."

Sonny's eyes got wide. "Snatch? You mean *kidnap*?"

"Yeah."

"Jesus Christ, Vince, why the fuck you wanna get into somethin' like that?"

Vince stared at him. "I got my reasons."

"Money? You askin' a ransom? They better ways—"

Vince interrupted: "I *said*, I got my reasons," starting to get angry.

"All right, all right, take it easy. Who the broad?"

"That ain't important."

Sonny laughed. "What you mean, that ain't important?"

Vince yelled: "What it means, you don't need to know! Now, you wanna help me or not?"

Sonny put up his hands, palms out. "Jus' chill, Vince. Man, you done turned into some kinda hardass, forget who your friends are." He picked up his drink, started sliding out of the booth. "I get you a car, you need one, but I don't wanna have nothin' to do with no kidnappin'. Now, if you excuse me, I gotta work on Miss Neon over there. I'm kinda wonderin' if her little bush orange, too. Ha ha!" and he winked at Vince, as if nothing had happened, and walked over to the girl.

★ ★ ★

The first thing he said afterwards, lying there, arms and legs intertwined, the blankets on the floor, was, "Jesus, you sure got over your fear of men." She laughed and kissed him.

It was great, the sex. The whole time, he kept thinking, "Damn, this is *good*," like he hadn't expected it to be like that, or like he hadn't remembered how much you could get into it. It had been a year and a half since he had a girl-friend. He'd gotten laid since then, sure, but it was always some one-night stand kind of thing, not anything special. This felt different. She was so eager—and aggressive, maybe even a little *too* aggressive. He liked women to be a little more submissive than that. But that's okay. It was something they could work out, as good as it all was. No, he was sure this was different, because he didn't want to go anywhere, and he didn't want her to leave. He wanted to be with her afterwards.

Now they were sitting back at the table, eating the rest of their dinner. He was in his underwear and an old sweat-shirt, she in his bathrobe, nothing on underneath. They kept grinning at one another, like a couple of high school kids, and she kept making noises, telling him how much she liked the food. The soup turned out really well—Enin was right, it was a great recipe, and very easy. The potatoes were definitely overcooked, but she didn't seem to care, and he didn't either, really. The Grand-Puy-Lacoste was fantastic, he knew it would be. She didn't ask him how much it cost.

They were eating the chops, when he noticed her frowning.

"What's wrong?"

"Oh," she said, "sorry. I was just thinking about you and your brother."

"Yeah? What about?"

"Just how mean he was to you earlier. That wasn't right. You were only trying to help him."

"I know. That's just the way he is."

"Doesn't make it right."

"No, I know. I'm used to it, though. He's always been kind of angry. He used to beat the snot out of me, growing up."

"That's awful!" she said, leaning over to touch his arm. "I'm so sorry."

"Oh, hell, that was a long time ago," he said. "Thing was, I could never figure out why he'd do it."

"Why he'd beat up on you?"

"Yeah. Didn't seem to be any sense to it usually. He'd just haul off and nail me."

"Didn't your parents do anything about it?"

"For a while they did . . . when I told them about it. See, his dad ran out on him and my mother when Vince was a baby. I've never seen the guy. I don't think my mother even saved any pictures of him. So then my mother married my father and had me, when Vince was five. So we grew up, living with our mother and my father, Vince's stepfather. I don't know the old man favored me. He was pretty cruel to both of us. Vince'd probably tell you a different story though. I think—I know, in fact—he thought the old man was mean to him and a lot nicer to me. So for a while when Vince'd beat up on me, I told my mother, and she'd tell the old man. But then the old man would kick the crap out of Vince, and I think she started feeling guilty, so after that she stopped telling him. She'd just have a talk with Vince, and of course that didn't do any good. He always told her he'd try and behave, but then he'd go on acting like he always did."

"And he ended up becoming a criminal."

"Well, it's not that simple," he said. He suddenly felt like he had to defend Vince. "He's not some kind of hardened case—at least I don't think he is. Or he wasn't before he went to prison this time. He's got a regular job, working in a garage. He's a good mechanic. You might not believe it, but he's really perfectionistic, has to do everything just right. It's just that something happened that twisted him up, I think, sort of sent him over the edge when he was younger. He always had a mean streak, but afterwards, he seemed to kind of withdraw into himself."

She said: "Yeah? What happened?"

"When he was nineteen, he was arrested for raping a fifteen-year-old girl."

"Oh, God. . . ."

"Well, it's not quite what you think. He was seeing the girl at the time. They were dating. He might have been a little too old for her, sure, but I think he really liked her. I know he did, in fact. She was about my age, and I remember her being selfish, liked having him buy things for her. The way the story goes, then, is she wants these shoes, really expensive things, something popular at the time, and he refused to buy them for her. They get into a huge fight, saying nasty things to each other, and he smacked her. This's what he told me happened. She was really mad, and swore she'd get even with him—"

"So she told everyone he raped her."

"Right. He got arrested, had to spend a few days in jail. Eventually, she dropped the charges, told everyone she'd been lying. But something changed in him after that. Like I said, he seemed to withdraw. I think it was after that he started getting involved in serious crime."

"*Serious* crime?"

"Yeah," he said, "you know, not kid stuff, stealing candy bars from the Seven-Eleven, or rolling winos, but three-to-five at the state penitentiary type crime."

She grinned at him. "Did *you* ever steal candy bars and roll winos?"

He grinned back, feeling self-conscious again. He realized he'd been talking too damn much, saying too much. "Well. . . ."

Playfully, she said: "Oh, you were a little hellion, were you? A little troublemaker?"

He laughed. "Yeah, I guess so. I guess you'd call it that."

She got up, came over, sat on his lap, her robe falling open, put her arms around his neck, started kissing him. "Then," she said, "why don't you show me how bad you can be."

CHAPTER 6

W hat Turner couldn't figure out was what the fuck the guy was doing in Camden in the first place. Right? Can you explain that? Yesterday's big news, cops citywide still talking about it: Dick Franks, *asshole* Dick Franks, *fuck-up* Dick Franks, stumbles onto a drug deal in Camden—he's there without permission, without authorization from Camden or South Division (hadn't even reported in that day)—and shoots John Franklin "Bootsie" Webber, one of the biggest drug dealers in the Northeast, wanted in at least four states for narcotics trafficking, extortion, murder, attempted murder, assault, etc., etc., and two of his known associates, after *they'd* just shot and killed two small-time Camden dealers, Derek Alan "Bam" Ash, and Michael Robert "Stones" Gordy. Webber and one of his associates killed, the other in critical condition. Franks *said* Ash was one of his snitches, he was going to hit him up for some info concerning an unrelated case, and just happened to stumble onto the drug deal. Walked in just as Webber capped Ash and Gordy. Yeah, and that explanation stinks like Auntie Jude's cabbage rolls. For one thing, Webber was shot in the street. If Franks just came in the door, how the hell did Webber get by him? And if Ash was involved in that kind of a deal, what was Franks doing associating with him in the first place? Jesus, ordinarily, acting without authorization would have meant his ass, Dick Franks hung up by the short and curlies. Hell, he'd been investigated by I.A.B. on three different occasions already, twice for assault, once for dereliction of duty. But the story made national news, and now the department didn't dare censure him. Commissioner Johnson must've punched a few walls over this one. Franks was *exactly* the kind of degenerate, renegade cop he was hired to get rid of. Now he can't touch him. Politics. Fucking politics.

It was Thursday, April 6th. Nick Turner sat in a booth at the Broad Street Diner, staring out the window, sipping his coffee. He was a 28-year-old police detective, from South Division, same as Franks. He was six-foot, 195 lbs., wore a crew cut, had brown eyes, and a big crook in his nose from a beating he took in a bar ten years ago. He'd just taken and passed the sergeant's exam—he was now Detective Sergeant Turner. Man, that was hard to get used to—still made him smile every time he thought about it. So now he outranked his 51-year-old partner, Dwight Wojcik. Wojcik was a fucking dinosaur, a racist Pollack with a short temper, but he wasn't a bad cop—and that's about the best you could say for him.

Turner was sitting there, thinking about Franks, waiting for Wojcik, who was in the can. Said he had to take a shit—this was their morning routine, the two of them. They'd stop for coffee, wherever they were headed, then Wojcik would say he needed to take a shit and disappear. Turner knew, and his partner knew that he knew. It was a little game they played.

The waitress came over, asked him if he wanted anything else, called him "hon." He said no, that was all. She left the check. Turner pulled out his wallet, dropped a couple of bucks on the table.

Wojcik walked up, asked if he was ready to go. Turner looked up at him, almost laughed. His fucking toupee was on crooked. Goddamn, that rug looked stupid, like something the cat coughed up. Turner didn't know why he wore it. He stood up. "Just a sec, partner," and he reached over and adjusted the toupee, got a whiff of Listerine and Jack Daniels.

Wojcik said: "On straight now?"

Turner said: "Yeah, let's go."

They walked out to the parking lot, got in the unmarked silver Plymouth Acclaim, Turner driving. He laid his blue suit jacket carefully across the backseat before he got in. Just bought the suit, after he passed the sergeant's exam. Thought he ought to work on his image a little. Wojcik kidded him about the new suit for a week, but what the fuck did he know? He wore the same wrinkled dark brown suit everyday, looked like it came from Sears & Roebuck 15 years ago.

In the car, Wojcik said: "What's the name?"

"The kid?"

"Yeah."

Turner pulled out of the lot, turning south on Broad.

"Kid's name is Wayne Anthony Reese. Grandmother's name is Elizabeth Young."

"I thought it was his mother."

"Nah, grandmother," Turner said. "He lives with her. The mother lost custody."

Wojcik said: "Probably some fuckin' crack whore."

Turner looked over at him, didn't say anything.

They pulled into the parking lot of Methodist Hospital, South Broad, between Wolf and Ritner. Walked in, flashed their badges to the nurse at the front desk, asked her who was treating Reese, Wayne Anthony. She told them: Dr. Wesley. Could she get Dr. Wesley down here, please? She paged, they waited.

There were pamphlets on health issues in a rack. Wojcik started going through a couple of them. "Hey, Nicky," he said.

"Yeah?"

"Maybe I ask the doc what he thinks about my stomach—you know, the pains I been havin'."

Nick was thinking he could tell Dwight what to do about those stomach pains: Cut out the fucking liquid breakfast he had every morning. He said: "Still bothering you?"

"Off and on. Feels better when I eat somethin'."

A woman in a white coat, stethoscope around her neck, stepped up. "Officers?"

Turner said: "Yeah?"

She said: "I'm Deborah Wesley. What can I do for you?"

Turner took a good look at her. She was in her late 20s, long dark hair pulled back, glasses. Attractive in an antiseptic kind of way. Wojcik said: "*You're* Dr. Wesley?"

She said: "Yeah, believe it or not, they let *girls* become M.D.'s now."

Turner laughed out loud. Wojcik blushed, stammered: "Nah, it's cause you're young—I didn't think. . . ."

Nick said: "I'm Detective Turner. This's Detective Wojcik. Sorry to bother you. You're treating Wayne Reese?"

"That's right," she said.

"His grandmother, Elizabeth Young, called us, said she thought he'd been assaulted."

"Yeah, I advised her to call you."

"So he *was* assaulted?"

"Well, I'd hate to think he did that to himself."

Wojcik said: "Did what?"

She turned to him. "He came in Monday night with lacerations and contusions on his face, and a big hole in his upper left leg."

Turner said: "What happened to him?"

She looked back. "He won't say."

"What's it look like happened to him?"

"Best guess? Somebody beat him up and carved the hole with a knife, or maybe did it with some kind of power tool, a drill maybe."

Turner and Wojcik looked at one another. Turner said: "Somebody took a *drill* to him?"

"That's what it looks like. He had to have surgery to repair the muscle. The surgeon and I talked it over, and that was our best guess, since he's not saying."

"Can we see him?"

"Sure," and she turned and started walking down the hallway. They followed.

Wojcik caught up with her as they reached the room. "Sorry 'bout that wisecrack," he said, standing over her. "I didn't mean nothin' by it. It ain't like I don't know there's women doctors," and he grinned at her. "Say, why don't you let me buy you dinner sometime, you know, make it up to you?"

She looked at him. "Or a *drink*?" Opened the door, walked in.

Still standing there, Wojcik said: "Yeah, sure, a drink sometime." He looked over at Turner and winked.

They walked in the room. A black kid was laying in the bed, late teens, cuts and bruises on his face, stitches over his eye, his leg bandaged up. An elderly black woman with thick gray hair and glasses was sitting beside the bed and stood up as they walked in.

The doctor said: "Mrs. Young, Wayne, these men are police officers."

Turner said to the old woman: "Please sit down, ma'am." She did. "I'm Detective Turner, this's Detective Wojcik."

She looked at the boy, then at Turner. "Thank you for coming."

Turner stepped up to the bed. The boy was avoiding looking at him. "Wayne, your grandmother's concerned about what happened to you, so she called us. Why don't you tell us about it?"

Still not looking at them, he said quietly: "Don't wanna talk to no cops."

Turner looked at the doctor. The doctor shrugged. Turner said: "You afraid to tell us what happened?"

The boy said, louder: "Ain't 'fraid a nothin'."

His grandmother said: "Don't be like that, Wayne."

He said, loudly: "Shut up! I didn' ask you call no fuckin' cops."

Wojcik stepped up. "You talk like that to your *grandmother*, you little shit?"

Turner put a hand on his partner's arm. "We can't make you talk to us—"

The boy looked at him, said: "You got that right. Now get the fuck on outta here."

His grandmother shook her head. "Oh, Wayne."

Turner said: "We can't make you talk to us, but we know somebody beat the hell out of you—Jesus, just look at your eye and that swollen lip. And we know whoever rearranged your face took a drill to your leg." He saw the kid shudder, and knew the doc was right about it being a drill. "So the question is," he said, "they do it for fun, 'cause they were pissed off at you, or for some other reason?" The kid was twisting the bed sheet between his long, bony black hands. Turner took a step around the bed, trying to catch his eye. "But, see, the way I'm thinkin', if a guy's crazy enough to use a drill—Jesus, a *drill*? God that musta hurt like hell—he's crazy enough to do somethin' like that, right, and if he was mad at *you*, specifically I mean, he'd a just capped you. Right?" He looked over at Wojcik.

Wojcik nodded. "Makes sense to me."

"So," Turner said. "We gotta figure either he was just some lunatic, that's the way he gets his kicks, or he wanted somethin' from you."

Wojcik repeated: "Yeah, makes sense."

"Now, I look at you, I see your one leg bandaged up, the other one's all right—see what I'm gettin' at? If this guy gets his kicks drillin' holes into people, why'd he stop with one leg? Why not do the other one?"

"Or his arm," Wojcik said.

"Yeah, or your arm," Turner repeated. "Hell, both arms, both legs, one in the head. On the other hand, if the guy *wanted* somethin', and maybe he *got* what he wanted," the kid shuddered again, "then I can see him stoppin' at just the one hole. Right? So what'd you give up, Wayne?"

"Maybe his sneaks," Wojcik said.

"Nah, not his sneaks. You don't drill a guy for his sneaks. Besides, who wouldn't give up his sneakers instead a bein' drilled, right? Guy *shows* you the drill, you give up the shoes."

Wojcik said: "I would."

"Yeah, me too. So it's gotta be somethin' *worth* gettin' drilled for—see what I mean? At least once. Ain't worth gettin' *both* your legs fucked up—excuse my French—but it's worth takin' the drill once. Lotta guys woulda cracked before that. Hell, I know I would," he chuckled. "Guy shows me a drill, I'll tell him anything he wants to know." He laughed.

The boy, still twisting the sheets, said: "'Cause you ain't no real man."

"Yeah, maybe," Turner said. "So, tell me, son: What'd you give 'em?"

He shouted: "Nothin'! I didn't give 'em nothin'!"

Turner said: "Come on, Wayne. What was it?"

The boy screamed: "Nothin'! I don't gotta tell you nothin'!" and he broke into tears, burying his head in the blankets. His grandmother reached over, started caressing the back of his head.

The doctor turned, motioning them out. They walked out of the room, into the hallway. "Nice try," she said, like she meant it.

Turner said: "Yeah, we'll come back, give it another shot. He's too freaked out about the whole thing right now."

She said: "Well, if you don't need anything else. . . ."

He said: "No, I'm sure you're busy. Thanks for your help." He smiled at her, wondering what she'd be like outside of the hospital, with her hair down, without those glasses, a little makeup. Might be okay.

She turned, started to walk away. Wojcik called to her: "Hey, doc! How 'bout that drink?" From behind they both saw her shake her head. He looked over at Turner. Turner shrugged, thinking, poor Dwight, he just doesn't fucking get it.

They started walking down the hallway. Wojcik said: "Hey, Nicky, you ever hear a spooks usin' a drill on each other?"

"No. You?"

"Never."

Then, thinking about it, Turner said: "I thought you were gonna ask her about those stomach pains."

Wojcik looked over at him, frowning. "What? Ask medical advice from some *girl*?"

Dick Franks was sitting in an unmarked Plymouth at the corner of 4th and Christian, next to Queen Village subsidized housing, a joint burning in the ashtray. He was eating an Italian hoagie, dripping oil and vinegar on his shirt, and reading about himself in the *Daily News* and laughing. Still couldn't fucking believe it. He capped Bootsie Webber, no witnesses to say what he was *really* doing there. The L.T. gave him a couple of days off, while they investigated. But he knew I.A.B. couldn't touch him. The Commissioner could kiss his ass, all he cared. Only thing was, he wished to hell he'd taken Bam's stash the other day when he had the chance. Now he was clean out and needed a taste bad.

He looked up to see a red Ford Explorer with tinted windows, a new one, pull up to the curb, stop. The passenger side door opened, a guy stuck his head out, puked in the street. Spit a few times, closed the door. The Explorer pulled away.

Franks looked back down at the newspaper, took another bite of the hoagie. A hot pepper fell on his pants. He cursed, picked it up, ate it. He reached over, grabbed the joint, took a long hit, then wadded up the hoagie wrapper, his napkins, tossed them out the window. Just as he did, three black guys turned the corner, his side of the street. One of them he recognized: Choosey Jenkins, small-time dealer. Him and Franks had an arrangement: Franks turned a blind eye to all his illegal shit and helped him out as much as he could with the narco boys, short of putting his own ass in the grinder, and Choosey supplied him with nose candy, and sometimes money. He called over to him: "Choosey!"

The three guys slowed down. The one in the middle, hair in dreads, black leather jacket, lowered his sunglasses, got a look at Franks, shook his head, said: "Oh, man."

Franks said: "Get in."

"Why you hasslin' me, man?"

"Hey, you're gonna find out what hassling really is, you don't get in the fuckin' car."

Choosey said to the other guys: "I'll catch you later," walked around, got in the passenger side. "Shit, Franks, you fuckin' my shit up, man."

"Yeah? You're breakin' my fuckin' heart."

Choosey looked over at him. "Goddamn, Franks, you look like shit, all amped out."

"What're you—my fuckin' doctor? Let's have it, Choosey."

"Have what?"

"Don't fuckin' play coy with me. I ain't got the patience."

"Oh, man, I ain't got shit. Case you ain't heard, market's all dried up right now. Ain't no zip to be had."

"Why do I get the distinct feeling you're fuckin' with me?"

"No, man. . . ."

Franks drew his 9mm, stuck it in Choosey's gut. "Now, motherfucker, give me what I want, or I'll cap you right now."

Choosey, starting to sweat: "Jesus, Franks, take it easy. Look, man, I ain't blowin' no smoke at you. Swear to God, I got no coke. Everybody's skin poppin' now, nobody's doin' blow no more. You want, I got some first class H, man, Chinese Red. I also got black bombers, dexies, reds, yellows, blues, some righteous crystal meth, a little kokomo, you want that."

"Ain't good enough. How much you got on you?"

"Only a couple hundred. I swear, Franks, times is bad right now. Case you ain't been readin' the paper, fuckin' cops been crackin' down. Your motherfuckin' narco buddies ruinin' the neighborhood."

"You're not makin' me very happy here, Choosey."

Then, sitting up in the seat, Choosey said: "Tell you what, man, I got some *info* you might be interested in."

"Yeah? Let's hear it."

"Didn't you have a hard-on for some cat named Vince, jewel thief?"

"Vince Kammer?"

"Tha's the one."

"What about him?"

"Little birdy told me he out."

"Released from Graterford?"

"Tha's the word."

Franks nodded and smirked. "No shit. Kammer's out."

Choosey said: "So, you happy now?"

Franks put his gun away, said: "Get the fuck outta here."

CHAPTER 7

It was Friday afternoon, Lenny and Mo were sitting in Lenny's copper-colored DeVille at Broad and Snyder, keeping an eye on South Philadelphia High School, waiting for school to let out, waiting for the two niggers who raped Anne-Marie. Mo got the guns yesterday from his "source," wouldn't tell Lenny who the guy was—like it was some kinda big fucking secret, like Lenny didn't have any business knowing. Jesus, the guy was a ball-buster sometimes. They were .38s, both of them, one a snub-nose, the other had a three-and-a-half-inch barrel. Mo took the longer barrel, *of course*, gave Lenny the snubby. Sitting there in the car, Lenny could feel the gun tucked in his belt, pressing against his stomach. It was uncomfortable. He wished he could just throw the fucking thing away, use his Smith & Wesson. But that wouldn't be smart, he knew it.

Since he got the names on Monday, Lenny'd

identified the two kids, found out where they lived, and followed them around when they weren't in school. Outside of picking up Billy Hope Jr. and shuttling Gina's ass around, that's what he'd been doing all week. Did a damn good job of it too—he knew their whole routine.

Johnny let them know this was top priority. They also had to find Vince Kammer, lean on him, get him in to see Johnny, but this was the first order of business. Mo'd been asking around, trying to find the guy, find out where he was staying, but hadn't come up with anything yet.

Lenny was excited, a little nervous. He'd been planning what to say to the kids before he capped them. He *had* to use his new nickname. Then when Mo heard it, saw Lenny do the job, heard what Lenny said to them, his rep would be sealed. The Italian ball-buster wouldn't say shit to him after that. Fuck, maybe he'd cap Mo while he was at it. Do the kids, turn around and pop him.

Lenny grinned, glancing over at Mo.

Shit, wouldn't that be something? It was just a joke, he knew, but it really would be something, wouldn't it?

What he was thinking about saying was something like, "You know who I am?" He'd have the gun in the kid's mouth or something, right? Say, "You know who I am? I'm Lenny Deuces," then *bam!*, put out his lights. Or, make the other one watch while he did the first one. The other one's watching, while he puts the snubby up against the kid's head, looks over at him, says: "I work for Johnny Stacks," or better: "I'm Johnny Stacks's right-hand man. *My* name? Lenny Deuces," and then cap the kid. Man, now that he thought about it, too fucking bad he had to whack both of them. If he could do the one, and let the other one go, you know, to spread the word, everybody'd fucking know who he was.

Now that he was moving up in the business, Lenny was thinking he ought to get rid of Gina. Jesus was he tired of her bitching. She was okay looking, I mean, she'd be passable if she'd just shut her damn mouth, maybe put on a little weight. And she wasn't even that great a lay. She didn't swallow, for Christ's sake. She'd go down on him— and he practically had to beg her to do that—but she wouldn't swallow, make him pull out. What the fuck? What the fuck's the good of a blow job if she don't finish it? Enough of her shit. Find himself a new girl, maybe a little younger—like Christina. She'd be fucking perfect, except she probably wouldn't want to go out with him after he broke it off with Gina. Shit always worked like that.

Lenny looked over at Mo, the chunky fucker sitting there with his sleepy eyes. Lenny was thinking he oughtta keep things cool with Mo, at least until this was over and Johnny heard what kinda job Lenny did on the two niggers. Lenny said: "Listen, man, I know you was only kiddin' around the other day."

Mo looked over at him. "What?"

"The other day? When you said all that Italian shit to Gina. I know you was only kiddin' around. All that shit, that whole situation was her fault. Just wanted to let you know, I didn't blame you or nothin', or take it serious."

Looking back out the window, Mo said: "So you know what these two niggers look like, can spot 'em?"

Jesus, like the guy didn't listen at all.

"Yeah, Mo, I been following them all week."

"We don' wanna kill the wrong ones."

Lenny shook his head. "Don't worry about it. I know what they look like." There was a pause, and Lenny said: "She's some kinda ball-buster, I gotta tell you. That fuckin' bitch don't know how to open her mouth without complaining. It wasn't like she was really comin' on to you—you know that, right?" Mo didn't say anything. "She was just bustin' my balls, trying to get back at me, you know? 'Cause she knew I wouldn't smack her in front of other people. I mean, alone, she don't say shit to me, I take care of business—know what I mean? So she thought, you know, in front of other people, she could get away with it. Man, I shoulda just capped her—fuckin' shot her through the heart, except she ain't got one."

Mo looked over at him now with his dead eyes, like he didn't get the fucking joke. Lenny gave him a half smile.

"I thought about it before, believe me, plenty a times, she makes me mad enough." Then, thinking about it, Lenny said: "What you think about Christina, anyway?" feeling him out, seeing if he had any interest, you know, was any kinda competition.

Mo said: "You think you know where they'll be going?"

Lenny sighed: "Yes . . . I mean no. I don't *think*, I *know* —after school they go play basketball, this outside court, a park at Sixth and Ritner."

Mo pulled out his pack of Camels, put a cigarette in his mouth, lit it with a silver Zippo. Lenny rolled down the window a little more. He said: "Make sure you use the ashtray, will ya? I just vacuumed the car."

Mo said: "School's out."

Lenny looked up to see kids streaming out the door.

He looked carefully, trying to spot the two they wanted. A minute passed. Then he saw them. "There!" he said, excited, pointing. "That's them. They're the ones!"

Mo sat up. "Where?"

"Right there! See the kid in the blue T-shirt, jacket over his shoulder? That's Tyrone Bucknor. The one he's walking with's Todd Ohal."

Mo said: "You sure?"

"Yes! Sure I'm sure. I *know* that's them," Lenny said, then added: "Young, ain't they? One's only sixteen, the other's seventeen."

They watched them walk out onto the sidewalk, cross the street. Lenny said: "Wait a minute. Where the fuck they goin'?" Mo looked over at him. Lenny said: "That ain't the way they usually go. They usually go down Snyder, all the way to Sixth. Wait here."

Lenny got out of the car, followed them on foot, around the bank at the corner of Snyder and Broad. They went into the McDonald's a couple of doors down. Lenny walked up, pressed his face against the glass, watched them get in line. He went back to the car, got in. "They just went to McDonald's. Gettin' somethin' to eat, then they'll go to the park. They'll be comin' this way. They never miss the park—you know how them niggers love basketball."

Mo looked over at him. "Your jacket was open, showing your gun."

Lenny looked down, saw the handle of the .38 sticking out of his belt, his jacket unzipped. "Shit. You think anybody saw it?"

Mo tossed his cigarette out the window, said: "Look at

you. You all excited, but you don' think. You get outta the car, chase those kids like you think you invisible, nobody see you, like they don' notice you running after them, a gun sticking outta your belt. You talk a lot, all I see you doing. The other day in the restaurant? Your woman come up to another man, act like she want him in front of you, like you some kinda *frocio*, she do whatever she want. She my woman? I don' talk about it, I beat her, right there, in front of everyone. She try anything like that a second time, I kill her, no question. But, course, if she my woman, she know better than to do that in front of me." He pulled out another Camel, lit it.

Lenny couldn't believe this fucker talking to him like that. Wasn't Lenny the one, drilled that kid on Monday? Got the names outta the little fucker? All talk, no action, huh? Lenny'd show him some fucking action. He sat up straight in the seat, adjusted the pistol sticking in his belt. He cleared his throat, trying to stay calm, telling himself, just get this job done, after this, he won't say shit to you.

"Look," he said, "I just didn't realize the jacket was open was all. No big fuckin' deal. Nobody saw it. I was outta the car, what? Thirty seconds? Nobody saw it."

Mo said: "That ain't the point."

Lenny, getting tired of this shit, said: "Yeah? What *is* the point?"

"Point is, you ain't careful. You don' think about what you doing. An' if you ain't careful, you fuck this up, get us caught. But I telling you right now, I ain't going to jail 'cause you fuck up."

"I ain't gonna fuck it up."

"Good," Mo said. "Make sure you don't. An' keep that

woman a yours, that *puttana*, in line. Next time she touches me, if you don' smack her, I will."

Lenny was going to tell him he didn't have to worry about Gina, Lenny could handle her all right, but the two kids came around the corner now, eating Big Macs, carrying sodas. Lenny, excited, said: "There they are!"

Mo said: "Yeah."

"Well? What do we do? How do we do this?"

Mo said: "Follow them—keep a good distance, though. Don' let them spot us. We get a chance between here and there, we get them. Otherwise we have to wait till they done playing ball."

Lenny started the car, had to wait a couple of minutes for traffic to pass so he could make a U-turn. He kept looking in the rearview, watching the kids, making sure they were still there. Finally he got a chance, pulled out, did the turn, started east down Snyder, following the kids. After a minute or so, they'd both finished the burgers, threw the wrappers into the street. Lenny shook his head, wondering if they'd never learned to use a fucking trashcan.

At 11th Street, Mo said: "You getting too close, they gonna see you."

Lenny slowed down, pulled over, let them get a little distance. Traffic passed, he pulled out again. The kids crossed the street, over to the south side now. Snyder was much too busy, all kinds of traffic, all kinds of businesses— coupla body shops, a Blockbuster, Seven-Eleven, a bank, check cashing agencies—they'd never get their chance here. If they'd get a chance, it'd have to be on one of the side streets, maybe going down 6th, maybe on Ritner, right there at the park.

Lenny was still trying to work out in his mind what he wanted to say to them, get it perfect. "This's for Anne-Marie, compliments of Lenny Deuces." Or: "You remember Anne-Marie, don't you? The girl you tried to rape? She's Johnny Stacks's niece, and I'm a good friend of Johnny's. My name? Lenny Deuces." Something like that. None of it sounded quite like he wanted, though. He wanted it to come off perfect.

He felt himself starting to sweat, getting all nervous and excited and shit. He felt the sweat dripping down his sides.

They got down to 6th, to the run-down part of Snyder, where all the niggers live. The kids made the right, down 6th. Lenny noticed they were laughing, kidding around and shit. He thought, man, they sure wouldn't be laughing, they knew what was coming.

At 6th and Jackson, Mo said: "All right, this looks good."

Lenny glanced around, his heart beating fast. "Christ, Mo, ya think? It's awful light out, ain't it?"

"No, this's good. Nobody 'round. We pull up, like we askin' directions, get 'em in the car."

"Oh, we ain't . . . we ain't gonna cap 'em here?"

Mo looked over at him. "No, we ain't gonna cap 'em here. We grab 'em here, take 'em someplace outta the way, do it. That all right with you, or you wanna do it Wild West style, shootout in the street, everybody watching?"

Lenny wanted to tell him, all right, enough with the fucking sarcasm. He said: "Yeah, course that's fine."

"Okay, then pull up to them. Don' let 'em see your gun at first."

Lenny hit the accelerator to catch up with them, went a little too fast, the kids turned and looked as they drove past. He pulled over to the curb just ahead of them. They were on Mo's side of the car. Mo opened the door, as they reached the car. He said: "Hey, I was wondering, you tell me where something is?"

The kids looked him up and down, giving each other elbows, laughing at his accent and his clothes—Mo always wore a powder blue suit that was small for him, the cuffs riding a little too high up his wrists. "Sure," the one said, blue T-shirt, Tyrone, "what the fuck you lookin' for?"

Lenny reached down, adjusted his piece, getting it ready to pull out.

Mo said: "Is a bar, 'round here somewhere."

The other one, Todd, said: "What the fuck the name a the place? They all kinds a bars 'round here." They laughed again, elbowing each other.

Mo said, "I got the name on a piece a paper, I can't read it so good, maybe you can read it," and he pulled a slip of paper out of his pocket.

The kids stepped up next to Mo, Tyrone took the slip, they both looked at it. Todd tried to read: "De-con . . . De-coon-gel."

Mo said: "*Decongelio*. Is Italian," and he had his gun out, stuck it in Tyrone's gut, said, "We taking a little ride."

The kids' eyes got wide, their jaws dropped, mouths open. Mo reached down, opened the car door, with the gun still in the kid's stomach. "Both of you, get in," he said, "or I kill him right now."

Without saying anything, the two kids climbed into the car. Mo got in beside them, his gun still pointed at them. Lenny had the snubby out now, in his hand, leaning over the back seat, his heart beating like fucking crazy.

Mo shut the door, looked up at Lenny, said: "Okay, now drive."

He glanced up in the rearview, saw the two young black faces scared shitless, pulled away from the curb, drove down 6th.

The whole time Lenny was thinking he wished he hadn't looked at their faces. Now he felt sick to his stomach, felt like he was going to puke. He wasn't sweating anymore, in fact he felt cold and clammy. Jesus, what the fuck was the matter with him? He tried thinking of little Anne-Marie, what these fucks did to her, trying to rape her, trying to stick their nigger cocks into her, telling himself they had it coming. They did this to themselves, he was only the messenger, for fuck's sake. Soon as they laid their hands on her, they did this to themselves, sealed their own goddamned fate. It was like they put the gun to their own heads. All he wanted to do was fucking get it over with. He'd feel better afterwards, after it was done.

Mo told him where to go. They were driving up Delaware Ave. Mo said he knew a place underneath the Ben Franklin, right near an I-95 overpass, where it was good and loud, secluded, right next to the river. Jesus Christ, saying that shit right in front of the two kids, both of 'em scared outta their minds, wondering what the fuck was going on, neither of them daring to say a thing, not asking any questions, nothing. Lenny wanted to yell at them, tell them what this was about, get his blood up, get rid of this queasy feeling.

They passed Arch St., then Race. Mo told him to pull over, right there, under the bridge. Mo was right. It was secluded, dark, and noisy as hell. The traffic from 95 and over the bridge was constant.

Lenny thought his goddamned heart was coming out of his chest.

Finally one of the kids spoke up. Tyrone, sniffling, said: "Man, what you want with us? We didn't do nothin'," ready to burst into tears.

Lenny wanted to yell, fucking scream at him, tell him it was his own goddamned fault, he shoulda never touched that girl. Didn't he know who she was? Didn't he know the kinda goddamned trouble he was getting himself into?

Mo said, quietly: "We just going to talk." Then to Lenny: "You get out first, come around, take that one," nodding at Todd Ohal.

Lenny got out of the car, the snubby in his hand, opened the back door, motioned for the kid to get out. The kid stepped out of the car, wobbly. His legs started to give, he fell against the car. Lenny saw a big stain on his pants. The fucker'd pissed himself.

Mo was getting out his side of the car now, the other kid, Bucknor, following him.

Lenny said, quietly: "Come on," to Ohal. The kid just stood there, leaning up against the car, whimpering.

Overhead the cars and trucks rushing across the bridge were loud, they drowned out every other sound.

Lenny said again: "Come on, goddamn it. Get this over with." The kid still stood there, crying.

Mo'd led Bucknor over toward the river bank. He looked back. Lenny knew he was waiting for him.

Lenny grabbed the kid by the arm, had to drag him

along. The kid knew what was coming, had to know. He was crying, pissing himself, couldn't fucking walk straight.

The kid stumbled once or twice, Lenny picked him up by the arm, dragged him along. Crying, he called out: "Tyrone!"

Lenny said, quietly: "Shut up. Just shut up."

Finally they made it over to where Mo was, standing over top of Bucknor, the kid on his knees, looking like he was in shock, not saying anything, just sitting there, eyes wide open, not making a sound.

Lenny looked over at Mo. Mo nodded his head, like motioning toward the ground. Lenny put a hand on the kid's shoulder, the kid wobbled; Lenny pressed, finally the kid fell to his knees. Soon as he hit the ground, he started rocking back and forth, crying.

Lenny looked back over at Mo. Mo, with his sleepy eyes, no expression on his face, lowered his pistol, one long, careful motion, to the back of the kid's head. A few seconds of silence. Then a big truck started lumbering across the bridge, making all kinds of fucking racket.

And: *Crack!* The muzzle flash, the kid fell face forward into the mud, the blood starting to come out of his face.

Lenny's nigger, Todd, started wailing, put his face down on the ground.

And Lenny could *not* for the fucking life of himself think of what he wanted to say to the kid. He knew there had to be something to say. He knew it had to be perfect. The kid had to hear it. Lenny had to say it. Otherwise what was the point?

It was like everything was going in slow motion. Lenny looked up at the bottom of the bridge, seeing the massive iron structure with the huge bolts and rivets, listening to the cars rumbling past overhead, then he glanced over at Tyrone Bucknor, laying dead in a pool of blood. And suddenly Mo was standing beside Lenny, boring into him with those half-closed dark eyes. Lenny looked back down at Todd Ohal, his face still in the mud, still crying, and he still couldn't think of what he wanted to say.

Mo leveled his pistol at the kid. Lenny didn't stop him. He fired.

CHAPTER 8

Morris sat up in bed, his heart pounding. He'd been having a nightmare and might've yelled out, he didn't know. He still had the images in his head: a river, black water flowing, something enormous and hungry underneath rippling the water, trying to pull him under, wanting to devour him. There were children that had turned to stone lying on the river bank, chalky white against the deep green grass, unable to help him. He looked around his bedroom, trying to get oriented. Sunday—he remembered it was Sunday, 5:30 A.M. He took a deep breath, then got out of bed, put on his sweats.

Downstairs, out the door, he went for a run. Up and down the streets of South Philly, east side of Broad Street, over to Delaware Avenue, from Oregon up to Washington, some blocks better than others, some black, some Asian, some Italian, some Irish. Most of it working class, some just poor, some drug and crime infested and filthy, others safe and clean. It looked different this early in the morning; it was quiet and peaceful. He saw Easter decorations in front windows. Here and there people dressed up, leaving for early Mass. The neighborhood reminded him of where he grew up in the northeast, his own block where his mother still lived filled with row homes and no trees, similar to where he lived in Brooklyn when he was going to cooking school in New York. There was just something about all that concrete, and the people, rough around the edges, some torn, that seemed to draw him, made him feel comfortable, at home. But as comforting as it was, the place held you down, kept you, ate away at you as long as you stayed there. If you stayed, you were one of them: found a girl from the neighborhood, got married, moved a few blocks from your parents, got a local job, went to flab, and got old there, died there. If you left, you cut any real ties and had to find or create a new world to live in, you became a different person. Holidays you came back to see the family, but it was never the same. You heard what they all said about the others who'd left before you, and you knew they said the same thing about you. Morris realized at some point that moving to Brooklyn, then South Philly, was his way of leaving but not really leaving, making a change, trying to get away but staying put. He figured it was probably something everybody wanted: for things to change and yet to stay the same. It was a contradiction, and that's one of the reasons why people were always so unhappy. But it was the desire itself, whether or not it could be fulfilled, that made us human.

Running, pounding the pavement, working up a good

sweat, he thought about Vince. His attitude, his demeanor hadn't changed since he got out of the joint on Wednesday. Maybe it was too soon to expect him to adjust, to start getting on with his life, but Jesus Christ the guy was a real pain in the ass, a real bastard sometimes. You try to help him out, cut him a break, and all he does is complain, walk around with that scowl on his face. Not only that, but anybody could see he was planning something, cooking something up. Remember the day he got out of prison? He said he had to take care of some problem. He said some things stay with you, some things you never forget. He was going to do *some*thing, and no doubt it was something illegal and maybe dangerous.

Morris kept telling himself it wasn't his responsibility, it just wasn't his goddamned problem, but he really didn't want to see anything bad happen to Vince. It was the damnedest thing: he couldn't stand being around him the way he was, and sure as hell couldn't wait for him to leave, move back into his own place, and at the same time he was concerned about him, wanted to help him if he could.

Okay, so what do you do to help the guy? Maybe get him to open up, talk about things, you know, talk about what went on in prison, he'll feel better, let go of some of that anger, not get himself into trouble. So feed him a decent meal—make him an omelet this morning. Let him spill his guts about what happened.

Morris stopped running, wiped off the sweat, took a few deep breaths, standing where he was, the corner of 13th and Mifflin, and headed for the Italian Market.

The place was packed, Sunday morning, a beautiful day, people already jamming the sidewalks. Checking out the stands, the fresh produce, walking up and down the market, Morris found what he wanted. He'd make two omelets: one with smoked salmon, sour cream, Dijon mustard, chives and tarragon. The other, shitake mushrooms, shallots, and Gruyere cheese. He found the best produce at two or three of the vendors, and the cheese at DiBruno's. He walked home and took a shower, then got the ingredients together, put on the coffee, toasted some bagels, and woke up Vince. It was 10:30.

Setting the table, waiting for Vince to come down, his thoughts turned to Vicky, how hungry he was for her. He'd worked every night, so they'd only managed to share a few stolen moments in the office at the restaurant this week, pawing at each other. Somebody'd knock at the office door, or they'd have to put the brakes on before it went too far, and afterwards he'd walk back to the kitchen, glassy-eyed, wiping off lipstick stains with his apron, sporting a huge erection, and have to try to make boeuf bourguignon that way. He grinned, thinking about her. She was different, no doubt about it, different from any of the other girls he'd ever gone out with. He reminded himself not to get too worked up over her, just play it cool, take it easy, things'll work out.

Vince came down in a few minutes, yawning and scratching, sat at the table. Morris poured a cup of coffee, walked into the dining room, handed it to him. "Black, no sugar, right?"

Vince nodded.

Morris said: "Get in late?"

"Late enough."

"You hungry? You want me to start the omelets?"

"Whatever you want."

Morris walked back into the kitchen, turned on the burners, started heating the pans, added the butter.

Looking over at the blank TV, Vince said: "Why don't you get cable?"

From the kitchen, Morris said: "Been meaning to. Just haven't gotten around to it," then listened to that sentence back in his head, asking himself if it sounded different, if it sounded like when they were kids in the northeast, if he was using his old accent. He couldn't tell.

"Oughtta get a VCR."

"Had one," Morris said. "It broke."

Vince took a sip of coffee. "So you don't watch TV, don't rent movies. What d'you do?"

Morris was sautéing the mushrooms and shallots. "I cook," he said.

"Yeah, that's work. What d'you do for fun?"

"I cook," said Morris, grinning to himself. He poured the eggs, chives, and tarragon into one of the skillets for the salmon omelet.

"You like it that much?"

"Yeah, I like it that much. Plus I'm good at it." Screw modesty. He knew it was true. He may have done a lot of stupid shit when he was younger—drugs, crime, all that stuff—and he may not have been any good at anything else, but he sure as hell knew how to cook, and he knew what good food tasted like.

In another minute, the mushrooms and shallots were done. He poured the eggs for the second omelet into the skillet, put the salmon and the mustard and sour cream in the first, folded it. Another few seconds, and the salmon omelet was done. He put it on a serving plate. "This's almost ready," he said. He put the mushrooms and cheese in the second one, folded it, let it cook a few more seconds, then slid it onto another plate.

Carrying the plates out to the table, he said: "You want some more coffee?"

"No, I'm good."

"This one's salmon, mustard, and sour cream; this one's mushrooms, shallots, and cheese," pointing to the two plates.

"That's cool," Vince said, taking a big spoonful of the mushroom omelet.

Morris buttered half a bagel, watching Vince take a bite of the omelet. The fork coming away from his mouth, he seemed to freeze a second, his mouth stopped moving, and a slight frown showed on his forehead. Then he started chewing again, speared a mushroom, put it in his mouth. Morris grinned to himself. Vince'd never say so, but that was the best goddamned omelet he'd ever eaten.

Morris said: "You remember when we were teenagers, living at home, after I started doing the cooking? One night I made omelets for dinner. Dad wasn't there. It was just you, me, and Mom. Remember? You got out the ketchup. Remember that?"

Vince looked over, shook his head.

"I told you ketchup didn't go on omelets, it wouldn't taste right."

"Yeah?"

"Yeah. Remember what you did?"

Vince shook his head. "No, what?"

"You threw the food on the floor—all the food, not

just yours, all of it, and said, 'Now it won't taste like any-thing,' and you got up and left."

Vince looked back down at his plate. He'd stopped eating.

Morris said: "I was afraid you were gonna ask for some ketchup just now."

Vince looked back over at him. "Yeah?"

Morris grinned. "Yeah. I don't have any."

Vince grinned back at him, started chewing again. Morris noticed his face seemed lighter. He wasn't scowl-ing. They ate in silence a few minutes, and then, eyes downcast, Vince said: "This don't need any ketchup."

Morris laughed out loud, letting go of the tension. "Goddamn, Vince. That's about the nicest goddamned thing you've ever said to me!"

Vince started laughing too. "Oh, shut the hell up," he said, seeming embarrassed. "It's just that, I don't know, you shoulda tried that fuckin' Graterford food, man."

"Yeah? Bad?"

"Oh, shit, bad ain't the word. Plus the fact you couldn't get no cheesesteaks, no water ice, no scrapple, least no decent scrapple. No, this's . . . this's first class."

Morris suppressed a smile. "Try the other one," pushing the plate toward him. Vince cut a big chunk of the salmon omelet, took a bite of it, started nodding his head. "Oh, man," he said. "Jesus is that good."

"You ready for more coffee?"

"Yeah, fill me up."

Morris got the pot from the kitchen, filled their mugs, sat back down. There was a pause, and then Morris said: "Got any plans today?"

Vince shook his head. "You?"

"Nothing. I'm off today. Seeing Vicky tonight, but this afternoon, you want to, we could go to the gym, shoot some hoops." Vince shrugged.

Morris took another sip of coffee, and ventured into it. "So Graterford was a bitch, huh?"

Still into the food, Vince was chewing and nodding.

"Tell me about it."

Vince took a bagel, buttered it, had a sip of coffee. Still enjoying himself, he said: "Nah, ain't nothin' to tell."

Morris said: "Then tell me about *it.*"

Vince was taking a bite of bagel, looked over at him. The lightness left his face, the scowl returned. "Ain't nothin' to tell," his voice hard again.

Morris leaned forward, elbows on the table. "Come on, Vince, what happened?" Vince shook his head. Morris said: "You said, some things you don't forget. Some things stay with you. What happened in the joint?"

"You don't wanna know."

Jesus Christ the guy was a hardass. "Yeah I do. That's why I'm askin'. So tell me 'bout it."

The anger returning, Vince said: "Ain't none a your fuckin' business."

Enough of this shit. Morris yelled: "Don't be such a goddamned prick, Vince! You got people around you, care about you, and you just shit on 'em."

Vince turned red. "All right. You wanna know? Then I'll tell you. Graterford cons got a way a doin' things. You either belong to a clan, or you're prey to every mother-fucker wants a piece a you. Niggers hang together, spics, even the chinks got their own little group. And Eddie the fucking Carp's head'a the whites. Only to belong to Eddie's crew, you know what you gotta do? Do you have any fuckin' idea what you gotta do?" Morris stared at him. "You gotta suck Eddie's cock. You gotta blow that big fat, ugly motherfucker, and *then* you belong, *then* you're one a them, protected. So I told Eddie when I got there, wasn't no fuckin' way I was suckin' his dick. I told him straight out, he stuck his fuckin' pencil dick in my mouth, I'd bite the fuckin' thing off. So you know what he done? He raped me. Had his boys hold me down, and he fucked me in the ass. Not once, not twice, half a dozen times, a dozen times, I lost count. I told him, before he done it, he touched me, I'd make sure he paid, I'd make sure he lost anything and everything meant somethin' to him. And he fuckin' *laughed* at me. He fuckin' laughed."

Vince sat back in the chair, his face flushed, spit on his lips.

"Now, ain't you glad you asked?" he said and stood up. He tossed down his napkin, and walked back upstairs.

Morris heard the bedroom door slam.

He sat there for a few minutes, looking at the food on the table, and knew he couldn't eat any more of it.

He got up from the table, carried the plates into the kitchen, and scraped the rest of the omelets into the trash. Bending over the sink, he ran water over the plates, slowly scrubbing at the bits of food with a sponge.

He paused a minute, watching the water pool in the sink and then run down the drain, and he felt like throwing up.

That evening: Vicky wasn't in the door two minutes,

they were kissing madly, biting, pulling each other's clothes off right there in the doorway, in the living room. She unbuckled his belt, stripped off his pants. He pulled off her skirt, lowered her to the floor, tore off her underwear, and entered her quickly. She moaned loudly, and he held her down, pinning her arms against the floor, thrusting furiously. She screamed, and they came together violently, both of them loud. It was very intense, and very satisfying.

Afterwards, sitting on the floor in a heap, their clothes in a pile beside them, Vicky said: "You've ruined me."

Morris grinned. "Yeah?"

"Yeah, I'm spoiled."

"So you liked that, huh?"

"You couldn't tell?"

"Yeah," he said, "you make some really wild noises—same as when you eat."

"No, not the same," she said, smacking him lightly.

"Similar."

"Well," she said, laying her head on his shoulder, tracing circles around his navel, "you sure know how to satisfy me."

"*Both ways*—in bed and in the kitchen?"

"Both ways."

He grinned. He knew there was something else he was good at besides cooking. "Speaking of the kitchen," he said, "I didn't buy anything for dinner. So we could go out or order in."

"What can you get delivered around here?"

"Mediocre Chinese or really good pizza."

"Good pizza?"

"Franco and Luigi's—best in South Philadelphia."

"That's quite a claim."

"Wait 'til you try it," he said.

"You're on," she said, then added: "Do you ever cook Italian?"

"I used to make a lot of Italian food, but I don't much any more."

She said: "I'm getting chilly."

"Put your clothes back on."

"But it's so nice being naked with you."

He kissed her on the top of the head. "We can be naked again later."

"I'll hold you to that," she said, reaching for her clothes.

They both got dressed, and Morris said: "You ready for a beer?"

"Love one."

He went to the kitchen, got the beers. "Want a glass?"

"Yes, please."

He brought out the beer and a glass for her. They sat down on the sofa, holding hands. "I used to make good eggplant parm," he said.

"Mmmm . . . that's one of my favorites."

"Let's see . . . osso bucco, manicotti, and I did a nice alfredo sauce."

"You're making me hungry."

"Basic Italian food's not as complex or interesting as French cuisine. You don't have the range of tastes, the delicacy of the flavors. But there's something very . . . satisfying about Italian cooking. It's much more simple and direct."

Morris stopped himself, listening to what he'd just said. He sounded like he was on NPR, for Christ's sake. There *was* a difference in the way he talked to Vicky and the way he talked to Vince. He wouldn't say anything like this to Vince. No, of course he wouldn't. But that wasn't bad, was it? Only thing was, he didn't want to turn into one of *them*. He met a lot of people when he worked at Le Bec Fin, but also at Le Tour, people who had money and could afford anything they wanted, but who had no taste at all. You could put Duck à l'Orange in front of them and they wouldn't know it from a Whopper. They'd swill a Corton Les Pougets like it was Kool-Aid. But the worst thing about them was that they would make a lot of noise, order people around, and anybody who didn't have money they treated like shit. And he saw too many people, friends from the old neighborhood and his classmates coming out of cooking school, get sucked into that. They'd get a little status, a little juice, and then start acting like those snobs, pushing people around, looking down on them, even forgetting their own friends and family. No matter what happened, Morris never wanted to be like that.

He said: "You know, there was always tension in my house when I was a kid, tension between me and Vince, between me and the old man, and especially between Vince and the old man. My mother, she was always the peacemaker. She wanted us to be this happy family, but it just wasn't gonna happen. When we were younger, she always wanted us to eat dinner together. She'd cook her awful meals, and call us all in. We'd sit around the table, hardly saying a word to each other. You could just feel the bad vibes, and half the time a fight would break out. Sometimes just words, other times things would get thrown, or one of us would get a beating. And my mother would end up crying. It made me so anxious, so mad, just thinking about it all day, the yelling and the fighting, I got so as I hated dinner. It would make me sick, sometimes I couldn't even eat."

He looked over at her. There were tears in her eyes. "What's the matter?"

She laid a hand on his thigh. "I'm so sorry you had to go through that."

"Oh, it wasn't that big a deal. You know, we grew up some, and Vince and the old man stopped eating together. It'd be me, my mother, and one or the other of them, usually my dad, sometimes Vince. Then it wasn't so bad."

He set down his beer, put his arm around her, and sighed. "I found out something today. I don't know if I should tell you or not. But I want to."

She looked into his eyes. "You can trust me, whatever it is."

"I know," he said, then wondered if that was true, whether he really could trust her. He thought he could. The thing was, he really *wanted* to. "It's about Vince. He was abused in prison."

"Abused?"

"Sexually abused . . . raped."

Her hand went to her mouth. "Oh, my God."

"Yeah, that's why he seems different, even angrier than before."

"The poor thing. . . ."

"He told me about it today, over breakfast. He didn't want to, but I sorta pried it out of him. I think he's embarrassed or ashamed of it."

He leaned over to pick up the beer bottle again, but hesitated, then sat back on the sofa.

"Vince swore he'd get revenge against the guy who . . . hurt him."

"What do you think he'll do?"

"I don't know, but I know it's been on his mind. That's what he's been occupied with these past couple of days. He's got something planned, and I'm sure it's something that'll get him in trouble."

There was a pause, and she said: "Do you think he could *kill* someone?"

"Maybe. I don't know. I never would have thought so before, but he seems mad enough, depressed enough. Yeah, maybe. I hope for his sake that's not it."

"What are you going to do?"

Morris sighed. "I don't know. I really doubt he'd tell me what he's got planned, and even if he did, what could I do? You can't go to the police with *possible* crimes that *might* be committed. And, besides, if I could do anything, I'd hope to keep him outta trouble, not get the police involved."

There was a pause. They sat there, caressing each other's hands, and Morris said: "You want me to order the pizza?"

"Sounds like a good idea to me."

"What do you want on it?"

"Mmmm. . . . Mushrooms and black olives."

Morris called Franco and Luigi's. Forty-five minutes, they told him.

Vicky said: "It makes me so sad to hear those stories about your family."

Morris looked at her, frowning. "There's nothing to be sad about. It's just the way it was."

"Well, it does make me sad. I feel like we were so fortunate. Everyone got along really well. My sister and I hardly ever fought, and my parents were always good to us."

"Was your mother a good cook?"

She smiled bashfully. "To tell you the truth, my mother didn't do the cooking."

"No?"

"No, we had a live-in cook."

Morris nodded. He felt stupid now for talking about those things, for telling her about his home life, telling her about his stupid little problems. The room suddenly seemed warm.

She said: "You remember the other night, our first date, you said you wanted to have your own restaurant?"

"Yeah."

"Were you serious about that?"

"Sure, I'd love to have my own place."

"Well, why don't you?"

He laughed. "'Cause it takes a hell of a lot of money to start a business."

She grinned at him: "I could come and manage it for you."

"Yeah. . . ? Then I'd be your boss. That might be interesting."

Head against his chest, she said: "Yeah, so? Why don't you do it?"

"I told you—I don't have the money." Jesus, it was like she didn't realize not everybody had that kinda dough, that some people actually had to work for a living.

"Well," she said, drawing out the word, "I *could* get it from my father. . . ."

"Your *father*?"

"Yeah, he's certainly got it. It would be a kind of investment for him, a business loan."

Morris couldn't believe she said that. What the hell was he, some kind of charity case? One of her stray animals she has to take care of? Was *that* what this was about? He set down his beer, took her by the chin so he could see her eyes. "Look, I don't want your *father's* money. I don't need any handouts."

The smile left her eyes, her face, looking at him. "I was only. . . ."

"Yeah," he said, standing up, feeling hot, suddenly pissed off, "I know what you were only trying to do. You think I'm some kind of fuckin' hard luck case, like those strays you take in, something to feel sorry for, something to take care of. Well, I'm not!"

Her voice turned cold. "I didn't mean to offend you. I was only trying to be *helpful*."

"You got no idea what it's like. You've had everything handed to you, your whole life. Your daddy bought you everything you wanted. Well, he ain't buyin' me!"

She stood up now, indignant. "Boy, you've got a real chip on your shoulder, haven't you? Somebody tries to do something nice for you. . . ."

"Nice!? Nice for *me*? No, no, sweetheart, that little offer, that gesture wasn't for me. That was for *you*. I'm just your latest project, your latest little stray animal, somethin' you feel like pitying, taking care of. A grand gesture of Main Line generosity, bestowed on one of us losers. You probably get a kick outta doin' guys from the other side of the tracks, guys who are *beneath* you. Makes you feel a little dirty. Right? Probably go home and wash your hands afterwards."

"I will tonight," she said. She grabbed her coat, walked out, slamming the door behind her.

Morris grabbed his beer bottle, saw that it was empty, and threw it at the TV.

CHAPTER 9

Lenny was pissed. It was Monday, pushing noon, he was on his way back from a Mexican joint with a carryout order for Little Johnny and Mo. I mean, Johnny runs the business out of a restaurant, for Christ's sake, and they send him to pick up *lunch*? No, they had to have burritos, just felt like Mex today. Lenny knew what this was about, of course. Mo told Johnny what happened with the two kids under the bridge, right? Probably said Lenny couldn't do it, couldn't handle the situation. No doubt. Well, Jesus, Mo didn't even give him a fucking chance—right? Mo caps the one kid, and Lenny barely had time to get the other one over there, the fucker cryin', pissin' himself, for Christ's sake. He had to drag him, practically. Just got the fucker on his knees, and there's Mo, gun in his hand, caps the kid before Lenny even had an opportunity. And now he was probably going around telling everyone Lenny didn't take care of business, Mo had to do it. That had to be it. Now Lenny was in the doghouse, back on shit detail.

Lenny pulled up in front of Dominic's, sat there for a minute in the Caddy, thinking about things. He was sick a this shit—being a gofer, sent on errands like some fuckin' nigger. Plus, he knew they talked about him behind his back when he wasn't there. Fuckin' guineas. Well, one thing was for sure, wasn't nobody gonna catch him with his pants down. They could talk all they wanted to, wasn't no fuckin' greaseball gonna put one in the back a *his* ear.

He reached inside his black leather jacket, patted the Smith & Wesson automatic in his shoulder holster, then reached over, opened the glove box. The .38 snub-nose was sitting there.

He closed the glove box, took the carryout, got out of the car.

Inside Dominic's, Johnny and Mo were sitting at a table, laughing, smoking cigarettes, drinking espresso. Lenny walked up to the table. There were dirty plates sitting there. They'd already eaten.

Lenny set down the carryout bags. "Here's your burritos."

Johnny said: "Sit down, Lenny."

"Ain't you gonna eat them burritos?"

"Later. Right now, sit down."

"Said you wanted Mex today."

"What—you bustin' my balls? You sound like my fuckin' wife now. You took too fuckin' long. We to have Donna make us some pasta. Now sit the fuck down."

Lenny said: "Sorry, Johnny," and sat down. He looked

over at Mo. The fucker was sitting there, staring at him with his dead eyes.

Fingering the gold chain around his fat neck, Johnny said: "This shit with Vince's takin' too long. The fucker's gotta be somewhere, so *find him*. He ain't got no girlfriend you know of, right?"

Lenny said: "Right."

"And you paid a visit to his mother?"

"Right."

"Well, what'd she say?"

"Said she don't know nothin' 'bout him, and don't wanna know."

"So where you gonna try next?"

"We thought we'd try the garage where he used to work, see if they heard anything from him, then he's got a brother, check with him."

"All right," Johnny said. "And if that don't turn up nothin', ask Billy where he's at. Now get the fuck outta here and find the son-of-a-bitch. Right?"

Lenny looked at Mo, then at Johnny. "Sure, Johnny. Only. . . ."

Exasperated, Johnny said: "Only *what*?"

"Only I ain't had any lunch yet."

Johnny pointed to the carryout bag. "You can eat that. Take it with you."

Lenny nodded. "Sure, Johnny. Whatever you say."

Morris felt like shit, and he had a bitch of a hangover. Last night, after Vicky stormed out, he drank everything in the house, the beer, vodka, a little bit of tequila left over from New Year's, and half a bottle of Jack Daniels. He was sitting on the sofa staring at his smashed TV. Every bottle he finished last night, he threw at the TV. It was the third or fourth beer bottle that finally shattered the picture tube. He was still mad at himself, couldn't believe he let himself get sucked in like that, so wrapped up, so involved with her, let her twist him up like that. He was acting like some kinda teenager, some high school kid, falls for the first girl who gives him a hand job. He knew from the beginning they were just too different, there was no way someone like that could be serious about him. It was okay playing around with her. I mean, she was a good lay, but he should've never let himself get so crazy over her, get so involved. It was just sex, for Christ's sake. Plenty other girls around. No way he needed her, no way he had to play her stooge, be some kinda puppy dog for her to play around with. No way.

There was a knock at the door. He slid himself to the edge of the sofa. Man, it hurt even to move. Got up slowly, made it to the door, wondering who the hell it could be, letting himself hope for a few seconds it was her. Opened it up, and he was disappointed and then pissed off at himself for thinking like that. There were two guys standing there. One dressed all in black, the other in a blue leisure suit too small for him. The second one was dark-skinned, had sleepy eyes. Morris said: "Yeah?"

The one in black said: "Vince here?" showing a mouth full of silver teeth.

Morris said: "He's sleeping."

The one in black looked over at Sleepy Eyes, looked back and said: "We'd like to talk to him."

"Yeah? Who're you?"

"I'm Lenny," said the first one. "This's Mo. Can we come in?"

Morris said: "Maybe you better come back. . . ."

Lenny stuck his foot inside the door, opened his jacket, showing a gun in a holster, said: "Maybe you better let us in."

Morris stepped back, feeling his heart beating, making his head ache worse than ever. "What's this about?"

The two of them stepped inside, closed the door behind them. Lenny said: "We got business with Vince's all. Just wanna talk to him." He grinned, flashing all that silver. "Sorry if we came off like a coupla hard-ons."

Mo said: "Where's he sleepin'?" with a thick accent.

Morris turned toward the stairs, said: "I'll wake him up."

Mo put a hand on his arm. "No, we'll do it."

Lenny said: "If you don't mind, of course," and the two of them went up the stairs, without waiting for Morris to say whether he did or not.

Morris sat back down on the sofa. He heard them talking upstairs, expecting a gunshot at any moment, wondering if he oughtta get the hell out of there. He could feel the blood pulsing in his eyes and ears. He heard somebody laugh, probably the one in black, Lenny.

In a few minutes they came back down. Vince was with them now, dressed. Morris noticed that Lenny had the gun in his hand. It wasn't pointed at anything, just at the ground, but it was *out*.

Morris said: "Vince?"

Vince said blankly: "I'm goin' out a while."

The three of them walked out. Morris got up, went to

the window, pulled aside the faded yellow curtains and, watched them get into a Cadillac, drive away.

Vince was wondering why the hell Johnny Stacks was so eager to see him. Maybe it was to thank him for not ratting, not telling on Johnny when he got caught for the jewelry store holdup. Maybe he wanted to pay him three years back wages for the time he spent in the joint. Yeah, fat fucking chance a that. Most likely he had some kinda bug up his ass. That's the only time he sent the hired help after you. Fucking Lenny thought he was cute, waking him up with that pistol, sticking it in his face while he was sleeping. Lame-ass Lenny. He used to be a sheet writer, just take the bets. So when did he get a promotion, get bumped to muscle work? Thought he was cute, wearing all black clothes like some kinda cowboy. From the back-seat of the Caddy, Vince said: "So what's this about?"

Lenny said: "You'll see."

"Meaning you don't know, right?"

"Johnny'll tell you hisself. I ain't authorized to devolve that info."

"Di*vulge*."

"What?"

"*Divulge* that information. You said 'devolve.'"

"Devolve?"

"Yeah."

"What's that mean?"

"It means like when you pass on some kinda responsibility or somethin'."

"I didn't say that."

"Yeah you did."

"How the fuck could I say it, when I don't even know what the fuck it means?"

"I don't know, Lenny. You just did."

Lenny looked over at Mo. "Tell him, Mo. What'd I say? Di-*vulge* or de-*volve*?" Mo glanced over at him but didn't say anything. "I know what I said. I said, 'divulge.' *Devolve*—never even heard the fuckin' word before. How the hell could I have used it?"

Vince was enjoying this. "So, Lenny, Johnny still got you pickin' up his laundry? Doin' the grocery shopping?"

Mo chuckled, kind of snorting.

Lenny said: "Just shut the fuck up, Vince."

"Maybe he gave you a promotion, got you cleanin' the toilets now."

Mo laughed out loud.

Lenny said: "Shut up, Vince. I'm warning you!"

"You got your own toilet brush and everything?"

Red in the face, Lenny drew his Smith & Wesson, started swinging his arm over the backseat, but Mo grabbed his hand, saying: "Put that away, *stronzo*, and drive the car. He just fuckin' with you."

Looking at Vince in the rearview, Lenny said: "You just watch it, motherfucker. I don't take that shit from nobody."

Mo said: "You don' pull your gun—never—unless you gonna use it."

Lenny said: "Yeah? Well, I *was* gonna use it."

"You was gonna shoot him? Right here in the car, in *your* car, with your gun you bought at the store, registered in your name? Kill him just like that?"

Vince said: "And before Johnny got a chance to see me."

Mo said: "Yeah, and before Johnny talk to him?"

Lenny said: "Who's fuckin' side you on?"

Mo said: "Ain't no side. I'm just telling you, you ain't bein' smart. You don' think."

They were quiet a few minutes, and then Lenny pulled up in front of Billy Hope's apartment building, saying: "You wait here. I'll get him," and got out of the car.

Vince called after him: "Try not to shoot anybody!" but he didn't know if Lenny heard him. Mo laughed out loud again. This was the first time Vince'd heard Mo laugh, ever. He figured it meant something. There was some shit going on between Lenny and Mo, some bad blood. He said: "He's some kinda putz, ain't he?"

Mo said: "He think he tough, some kinda tough guy, but he just a *stronzone*."

"Yeah? What's that mean?"

"It means, he this big piece of shit."

Vince started laughing. "Stronz—"

Mo said: "*Stronzone*," gesturing with his hand.

Vince repeated: "*Stronzone*," making the gesture too.

"Yeah," Mo said, "or, *cazzo, un cazzone*."

"*Cazzo?*"

"Yeah, that mean like 'dick' or 'asshole.' You also say, *testa di cazzo*."

Lenny and Billy were walking toward the car now.

Vince repeated: "*Testa di cazzo*."

Mo said: "Yeah, that means 'dickhead.'"

Lenny opened the door, got in. Vince said: "'Bout time you got back, *testa di cazzo*. We don't wanna keep Johnny waitin'." Mo chuckled.

Billy got in the car. Soon as he saw Vince, his face started going into spasms.

Turning around in the seat, Lenny said: "What? What the fuck you call me?" Mo chuckled again.

Billy said: "How you doin' Vince?" It was the first time they'd seen each other since the night of the robbery, three-and-a-half years ago.

"Billy."

Billy started: "Man, Vince, I'm really—"

Vince put up a hand, cutting him off: "We'll talk about it later."

Looking at Mo, Lenny said: "What's that mean? *Testa* what? What the fuck's that mean?"

Mo said: "Let's go."

Lenny started the car, looked at Vince in the rearview. "Don't think I'm gonna forget this, Vince. I don't forget shit like this." Vince just nodded, looked away.

Inside Dominic's, Johnny Stacks was sitting at a table. The four of them walked in. Mo took a seat next to him, lit a cigarette. Lenny went to the bar, sat on a stool. Billy and Vince stood in front of the table, not looking at each other.

In his cigarette voice, Johnny said: "Welcome back, Vince. Been awhile."

"Three years."

Johnny was fingering his gold chain. "Graterford treat you all right?"

"I got through it."

"We had a little trouble trackin' you down."

"Been at my brother's."

"Yeah, we know that *now*. I woulda figured you'd come and see me by now."

"Only been five days."

"So I guess your partner probably told you why we're so anxious to see you?"

Vince glanced at Billy. "No, we ain't talked."

"Well, then, let me enlighten you. I want my half a them diamonds, either that or half the fence, which I figure oughtta be thirty-seven five."

Vince couldn't believe what he was hearing. "You want the *money*?"

"Or the diamonds. Don't make me any difference."

"I just did three years at Graterford for you, and you want some fuckin' *money*?"

"That's just the hazard of the job, gettin' caught. Don't mean shit to me. All I want's what we agreed to—half the take, thirty-seven five."

Vince put his hands on the table, leaned forward. "Well, let me enlighten *you*. I ain't got them diamonds. I didn't get 'em that night, I never had 'em, and I ain't got 'em now. Cops showed up before we could get 'em. Billy split, then I split. One a the cops recognized me. I got away from 'em, but they caught me at home, with the tools, glass fragments on my pants they matched to the jewelry store. But no fuckin' diamonds. I—"

Johnny put up a hand. "Don't tell me your fuckin' sob story. Marty Cohen went to his grave, insistin' them diamonds was stolen. Even under a great deal of, let's say, *duress* in his final moments, he insisted he didn't have them stones, that you got away with 'em."

Vince straightened back up. "Well, I don't know what

to tell you, Johnny. I ain't got 'em, and I sure as hell ain't got thirty-seven five."

"You know, Vince, you're startin' to give me indigestion here," he said, then shouted: "I don't wanna hear no excuses! You get me that money, or that's your ass!" and he started rubbing his fat stomach, like it was upset.

Vince glanced at Billy again, then said: "How? If I ain't got it, got no job, then how'm I gonna pay you?"

Johnny took out a handkerchief, mopped his forehead, and said: "All right, we'll work somethin' out. You pull another job, make up for this one."

Vince put his hands on his hips. "You want us to pull *another job*? After I just got outta the joint?"

"Yeah, either that or Mo cuts your fuckin' balls off, feeds 'em to you. Your choice."

"Don't sound like much of a choice to me."

"I thought you'd see things my way."

"What kinda job is it?"

"A bar—down near the stadium. They get lotsa business weeknights from the packing plants down there. And every other Friday the workers come in with their paychecks."

Vince said: "So the bar owner's got a lotta cash on hand, cash the checks, so they'll do their drinkin' there."

"Bingo. Plus security's lax. Keep the money in a safe, but the bartender has the combination, and all he's got to protect him's a .357 behind the bar."

Vince sighed. "All right, give us a minute to talk it over." He motioned to Billy, and the two of them walked across the room, sat down at a table.

★   ★   ★

Billy's face seemed to have calmed down a little. Vince said: "I don't suppose you got thirty-seven grand laying around?"

"No. Sorry, Vince."

"Then it don't look like we got any choice, does it?"

"No, but it sounds like an easy job, easier than most."

"All right, so we'll do it, get it over with, then tell that fat guinea prick to go fuck himself."

There was a pause, and Billy said: "Thanks, Vince."

"For what?"

"For not rattin' me to the cops—you know, about the jewelry store."

"Well, wasn't no reason both of us should get sent up."

Billy leaned forward. "I had to leave, Vince. I *had to*. Them cops came 'round the corner, and if I'd a stayed, I'd been a sittin' duck, for sure."

Vince nodded. "Forget about it."

"I know what went wrong."

"What d'you mean?"

"That night, the robbery—I know what went wrong."

"Yeah, the fuckin' cops showed up. That's what went wrong."

"Yeah, but why did them cops show up, why'd that happen?" Vince shrugged. "It's because it was the *thirteenth* job."

Vince rolled his eyes. Billy and his fucking superstitions. "C'mon, Billy, that's a load of bullshit. Them cops drivin' by was a coincidence."

Billy was shaking his head. "No, wasn't no coincidence. You never pull thirteen jobs with the same guy—I heard lotsa other guys say the same thing. Somethin' always goes wrong. You remember Arch Stanton? He told me this story one time—"

Vince cut him off: "Besides that wasn't number thirteen, anyway. There were the two liquor stores in Jersey, that's two; the gas station, three; two check cashing agencies, four and five; those four bars in the northeast, that makes nine; the grocery store in Wildwood, ten; the nightclub in Chester, eleven; and the jewelry store. That's *twelve*, not thirteen."

Billy counted on his fingers, then counted again. Then his eyes got wide "Shit, that means *this one's* thirteen!" and his face started jumping again. "We can't do it, Vince. We gotta tell him we can't do it!"

"Jesus, relax, Billy. That don't mean shit. Just a superstition. There's other shit you do thirteen times, right? You ever banged some broad thirteen times?"

"Not in a row."

"No, I don't mean all at once. I mean, you ever go out with some broad long enough, you banged her thirteen times?"

"Well . . . yeah."

"So? Anything terrible happen the thirteenth time? Your dick fall off? Your balls shrivel up?"

"No. . . ."

"So, what's that tell you?"

"Well, maybe it just means I dodged a bullet that thirteenth time. I caught a break."

"Yeah, and maybe it means there ain't nothin' to them superstitions—it's just a bunch a shit."

"But you can't prove it ain't true. You can't *prove* nothin' bad's gonna happen."

"Jesus, Billy, you can't prove your dick ain't gonna fall off the next time you bang some chick the thirteenth time, either. But I bet that won't stop you from doin' it. Look, there's somethin' I wanted to talk to you about. Maybe this'll make you feel better. I want you to help me do somethin' special."

"A job?"

"Yeah, a kinda job. Figure you owe me, right? For leavin' me at the jewelry store." Billy nodded. "Okay, then you'll help me with this." He lowered his voice. "I wanna snatch somebody, a broad."

"You wanna kidnap some broad?"

"Yeah."

"Jesus, we ain't never done nothin' like that before."

"I know. What I said—somethin' special. So we do the two a these jobs, and it's like we skip thirteen, go right to fourteen."

Billy ran his hand over his bald head. "I don't know, Vince. I ain't sure it works like that."

"Yeah, well, trust me, it does."

"What you gonna do with the broad after we grab her?"

Vince leaned back in the chair. "I ain't sure yet. Haven't decided."

"Well, who is she?"

"I'll tell you later. Right now, let's tell fatso we're gonna do the job, get outta here, get somethin' to eat."

Billy nodded, and they both stood up and walked over to tell Johnny they were in.

CHAPTER 10

Nick Turner was sitting in a booth at the Melrose diner, 15th and Snyder, staring at half a Reuben. They were having a late lunch. Wojcik wolfed down a B.L.T. and said he had to take a shit. He was in the can now. His trips to the john were becoming more frequent.

This morning they got a missing persons call, two of them in fact. First: Todd Ellis Ohal, black male, age 16, reported missing by his sister, Tanya Ohal. Second: Tyrone Jeffrey Bucknor, black male, age 17, reported missing by his stepfather, Alan Null. Ohal and Bucknor were best friends, lived a block apart, Jackson and 7th, Jackson and 6th, last seen Friday afternoon. Why the hell weren't they reported missing before now? Ohal's sister said she assumed he was at Bucknor's. Bucknor's stepfather said the same thing. They were in school Friday. Neither one of them came home all weekend. Ms. Ohal started to wonder about her brother, called the Bucknor/Null residence. No, they hadn't seen him, either one of them, all weekend. She called it in.

This morning, Turner and Wojcik visited the families, started getting a picture of the two kids. They were both average to below average students at South Philadelphia High. They both loved basketball, played everyday after school at an outdoor court on 6th Street, south of Snyder. Had they ever skipped out before without telling anyone? Once or twice, just overnight, never a whole weekend. Do they make a habit of ditching school? A day here, a day there. Were they into drugs? Ms. Ohal: No, she didn't think so. Mr. Null: Probably. Ain't all kids these days?

Turner got a list of names, kids the two boys knew, hung around with. First step: Interview the kids on the list, find out if Bucknor and Ohal were in trouble or had plans to run away. Find out if they were into drugs or any kind of criminal activity.

He took a bite of the Reuben, forced it down. Just wasn't hungry the past couple of days. Not sure why. Didn't feel much like eating.

When they got the chance, they oughtta stop back at Methodist, check on Wayne Reese, see if he's ready to talk about what happened to him. Funny: Turner'd been thinking about the doctor, Dr. Wesley, Deborah, the past couple of days, imagining her outside of work, her hair down, wondering if she was married. He didn't think to check for a wedding band before. Yeah, but would she even want to go out with a cop? She was a doctor, for Christ's sake. But there *was* something in her voice when she said "nice try," after he interviewed the boy—call it admiration. She was impressed. Sure, but being impressed is a whole lot different from being—what? Interested, romantically interested, attracted to you. Thing is, Wojcik probably fucked the whole thing up by coming on to her. Now how would it look, you asking her out? Like another hard-up guy on the make, except this one wouldn't have booze on his breath. Can it, it's a stupid idea.

Turner checked his watch. School would be letting out soon. They needed to get over there, talk to the kids on the list. He took a sip of coffee—cold and bitter, then put money on the table, walked over to the restrooms, knocked on the men's.

Dwight's voice: "Occupied."

Through the door: "We gotta get goin', partner."

"I'll be out in a sec, Nicky."

Toilet flushed, water running, gargling sounds. The door opened, Wojcik walked out. "Ready to roll?" Jack Daniels on his breath.

Nick: "I'm ready. But partner?"

"Yeah?"

"Eat a fuckin' mint, will ya?"

Standing outside the doors, South Philadelphia High School, corner of Broad and Snyder, badges open, kids streaming by them, asking for Marc Spotts, Thomas Conroy, Tamika Houser, Amber Benson. Anybody seen them? Getting lots of stares, some laughs at Wojcik's rug. Found Spotts and Houser, both black, both about 16, 17. Pulled them aside. Benson was absent today, Conroy probably went out another exit.

Nick: "I'm Detective Turner. This's Detective Wojcik."

The girl: "What the fuck kinda name that, 'Wojcik'?"

Dwight: "It's Polish, if it's anything to you."

"Polish? You a Pollack?," she laughed. "I heard a joke—"

"Yeah, I'm sure you did. What the fuck kinda name's 'Tamika'?"

"It's *African*."

"What, like Kunta Kinte?"

The girl said: "Who?"

Turner stepped in before it got any worse. "We're looking for Todd Ohal and Tyrone Bucknor. We understand you're friends of theirs. They're missing. When was the last time either of you saw them?"

The boy said: "Friday. They was in school Friday. Ain't seen 'em since."

Turner to the girl: "Was that the last time you saw 'em, too?" She nodded. "Do either of you know where they might be?" They both shook their heads. "I understand they play basketball after school. Either of you know if they were planning to play Friday?"

The boy: "Yeah, they said they was gonna play. I was there, they didn't show up."

"You were there at the park on Friday, and they didn't show?" The boy nodded. "Either one of 'em into drugs?"

The two of them looked at one another.

Turner said: "We ain't narco. We're just tryin' to find 'em."

The girl: "Just a little weed, nothin' big."

Turner: "Do you know if either of them was in trouble in any way?" They both shook their heads, then the boy suddenly stopped, like he remembered something. "What is it?"

The boy said: "Nothin'."

"Don't hold out on me. They could be in trouble."

"Well. . . ."

Wojcik, angry: "Spill, goddamn it."

The boy looked over at the girl, then at Turner. "I talk to you in private?"

Turner: "Let's take a walk," and he put a hand on the boy's shoulder. They started walking across the parking lot. Broad Street was busy: cars and buses jammed, horns honking. Early afternoon rush.

The boy looked back at Wojcik and the girl standing there. "I didn't wanna say nothin', front a her. She go out with Tyrone, you understand."

"Yeah, sure. So what is it? What's going on?"

"Well, Tyrone and Todd, they was into some shit last week, maybe the week before."

"What kinda shit?"

He lowered his voice: "They grabbed this girl, was gonna try an' do shit to her."

"What girl?"

"I don' know. Wasn't here, outside a Catholic school."

"They were gonna rape her?"

"Nah, they was jus' playin' 'round. I wasn't there, but I heard this girl was flirtin' with 'em and shit, over at McDonald's, coupla days after school, week before last. She wear that uniform, so they know she go to Catholic school, and they was gonna grab her after school, you know, make her do things."

"So what happened? They grab her?"

"Yeah, what I heard. They grab her, tear her clothes, and the cops showed up, they took off."

"They didn't get caught?"

"Nah, and they was worried and shit the cops'd come

after 'em, but she didn't know their names or nothin', so maybe they got away with it. Least that's what I heard."

"Do you know who the girl was? Her name?"

"Nah, didn't hear that."

"When did it happen?"

The boy thought about it a moment. "Ain't sure. I think maybe Thursday or Friday."

"Last week?"

"Week before."

"So who told you about this?"

"Wayne."

"Wayne who? What's his last name?"

"Reese."

Turner felt his heart jump. "Wayne Reese?"

"Yeah."

"You know he's in the hospital?"

"Yeah, I heard."

"You know why?"

"I heard he got hit by a car."

"When did he tell you about it, about the girl?"

"Last weekend, Sunday. Said I shouldn't tell nobody."

Turner suddenly realized that Wojcik and the girl were yelling at one another. He couldn't hear what it was about over the traffic. He said thanks, left the boy standing there, and walked quickly toward them, before his partner did anything stupid.

Wojcik was yelling: "How can you say that?"

The girl shrugged her shoulders defiantly. "Just the way it is."

"You don't know what the hell you're talkin' about!"

"Oh, and *you* do?"

"Hey, don't give me that mouth, you little bitch!"

"Bitch?! Who you callin' bitch, *bitch*?"

Turner reached them, saying, "What's going on?"

Wojcik said: "Twenty-six *thousand* points. Celtics' all time leading scorer. Thirteen consecutive all-star games, eight NBA titles."

Hands on her hips, the girl said: "Yeah, an' he some big ugly *white* dude."

"What's that got to do with anything?!"

Turner repeated: "What's going on?"

The girl said: "Magic Johnson won a gold medal at the 'lympics. He practically invented the triple double. Only reason he didn't have more points an' rebounds, he got sick, only played thirteen seasons."

Wojcik threw up his hands. "What d'you even know about the game?! You're fifteen years old, for Christ's sake!"

"Sixteen!"

"Magic Johnson retired when you were still in diapers!"

"I got ESPN. I seen clips from them old games!"

Wojcik looked at Turner: "This little brat, never even fuckin' heard of Havlicek. . . ."

She said: "I heard of him!"

"She's sayin' Magic Johnson's better'n John Havlicek. You believe that? Can you fuckin' believe that?"

Turner cracked a smile. "C'mon, we gotta go."

Walking away, shaking his head, Wojcik said: "Kids these days. Huh, Nicky?"

★   ★   ★

Turner filled his partner in on what the boy, Marc Spotts, told him. They called the communications center, police HQ, where they take the 911 calls, asked if anything came in on Thursday, March 30th or Friday, March 31st, attacks on juvenile females, around St. Maria Goretti High School. Yes, there was a call on Friday that fit the description. Assault, attempted rape. Victim: Anne-Marie Decongelio, white female, age 15. Two unidentified black assailants, both teenagers, fled the scene. The case went to Special Victims—they handle all sex crimes. Turner got hold of the detective in charge. Interesting: After the initial report to the uniforms, the Decongelios refused to cooperate, wouldn't allow their daughter to be interviewed, said they wouldn't press charges if the punks were apprehended. So what happened between the time the patrol car responded and Special Victims got the call?

They were in the unmarked Plymouth, on their way back to Methodist to re-interview Wayne Reese and ask him about the attack on Anne-Marie Decongelio. Turner said: "So why did the parents refuse to let the daughter be interviewed?"

Wojcik replied: "I don't know. They hate cops, maybe."

"Or they're protecting the girl, don't want to put her through that."

"Yeah, but you'd think they'd wanna protect her from the fuckin' animals, did that to her."

"Like, who's to say they won't do it again?"

"Sure."

"But they didn't know the punks singled her out. Coulda been random, all they knew."

"Yeah, but they don't know they *didn't* single her out."

"So maybe they got some other way a protecting her?"

Wojcik said: "You know them fuckin' guineas."

Turner nodded, thinking about it, as they pulled into the Methodist parking lot. They got out of the car. He took his suit jacket from the back seat, put it on.

"Hey, Nicky—"

"Yeah?"

"Maybe I get somewhere with this lady doctor, what d'ya think? Last time she said we should have a drink. She ain't bad lookin', right?"

Turner, suddenly angry: "Just give it a rest, will ya?"

"Why? What? What'd I say?"

"I think she was just yankin' your chain's all."

They walked into the lobby of the hospital. Wojcik said: "Really? You think she was just fuckin' with me?"

Turner said: "Yeah."

"Well, shit."

They took the stairs, walked down the hallway. Approaching the kid's room, the door opened, Dr. Wesley walked out. She saw them, folded her arms across her chest—Turner didn't know what to make of that. She said: "Detectives."

In his business voice, Nick said: "How's he doin'?"

"Physically, he's healing. Mentally, emotionally, he's still a mess. That just might be the way he is, though."

"All right if we talk to him?"

"Sure," she said. "I don't know if you'll get anything out of him, but you can try."

Turner stood there looking at her, trying to think of something else to say, and felt the seconds pass. He said: "Well. . . ."

"Do you want me to be there when you talk to him?"

"Only, you know, if you want to."

"Well, I've got a lot to do. . . ."

"Yeah, sure. No problem. Maybe we'll see you later, then."

She raised an eyebrow. "Yeah, maybe," and she turned, walked down the hallway.

Wojcik sidled up to Nick, both of them watching her walk away, said under his breath: "Fuckin' bitch."

Nick sighed, pushed the door open. They walked in.

The boy was alone in the room this time, laying in bed, watching TV, a daytime talk show. He glanced over at them as they walked in, then turned his attention back to the TV. Friendly, Turner said: "How ya doin', Wayne? Feelin' any better?" The boy didn't say anything, still wasn't looking at them. Nick walked over to the head of the bed. "They feedin' you that hospital food? Man, that shit'll kill you, won't it?" He turned toward the TV set. "What you watchin'? Sally Jessy?"

Wojcik said: "Yeah, I seen the previews for this. They got these broads on, don't know their husbands are queers. See that one? Yeah, watch this, her husband's gonna come out dressed like some fag, all in black leather. You imagine?"

Nick said: "Maybe we can turn it off a minute, talk a little bit. What d'you say?"

Still staring at the TV, the boy said: "Ain't got nothin' to say."

"Well, let's turn it off anyway," said Nick, and he walked over and shut the TV off. He started walking back to the bed, and the kid hit the remote control switch and the picture came back on. Nick turned around and unplugged the TV.

"Enough of that shit. We're *gonna* talk. You don't wanna say anything, then you can just listen to me, 'cause I got somethin' to say. First: Why don't you tell us what happened to you? Who beat you up, took a drill to your leg?" The boy was silent, staring out the window at the overcast skies. "Okay, fine. Then lemme ask you this: You talk to Tyrone or Todd recently?" The boy quickly turned his head this way, his eyes wide. "Oh, so you know who they are?" The boy was working the sheets between his hands, his jaw clenched. "Buddy a yours—Marc Spotts— said you told him Tyrone and Todd got themselves into some trouble week before last. Said you told him they tried to do some little Catholic girl. How 'bout it?"

Angry, the boy said: "He a liar!"

"Yeah?" said Nick. "Turns out a girl *was* attacked by two black kids outside Maria Goretti Friday before last."

"Don' know nothin' 'bout that."

"Well, it's kinda interesting, don't you think? Here you go and tell this story to Spotts, he tells it to me, it turns out to be true, and now you're sayin' you don't know anything about it. Kinda fishy, wouldn't you say?"

Wojcik said: "If it stinks like shit, and it tastes like shit, then it's shit all right."

Turner looked at his partner. "Well put." Then to the boy: "So you're telling us you don't know anything, what happened to that girl?" The boy shook his head. "You didn't go around, telling people about it?" Shook his head again. "Well, then," Nick said, "maybe you can tell us what happened to Todd and Tyrone."

The boy looked up. "What happened?"

"That's what we'd like to know," leaning in close and lowering his voice. "They *disappeared*. Nobody knows where they are."

His eyes started filling with tears, and he shouted: "I don't know nothin'! I don't know nothin'!" burying his face in the covers, smacking himself on the head.

Wojcik shouted: "What'd you do?!"

"No!" The boy screamed, thrashing around, hitting himself violently over the head.

Nick started trying to grab his arms, trying to restrain him. He shouted to Wojcik: "Get the nurse!" Wojcik ran out of the room.

Nick got hold of the kid's arms, held him down, the kid fighting, thrashing in the bed.

In a moment, Wojcik ran back in, followed by a nurse and Dr. Wesley. The nurse was carrying a syringe. The doctor helped Turner hold the boy down, while the nurse swabbed his arm and injected him. In another moment the boy stopped fighting and fell back against the pillow. Nick let go of his arms, took a deep breath.

The doctor said: "That's some bedside manner you've got."

Nick didn't get her tone, whether it was angry, sarcastic, what. She was hard to read. He said: "He feels guilty. He's done somethin', and he don't wanna say what it is. Feels too guilty about it."

The doctor said: "Well, try to take it easy on him. He's been through enough already, for God's sake," and Nick heard the anger this time.

"Look, I got two missing kids, might be in danger, and

he knows something about it. I ain't got time to sit around, hold his hand, till he feels like talkin'."

"Well, he certainly doesn't need to be bullied by a couple of—"

"Coupla a what?" Nick stood up, his chest swelling, looking down at her.

She folded her arms across her chest. "Oh, what? Now you're going to brow beat *me*? Take out the rubber hoses and brass knuckles?"

"Rubber hoses? Brass knuckles? What year you think this is? You been watchin' too many old movies."

Wojcik laughed.

She said: "Yeah, well I saw what happened to Rodney King in Los Angeles, or Amadou Diallo in New York."

"Well, this ain't Los Angeles or New York," said Nick. "And we ain't all bullies or—"

"Drunks?" she said, looking over at Wojcik.

Wojcik took a step toward her, fists clenched, and Nick put out a hand to stop him. "You know," he said to her, "I thought you were okay. In fact, I was thinkin' 'bout askin' you out, but now, forget it. You're some kinda cop-hater." Then to Wojcik: "C'mon, let's get outta here."

They walked out the door. She followed and said: "You got a lotta nerve! What makes you think I'd go out with *you*?"

Nick turned around. "'Cause I'm a nice guy, I'm honest, and I treat people with respect."

Even in the dim fluorescent lighting of the hallway he could see her face turn red.

He turned back around, and they left her standing there.

In the parking lot, Wojcik said: "You was gonna ask her out, Nicky?"

Turner said: "Shut up, Dwight."

CHAPTER 11

Monday afternoon Morris was sitting around, nursing his hangover, waiting for the cops to knock on his door, wanting him to come down to the morgue, identify Vince's body. He figured those two thugs probably shot him and dumped him somewhere. He figured at least that'd be the end of it, and he could wash his hands of the whole thing, but Vince finally showed up with some sloppy looking guy named Billy. And man, it was clear they were up to something. This Billy guy was nervous, had this tic, a facial spasm, like he was winking at you all the time. Made him look suspicious, like he was guilty or something. Morris didn't even bother to ask them what was going on, knowing Vince'd just tell him to mind his own goddamned business. Vince just said they'd come back for something, and they left again. Tired of not knowing, and just curious, Morris grabbed his jacket and was out the door, followed them.

They walked straight down 2nd Street, down to

Oregon Avenue, went to a diner. At the house, Vince said they'd already eaten, so maybe they were meeting somebody, someone who had something to do with whatever Vince was cooking up. Morris gave them a couple minutes, followed them inside, sat down in a booth so he could watch them. Ate a piece of cherry pie, wasn't half bad, choked down battery acid coffee. Vince and Billy just sat there, drinking beer, not really even talking much. The dinner hour passed, people coming and going, Morris wondering what the hell he was doing here, wasting his time like this, when he caught Vince and Billy checking out one of the waitresses. At first he thought maybe they were just into her, but she wasn't that great looking, not the kinda girl Vince'd normally go for, and then when she got her coat, Vince and Billy were up, out of the booth, followed her out the door.

Morris followed them out. It was dark now, easy to keep outta sight. They walked west on Oregon, a block or so behind the woman, then went down 5th to Shunk, and west on Shunk a couple of blocks. Eventually, she made a right on 8th Street, walked half a block, and went into a house. Vince and Billy stood there, watching her disappear. The door closed, lights came on inside the house. They started walking again, turned the corner at the end of the block and were gone. Morris crossed the street, walked up to the woman's house. He stood there, looking up at her lighted windows, wondering who she was, and whether he should knock on her door and find out. But what would he say to her: My brother's following you? It was too messed up, she'd think he was nuts, so he memorized the address and went home.

So today, Tuesday, noon, sloppy Billy showed again and picked up Vince in an old black Lincoln. Morris was out the door, hopped into the Nova, but lost them at a stoplight. He drove around a while, ended up back at the woman's house on 8th. Sitting in the car across the street, he was debating whether he oughtta just knock on her door.

Think about it: Why was Vince following this woman? It was a good bet whatever revenge he was planning had something to do with her. No other reason he'd be following her like that, right? What's that mean, though? Means they're going to hurt her. Yeah, but why? What's she got to do with anything? That's what Morris had to figure out.

Across the street her door opened, and she came out. He watched her walk down to the end of the block and go into a carryout. He got out of his car, walked down to the corner, followed her into the store. The place was little, crammed with shelves, racks, and coolers. There was a fat girl behind the counter, late teens, doing a crossword puzzle, watching the soaps on a portable TV. The woman got a soda from one of the coolers. Morris pretended to check out the Tastykakes, got a good look at her. She was in her early to mid-20s, average height, kinda chunky, dark blond hair with a ton of hairspray. She had on tight jeans and a pink T-shirt with teddy bears on it. She walked passed him, put the soda on the counter. "Dollar," said the girl.

The woman gave her the money. "How ya doin', Debbie?"

"Tired," said the fat girl, punching the numbers into the cash register. "You workin' tonight?"

"Yeah, unfortunately." She took the soda and said: "Tell your brother I said hi."

The girl laughed. "I will. See ya."

The woman left without saying anything else.

Morris grabbed something from the rack, put it on the counter. The girl said: "S'at all?"

"Yeah."

"One forty-nine," she said, ringing it up.

He handed her two dollars. "That girl that was just in here . . . she works at the diner, doesn't she?"

"Jeanette? Yeah." She handed him the change.

Morris said: "Thanks," walked out.

Outside again, he watched her go back down the street and into the house. He threw the Tastykake in somebody's garbage, got in the Nova, drove back to the diner. It was mid-afternoon, and he was already late for work, so he found a payphone just inside the foyer, called Enin, lied and said he was still sick, wasn't going to be in tonight. Enin was quietly pissed, you could tell. But screw it, he had too much time invested in this thing already. He wanted to find out what was going on, and help out Vince—keep him from doing something stupid—if he could.

The diner was mostly empty. The place was dark, dark floors, dark wood paneling on the walls, heavy brown curtains on the windows—felt really depressing even in the middle of the afternoon. There were bad paintings of Sinatra and Frank Rizzo hanging on the wall—very South Philly—and the jukebox was quietly playing an old Frankie Valli song.

Morris sat down in a booth. A waitress came over, handed him a menu, set a glass of water on the table, disappeared. He was hungry, but most of the food was shit. No idea why anybody'd eat this way if you didn't have to.

The waitress came back, pad in her hand. "What can I get you, hon?"

Morris looked up at her. She was late 20s, had dark, almost black hair in a bob, just underneath her ears, good looking, soft features, but she had the Philadelphia accent, and had it bad, so that her voice almost contradicted her face. She was wearing a blue dress and a white apron. "What's your name?" he asked her.

"Eva," she said flatly, like a hundred guys had already asked her the same goddamned question today.

"Eva what?"

"Beal."

"Eva Beal?"

"Yep." Career waitress: tough, efficient, and just the right amount of attitude. Flirted with the old guys, was chummy and non-threatening with the women, took shit from nobody.

"Great name," he said.

"Yeah? I always thought it was kinda old fashioned, like somebody's grandma."

"That's what's cool about it."

She shrugged. "So what'll ya have?"

"What's good?"

"Me, I like the fried chicken."

"What else?"

"Meatloaf's not too bad."

"How's the house salad?"

"Good."

"What're you gonna say, right?"

"Yeah," she said, with a hint of a smile, "it sucks, don't get it."

"All right, I'll have that."

"Just the salad?"

"Yeah."

"You on some kinda diet?"

"I look like I need it?"

"No, that's why I'm askin'."

"I just feel like some greens is all."

She scribbled on the pad, and at the same time, said: "French, blue cheese, Thousand Island, Russian, or vinaigrette," as if it were one word.

"Vinaigrette."

"Anything to drink?"

"Just the water."

"I'll be back," and she walked away, with such a conservation of movement and energy that it seemed effortless.

Okay, so what to do here? Maybe ask the waitress, Eva, about this woman, Jeanette, who she is. He had to try and figure out why Vince's following her around. Yeah, but would she even answer those kinda questions? You got to admit it does sound pretty weird.

In a few moments, she came back to the table, set down a small plate with a roll on it and two tabs of butter, and the "salad": iceberg lettuce and one cherry tomato. There was nothing green about it, and it looked like it'd been sitting shrink-wrapped in the refrigerator for a few days. He grinned, looking at it sitting there, and said: "How long you worked here?"

"Six years."

He looked up at her. "You like it?"

She shrugged. "Pays the bills."

"Ever think about gettin' a better job?"

"Yeah, like what? I didn't go to college or nothin'."

"I mean a better waitressing job."

"Like where?"

Tell her about the restaurant, get her interested. "Ever heard of Le Tour de Cochon?"

"No," she said, "what's 'at?"

"It's a restaurant. I'm a chef there."

"Where's it at?"

"Here in South Philly—right off South Street."

She rolled her eyes, "Yeah, right. Nice try, buster. You're gonna offer me some sweet job, and all I have to do is come back to your place tonight, right?"

Man, she was quick, smart. He was starting to like her. "Actually, I did want something, but it's not what you think."

She raised an eyebrow. "Yeah?"

"Yeah, I need some information."

"Information? You some kinda cop or somethin'?"

He laughed. "No, I really am a chef."

"What kinda information? You wanna learn how we make our pork chops?"

He laughed again, not sure if she was kidding. "No, it's about somebody who works here. She's another waitress."

She shook her head. "Nah, I'm not gonna get somebody I work with in trouble."

"It's nothing like that," he said. "In fact, it's the opposite. I'm trying to keep people outta trouble." There was a pause, she stood there frowning at him. He said: "Just give me a chance to tell you what it's about, will ya?"

"All right," she said, "I got a break in about fifteen minutes," and walked away.

There was a bench outside the carwash next to the
diner. They sat down there, watching the cars come out
dripping wet, a crew of Mexicans wiping them down with
rags. Eva looked even better out here in the sunlight, and
somehow she reminded him of an old girlfriend, though
he wasn't sure what it was about her. She took out a pack
of Marlboros, put a cigarette in her mouth, lit it. She kept
staring at Morris, like she was trying to figure out if he was
for real. She had sensual green eyes, and the way she was
looking at him excited him a little. He said: "I like your
hair."

She reached up, touched the ends lightly with her
fingers. "Yeah? It was real long, 'til 'bout three months ago.
I wanted somethin' different, so my girlfriend cut it for
me. I been thinkin' 'bout gettin' a rinse, red maybe."

"I wouldn't."

"No?"

"No, that color's nice—suits you."

"Thanks." She drew on the cigarette, blew out the
smoke. "You know, I don't get you. Minute ago, I thought
you were tryin' to pick me up, now I'm wonderin' if
you're queer or somethin'."

Jesus! Queer? Morris felt himself turn red, and he forced
a laugh. "Why—just 'cause I said you got nice hair?"

"Well, most guys—you know, normal guys—don't talk
about the color of a girl's hair. They'll tell you you got nice
tits or a great ass or whatever, but they won't say your
natural color suits you."

"Maybe you been hanging around with the wrong kinda guys."

"Jesus, you got that right."

"I just think you got nice hair's all. I'm not gay."

"I don't care," she said. "Don't bother me none. This guy I went out with once in high school turned out to be queer. He got AIDS, though, and died. You don't look queer—but you can never tell, right?"

"No, I only like women—believe me." She shrugged, and he said: "Could I bum a cigarette?" She took out the pack, gave him one, then lit it for him. "Thanks," he said, taking a drag on it. It was the first one he'd had in a week and a half, maybe two weeks. He'd been trying to quit. It felt and tasted great.

"So let's have it," she said. "What's the mystery?"

"You know a girl named Jeanette, early to mid-twenties, dark blond hair, kinda heavy, works at the diner?"

"Yeah, sure."

"What's her last name?"

"Carpioli."

"Jeanette Carpioli?"

"Yeah."

"Where's she live?"

Eva knocked the ash off her cigarette. "Not sure."

"Eighth Street?"

"Could be."

Then it hit him: 'Carpioli.' Eddie the *Carp*. He said: "You know someone named *Eddie* Carpioli?"

"Yeah, that's her dad."

"You ever seen him? He come into the diner?"

"Not for a while," Eva said. "He's in jail. Jeanette's

always bitching about having to work, 'cause he's in prison." She paused, drew on the cigarette, said: "What's this about, anyway? You mixed up with her dad somehow?"

"Mixed up, how? What d'you mean?"

"Eddie's mob. Him and Joey Spinoza run Philly."

"No, nothing like that," said Morris.

"Then what is it? You got a thing for her?"

Morris laughed for real this time. "She's not my type."

"So you don't like men, you don't like fat Italian broads. What *do* you like?"

Was that an invitation? He grinned at her. "How 'bout having dinner with me tonight?" She narrowed her eyes at him. "I wanna find out if I can trust you," he said.

"Trust *me*? You're the one askin' all the oddball questions."

"Okay, so maybe I need to prove you can trust me too."

"What—you wanna take me to that place where you work?"

God, imagine bringing her to the restaurant, showing her around and running into Vicky. "No," he said, "not yet. . . ."

She dropped her cigarette stub on the ground. "So that business about gettin' me a job was just a line?" Ground it out with her heel.

"No, it's not that. . . ."

"Where then?"

"Why don't you let me cook for you?"

"At your house? I don't even know your name, for Christ's sake."

"Morris," and he stuck his hand out to her. Still eyeing

him, she took his hand and shook it lightly. "So what d'you say? I'll make whatever you want."

"Lasagna?"

He smiled. "Sure, if that's what you want."

"Okay," she said. "I'll come—'cause I like mysteries, and I love lasagna, but only if the place seems safe. I don't like it, I ain't stayin'."

"Deal," he said. "What time you get off?"

"Seven."

He had a notepad in his pocket. He tore out a sheet of paper, wrote his address on it. Looking at it, she said: "I gotta get back to work now," and she stood up. "I'll be there 'bout eight or so."

He grinned at her. "Okay. See you then."

She started walking away, then looked back and said: "I hope you ain't lyin' 'bout that job," and before he could say anything, she added: "*and* I hope you ain't queer," and turned and walked back to the diner.

At 8:00 the lasagna was in the oven, spinach salad was made, and he'd decanted a bottle of '90 Amarone della Valpolicella, a nice Italian red. At 8:25 there was a knock at the door. He opened it, Eva was standing there, arms folded across her chest, like she was telling him she wasn't putting up with anything—no surprises, no nonsense, no bullshit. She stuck her head inside the door, checking out the place, then came on in. She was wearing blue jeans and a red turtleneck sweater—looked cute, but she wasn't dressed up. Morris felt kind of stupid all of a sudden, standing there in a pressed white button down and his sport jacket, maybe he looked like he thought it was a date or something. Shit. Too late to change now. Maybe lose the jacket.

Giving him the once over, she said: "You look nice," and he felt better and decided to keep the jacket on.

"Thanks. C'mon in." Closed the door behind her.

"Sure smells good in here."

He motioned toward the sofa. "Dinner won't be long. Get you something to drink?"

She sat down, arms still folded. "What d'you got?"

"Beer, gin, or the wine we're having with dinner."

"Yeah, that's fine."

"What—the wine?"

"Yeah."

He went to the table, poured a glass of wine, brought it back to her. "Thanks," she said. "That's a pretty glass."

"I hope you're hungry."

"Starved."

He took a drink of beer, set the bottle down, then went over to the CD player, hit the button. Tony Bennett started singing "Don't Get Around Much Anymore." Morris sat back down, and there was a long pause. He was checking her out, thinking, damn, she is good looking. But it felt a little strange having her here, like they were doing something wrong.

She said: "Who's 'at?"

"The music?"

"Yeah."

"Tony Bennett."

"Oh, yeah? My dad used to listen to him. Hey— where's your TV?" she said, looking around.

He'd taken the broken set down to the basement. "Oh,

it broke. I need to get a new one. I don't watch it much anyway."

She took out the pack of Marlboros. "Mind if I smoke in here?"

"Go ahead." She lit the cigarette, blew out the smoke, put away the lighter. He said: "So, tell me a little about yourself."

"Like what?"

"I don't know. What d'you do for fun?"

"Got an ashtray?" He nodded, went to the bureau, took one out of a drawer, brought it back to her. She said: "I hang out with my girlfriends, go to the movies, see a Flyers game once in a while. What about you?"

"I work a lot, so I don't have a lotta spare time."

"That sucks."

"No, I like it. I love cooking."

"Really? That's great. Wish I had a job I liked."

He said: "Since you're so hungry, we could start on the salad."

She shrugged. "Yeah, sure."

They got up, went to the table. He watched her expression, looking at the place settings. She seemed impressed, but didn't say anything. He served the salad, and they started eating. He said: "So, how well do you know Jeanette?"

"Pretty well. How well do *you* know her?"

"Never met her." She looked over at him and frowned. There was a pause, both of them eating, and he said: "Okay, let me level with you."

She set down her fork, took a drink of wine. "Okay." Waiting for him to spill it.

Man this girl's hard to read. The whole time this afternoon, and now, he couldn't quite figure her out. She seemed interested in what he had to say, but no telling whether or not she'd help him keep Vince out of trouble. And she kept looking at him with those green eyes in ways that, well, made him a little nervous. "I got a brother," he said, "a half brother, who's kinda . . . mixed up."

"Yeah?"

"Yeah," he said, getting up. He went into the kitchen, took the lasagna out of the oven, set it on the counter to cool. Coming back to the table he said: "We grew up in the northeast."

"I was kinda wonderin' where you was from. Sometimes you sound like you're from Philly, and sometimes you don't."

Funny, that's what Vicky said. "Yeah, the northeast," he said. "Anyway, we both got into a lotta trouble growing up, and my brother, Vince's his name, he sorta stayed in trouble. I went straight."

"Became a cook."

"Yeah, a chef. But Vince got involved with some bad people." Morris took a drink of wine.

She said: "What's all this got to do with Jeanette?"

"Thing is, Vince just got outta prison. He was up at Graterford, and he was attacked in prison by—"

"Eddie?"

He nodded. "Yeah, it was Eddie, attacked him. And Vince swore to get even with him. And now I think he wants to hurt Jeanette."

"To get even with what Eddie did to him?"

"Right."

"How d'you know that?"

Morris stood up, took their salad plates into the kitchen. He told himself: You're rushing things, slow down. He took a breath and said: "Well, I don't know for sure, but I saw him following Jeanette, him and this other guy."

"What d'you think he's gonna do?"

From the kitchen, Morris said: "Not sure." He was cutting the lasagna, putting it onto the plates. He carried them out, put them on the table. "What I wanna do is keep him outta trouble, if that's possible—and keep Jeanette from getting hurt, of course."

They both started eating, carefully, letting the lasagna cool. Morris refilled her wine glass—she was drinking fast—and poured some for himself. She said: "So what's this got to do with me? Why don't you talk to him—or maybe to Jeanette?"

He nodded. "Yeah, I thought about that. But Vince'd just tell me to go screw myself, mind my own business, and I'm afraid if I talked to her, she'd just call the cops, and he'd get in more trouble—it'd be some kinda parole violation, you know, conspiracy or something."

"More likely she'd just tell Eddie. The mob likes to take care of their own problems."

"Yeah, of course. That'd be even worse."

"So what d'you want me to do?"

He watched her eating the lasagna, sort of waiting for her to say something—how much she liked it, something like that, the things people usually say. She didn't say anything. He said: "Well, here's what I wanna do: I thought we could keep an eye on the two of them, watch them, make sure nothing bad happens, and keep him outta trouble."

She wiped her mouth on the napkin, and sighed. "I don't know, Morris. It all seems kinda crazy to me. But I guess you're on the level. This'd be some elaborate pick-up scheme."

He laughed. "Yeah, I guess it would."

"Besides you're way too cute to have to go to all this trouble to meet girls . . ." He felt a little tingly rush when she said that, and he washed it down with a drink of wine. "So I guess it's okay—we can try it."

"Thanks," he said, relieved. "I owe you one."

"Yeah, you do," she winked at him. "Only thing is, if it looks like Jeanette's gonna get hurt, I'm gonna say somethin'. I ain't gonna let anything bad happen to her, just to keep your brother outta jail."

"No," he said, "I won't either."

They drank one bottle of wine with dinner, and were almost through the second one, sitting on his sofa, both of them kind of drunk, laughing, getting chatty. Morris was telling her about Enin, what a temper he had. "He's a great chef—he can make the simplest things come alive, make them really interesting, but if anybody makes a mistake, he really goes off on 'em." He paused to take a drink, then said: "The other day he was arguing with the laundry man about some stains in the table cloths, and the guy called him a frog." Eva laughed, head back, Morris started laughing with her. "So he chased the guy out of the restaurant with a meat cleaver."

"Oh, God!" she said. "I seen one of our busboys pull a switchblade one time, but never seen anybody chased with a cleaver. So what happened?"

"Oh, I don't know," Morris said, calming down. "I wasn't really there. Somebody told me about it." He reached over, took the bottle from the coffee table, filled their glasses, killing the rest of it.

"It's good wine," she said, taking out her pack of Marlboros.

"Yeah, it's not bad."

She put a cigarette in her mouth, took out her lighter. "You want one?" offering him the pack.

"Yeah, sure."

She gave him one, lit it, then lit her own.

He took a drag on the cigarette, very deep, let the smoke come out his nose—it felt great, very satisfying, like the one this afternoon, maybe better.

He glanced over at her, thinking she was the kind of girl he would've gone out with when he was younger, before he became a chef, before he changed his life, his direction. In fact he'd gone out with a lot of girls like her, girls from the old neighborhood that looked and talked like her.

He watched her set the cigarette down on the edge of the ashtray, then lean over towards him. "Come here," she said in a warm voice.

He hesitated, looking into her eyes, then down at her mouth. Her lips were stained purple.

She put a hand on his cheek, and drew his face to hers, and kissed him, her tongue flitting into his mouth.

His head was spinning from the wine, and he felt himself getting hard, and he told himself that maybe he shouldn't be doing this, but he didn't pull back.

She bit his mouth, his lips, and ran her hand along his thigh.

He leaned into her. He was giving in, he knew he was giving in, and he pulled her closer, enjoying the feel of her body, her tits rubbing up against his chest.

The phone started ringing. Four times. Five times. Six times. The image of Vicky flashed through his mind, and he tried hard to push it away, concentrating on the way Eva's mouth felt, focusing on her tongue moving against his, and feeling the touch of her hand on the back of his head.

He paused, pulling away from Eva, thinking maybe he should get the phone, but when he reached for it, it stopped ringing.

He turned back to Eva.

She put a hand on the back of his neck, pulled him forward, and kissed him again.

CHAPTER 12

Fingering the gold chain around his neck, Little Johnny said: "You sure?"

"Sure, I'm sure. That fucker won't say shit."

"What'd you say to him?"

Lenny said, for the second or third time: "I told him, he said anything to anybody 'bout us, 'bout them two kids, he was dead."

Lenny was on the hot seat today. It was Wednesday, noon, at Dominic's, Johnny, Lenny, and Mo sitting around a table. Johnny'd spotted a silver Plymouth Acclaim, looked like a South Division unmarked across the street earlier. Maybe coincidence, maybe not. He asked Lenny what he told the kid in the hospital, the one who spilled on his friends, after he drilled him.

"That all?"

Lenny sighed. "I told him we know where he lives. He talks, we'll find him, pop a cap in his ass."

"And you blindfolded him again, takin' him outta here—he didn't see nothin', 'cept the basement?"

"Right. We took him out blindfolded, dumped him down near the stadium."

"Tell me again why you took off the blindfold in the first place."

"I didn't take it off!" Lenny yelled, getting hot now. "Mo did. When I got here, the blindfold was off!"

Johnny leaned forward, elbows on the table, still only looking at Lenny, like any trouble was Lenny's fault. "And you didn't use no names?"

"No, no names. . . ." Then, thinking about it: "Wait a minute. I think Mo used my name." He looked across the table at Mo, the sleepy-eyed fucker, sitting there. "Didn't you? You used my first name, right—when I first got here, front a the kid?" Mo didn't say anything.

"But you didn't mention *my* name?"

"No! Why would I?" Lenny was seriously getting pissed now.

"Mo says you used my name, told the kid Anne-Marie's my niece."

"I did not!" Lenny was starting to sweat. "I swear, Johnny, I didn't say no such thing."

Mo said: "Yeah you did, *stronzo*. You told the nigger the girl is Johnny's niece."

"That's a lie!" Then Lenny started wondering, maybe he did say that. He couldn't remember now. "Anyway, even if I did, he ain't gonna say nothin' to nobody. I told him, he did, he was fuckin' dead!"

Johnny leaned back in the chair, rubbing his fat stomach. "Yeah, you better hope he don't say nothin'."

"He won't, Johnny. Trust me. You want, we could whack him, you know, just to be sure."

Johnny said: "You let us worry 'bout that."

Lenny's heart sank. It was like he was out of the club now—maybe for good. "Sure, Johnny." There was a pause, and he said: "So, what d'you want me to do?"

Johnny sighed. "Go to the store, get me some cigars, will ya?"

Lenny slowly stood up. "What kind you like?"

"I don't know—them Excaliburs, I guess."

Lenny walked out without saying anything.

Mo said: "You see? He don' know what he's doing. Why you put up with him?"

Johnny nodded. "Yeah, he's kind of a fuck-up, but he might be still useful. I'll think about it. Maybe we can use him to tail Vince, keep an eye on him."

"No way," Mo said. "Vince's too smart. I thought you wanted to whack Vince, anyway, kill him during the robbery."

"Not now. If them cops are watchin' us, we can't do it now. He's got too many ties to us. They'd trace him back here in no time."

"So you wanna call off the robbery?"

"Nah, let's go ahead with it. We need the dough."

"You still want me to be there?"

"Yeah, I already told Vince you're in. He was pissed, but fuck him. Now, I tell him you ain't comin', he's gonna get suspicious. Besides, I want you there, keep an eye on things, and keep an eye on *him*. If somethin' fucks up, go ahead and whack him, instead of lettin' him get caught. I don't think Vince'd do two falls for us. But, listen—if you do whack him?—make sure you put his body somewhere it won't never be found."

Mo nodded. "What about the other problem?"

"Yeah, I don't know. I don't think they're gonna do nothin' 'til after the robbery, so we got 'til then to think a somethin'."

"You can't let nothin' happen to her."

Johnny said: "I know. We'll figure somethin' out," standing up. "Right now I gotta use the can," and he walked down the hallway, to the bathroom.

Morris was lying on his sofa, sleepy, staring up at the cracked paint on the ceiling. It was afternoon already, and he kept telling himself: You oughtta get up, do something. Then he'd close his eyes and images of Eva would come to him, the way she looked and felt last night. You couldn't really tell when she was wearing her waitress outfit, but naked she was almost voluptuous, she had hips, and her tits were big and firm. The whole scene kept replaying in his mind: The way she unbuttoned his shirt, kissed his chest, undid his belt; the way she pulled off her sweater, then peeled out of her jeans, nothing but the little black thong underneath. After that there was no way he could hold himself back, and the sex felt dirty, like meeting someone at a bar and doing it in the public toilet, and that made it exciting. And now, thinking about it, he was getting aroused again.

She spent the night and left midmorning. He put together a nice breakfast for her, and she still didn't say anything about his cooking. It was odd—she didn't seem to, you know, appreciate how good it was. It bugged him a little. And it felt a little weird, all of it happening like that, so fast, meeting her at the diner yesterday, doing her last night, but as soon as she left this morning, he started thinking about her. He hadn't showered yet, and he could still smell her sex and taste her in his mouth. And he loved that sensation—the smell and the taste the morning after.

Bad thing was, his stomach didn't feel so great today—maybe it was nerves, and maybe the lasagna last night gave him indigestion. He knew he wasn't going into work again tonight, and not just because he felt bad. He'd decided sometime last night to tell Enin he was taking some time off. He hadn't taken any vacation since the restaurant opened, three years ago, so he was due. No way Enin could refuse. He picked up the phone, dialed Le Tour.

Somebody picked up. A voice said: "Hello, Tour de Cochon." It was Vicky. Morris sat there, silent, holding the receiver. "Hello. . . ? Hello?" and she hung up.

He slowly, carefully put the receiver back. He felt stupid now, like some kinda coward, avoiding her. God, how could he have let himself get so twisted up? What was he going to do—never go back to the restaurant, just to avoid seeing her? That was kid's stuff, really stupid. He told himself: You're gonna have to figure out what you want, to work things out with her or just let it go.

The phone rang, and it made him jump. He stared at it, letting it ring a few times. He answered, almost breathless: "Hello?"

A woman's voice: "Morris?"

"Yeah?" his heart pounding, ready to come out of his chest.

"It's Eva."

Disappointment hit him. "Hi."

"That's all you got to say—after last night? 'Hi'?"

He laughed, maybe forcing it a little. "How you doin'?"

"I'm great," she said, and he could hear her smiling. "It just so happens, I got my clock cleaned last evening."

"No kidding?" he laughed again, this time for real.

"Yeah—some guy I met yesterday, in fact, seemed to really know what he was doin'. How're you?"

"Okay. My stomach's a little upset. I think it was the lasagna. How d'you feel?"

"Fine—didn't bother me at all."

"Good. You at home?"

"No, I'm at work already. I wanted to tell you, Jeanette's here, so she's okay."

"Good. Vince's still sleeping."

"Yeah? I heard him come in last night—least I think that was him."

"Yeah, I heard him too. I'm gonna see if I can find out what he's up to today."

"Well, let me know if you find anything out."

"I will."

"I better get back to work," she said. "Just wanted to say hi."

"All right." The image of her underneath him, the way she felt, the way she tasted, was running through his mind. He was getting very hard. "Say, Eva—"

"Yeah?"

"You interested in maybe. . . ."

"What?

"I don't know, I just. . . ."

"Want another taste, do ya?" she said, her voice dropping, getting husky.

"Yeah, I think I would."

"You keep makin' lasagna, I'll keep comin' over."

"Okay," he said and hung up.

He lay back down on the sofa for another half hour, then told himself to get his ass up, make some coffee. He didn't like just lying around, being idle, had to keep busy, doing things. He went into the kitchen, ground the beans, poured the water. There was a knock at the front door. He walked into the living room, looked out the window, didn't want to be surprised by those two thugs. It was Billy, standing there on the stoop. Morris opened the door, told him to come on in, said Vince was still sleeping.

Billy came in, closed the door behind him. "I hate to wake him up, but he said to come by around two. What time is it, anyway?"

Morris looked up at the wall clock. "Quarter past. You want some coffee? I just put some on."

Billy stood there, rubbing his belly. He looked unkempt, just like the other day, dressed in dark blue polyester work pants and a stained white short-sleeved shirt, untucked and unbuttoned over a Phillies T-shirt. "Yeah, I guess so. Sure."

Morris went into the kitchen, poured two mugs. "How do you take it?"

"Black's fine."

He came out, handed Billy the mug. "Sit down. I'm Morris, by the way. Vince's brother—half brother, really. We didn't meet the other day."

Billy sat on the sofa. "Yeah, Vince said he's stayin' with

you." He took a sip. "That's good coffee—way better'n I make."

"Thanks."

They sat there for a moment, looking at each other. Morris reached over to the coffee table, grabbed a pack of cigarettes Eva left behind, put one in his mouth, lit it. He was wondering if he could pump this guy for some information about what's going on, what Vince was planning. Billy said: "So, you're a cook?"

"A *crook*?"

Billy laughed. "No, I said *cook*."

"Oh, *cook*," and Morris laughed too. "Vince tell you that?"

"Yeah."

Morris was surprised. He wouldn't have thought Vince'd talk about him to his friends. "I'm a chef," he said.

"A chef? Oh, he said cook."

He took a drag on the cigarette, blew out the smoke. "I don't think he really knows the difference."

"Yeah, prob'bly not. Vince'd just as soon eat Twinkies as anything else. Where d'you work?"

"At Le Tour de Cochon."

Billy whistled. "No kiddin'. I heard a that place—my parents used to eat there. They always said how nice it was."

"Yeah? Who's your parents. Maybe I know 'em."

Billy's cheek twitched. "Uh. . . . My dad, he's dead now . . . he was William Hope?"

"Oh, the surgeon. Yeah, I knew him . . . wait a minute, didn't he—"

"Yeah," said Billy, "he killed himself."

"Oh, I'm sorry, sorry for bringin' it up."

"S'okay." Billy took a sip of coffee. "So, you like it?"

"Like what?"

"Workin' at that restaurant?"

Morris reached over, pulled the ashtray toward him. "Yeah, I like it. I've got a lot of freedom there to experiment with my cooking, play around, come up with new things."

"You like to make up new things when you cook, not just, like, follow a recipe?"

"Yeah, that's the best part of it. Actually, I'd like to have my own place, so I could experiment all the time, continually change the menu. People get tired of eating the same thing over and over again. You need to have variety, you know, somethin' different once in a while."

"When were you born?"

"When was I born?"

"Yeah, when's your birthday?"

"February Fourteenth."

"No kiddin'? Valentine's Day. You're an Aquarius. That makes sense. Aquarians are very creative."

Morris grinned. "Yeah?"

"Yeah. And they're idealistic and independent, sometimes aggressive, and they like to argue."

"So you're into astrology, huh?"

"Yeah, mostly just for fun, though. When I want real advice, I don't bother with it."

"No?"

"Nah, then I go to Wilhelmina—she's a psychic."

The guy was *serious*. Morris dug his fingernails into his palm to keep from laughing. There was a pause, and they could hear Vince overhead, moving around. Morris took another drag on the cigarette, knocked off the ash. "Sounds like he's up." Billy nodded. Morris glanced up the stairs and lowered his voice: "So what's Vince been up to these past coupla days?" and he noticed the left side of Billy's face start jerking again, like he was winking, involuntarily. Man, something was going on.

"Maybe you oughtta ask him 'bout it."

"He won't tell me, and I don't want him to get in trouble."

Billy shrugged nervously and looked away, taking another sip of coffee.

In a couple of minutes, Vince came down the stairs, dressed. "Shoulda woke me up," he said to Billy.

"I only just got here."

Morris said: "You want somethin' to eat?"

Vince was putting on his jacket. "Nah, we gotta get goin'."

Billy said: "Where we goin' first?"

Vince said: "The Greek's, get things ready."

Billy said: "I gotta get some gas."

"We'll do that on the way."

Morris watched them starting to walk out the door, and he was debating whether to follow them. He had an idea who "The Greek" was: Ted Cosmatos, an old friend of Vince's, owned a TV repair shop. Why would they be going there? Maybe it had something to do with what Vince was planning. Yeah, and maybe he was just fixing Vince's radio or something—or Vince was going to ask him for a job. Let's hope.

Morris went to the window, watched them get into

Billy's Lincoln, looked over at his jacket hanging there, wondering if he should grab it, follow them, when his phone started ringing. He answered it: "Hello?"

"Morris?" It was Enin's voice, that high-pitched, nasal French accent.

"Hi, Enin."

"You coming into work tonight?"

"I was getting ready to call you. I want to take a few days vacation time."

"Vacation? We're too busy. It's not a good time—you know that."

"Yeah, well, I need the time off."

Enin's voice seemed to go up an octave: "You're avoiding Vicky aren't you?"

"What?"

"What did you do to her? She's been angry, *très abattue*—how you say?—depressed, very bitchy lately. What did you do to her?"

"Look, Enin, I don't wanna go into—"

"Let me tell you, you better get in here, straighten out things with her, and get back to work!"

Morris was starting to get pissed. He didn't like to be told what to do. "Yeah? Or what?"

"Or you find another place to work—*tu comprends?*"

Angry now: "Yeah, I understand. Go fuck yourself," and he slammed down the receiver.

CHAPTER 13

It was late, and Franks was edgy. No sleep in 48 hours, and he hadn't done any blow in—how long? A week? Couldn't even fucking remember now. He was jonesing bad, kept himself going popping bennies, smoking crack. He was running out of snitches and junkies, people to lean on for the coke. If it went on any longer he was just gonna have to go to New York and fucking *buy* the shit. But that would take money— real money, which was scarce right now, too. That's why he needed to find Vince Kammer. The fucker had those diamonds from Cohen Jewelers, from the robbery four years ago. Two hundred and fifty grand worth. If Franks could get his hands on them, that'd be a happy fucking payday. Buy a lotta shit with that kinda money.

He was cruising North Philly, up past Temple Hospital, no man's land on a Thursday night. Bums, winos, whores walking the streets, here and there some psycho shouting about Jesus. He was looking for a couple of dealers he knew, worked this neighborhood. Chances are they'd be dry too, but it was worth checking out. He pulled over to the curb, took his pipe out of the glove box. Only two rocks left, he put one in the bowl, fired it up. His hand shook holding the lighter. Jesus Christ. This shit eats your fucking brain. Gotta score some of the good stuff. Gotta score them diamonds.

He finished the rock, put the pipe back in the glove box. Laid his head back on the rest. Tried to close his eyes, but his heart was racing, and those images came back to him—evil shit, knives, blood, heads blown apart, shredded flesh. He shivered, then opened his eyes, sat back up straight. It was just the dope talking, but it was pretty fucking ugly, kept him up.

There was a knock at the window. He looked over. Some black whore, round here they call them Rockettes or Rock Stars, glittery gold mini, purple tube top, knee-high vinyl boots, a Supremes wig. He rolled down the window, she leaned on the door edge, sniffing the pipe smoke. "Hey, baby, wanna party?"

Yeah, right, a $20 junkie whore with HIV written all over her. He said: "Know where I can get some blow?"

She smirked. "Shit, sweetheart, where you think you at? This ain't Society Hill."

"You know Nathan Crawford, calls himself Naughty Nate?"

"Yeah, I know him."

"Seen him around?"

"He got busted, baby. Doin' hard county time."

"Shit. How 'bout Ronald Wilson?"

"Don't know the man. C'mon, why don't you and me have a little party, all by ourselves, make you feel good."

"Beat it." He started the car.

Desperation in her voice now: "C'mon, just lemme smoke a little with ya. I need that kryptonite bad."

He looked back over at her. "Yeah, how bad?"

"Real bad. I do anything, baby."

"*Anything?*"

She grinned. "You know it, sugar."

He grinned back. "All right." He looked around then pointed out toward the sidewalk. "See that dog shit layin' there?" She glanced over, then nodded. "Pick it up."

"What you talkin' 'bout, baby?"

"You heard me—pick up that dog shit, bring it over here."

She crinkled her nose, looked at him incredulously. He nodded to her, and she walked over and picked up a dog turd, brought back over to the car. He said: "You'll do anything for it, right? So eat that dog shit."

"You jokin'!"

"No, I ain't. Ain't you never heard a scatological fetish?" She shook her head. "That's when a guy gets off watchin' chicks play around in shit, eat shit, whatever. That's me."

"Ah, c'mon. You ain't serious, baby."

He took out his stash, showed it to her. "Only one rock left, and sweetheart it's a white fucking tornado. You eat that shit, it's yours." He rattled it around in the vial.

"C'mon, ain't there somethin' else I could do? You wanna fuck me in the ass?"

"No. Nothin' else I want."

She looked at the dog turd. "Ah, man."

"Thought you wanted it," and he started to put it away.

Desperate: "Wait a minute. Okay, I'll do it."

He grinned. "All right, but you gotta swallow it."

"What if I get sick?"

"You ain't gonna get sick," and he rattled the vial again. She frowned, then raised the dog shit to her mouth, bit into it, cringed, gagged. Franks, laughing, said: "All of it!" She put the rest in her mouth, chewed, gagged, swallowed.

Walking around in a circle, spitting, she said: "Ah, god-damn! That's some nasty shit! I think I'm gonna puke."

Franks laughed, head back. "All right! Good for you!" He pulled his badge, showed it to her. "By the way, solici-tation's a no-no. Consider yourself lucky—next time I'll bust you," and he put the car in gear and pulled away. He heard her running after him, screaming: "You asshole! You fucking asshole!"

He laughed again, shook his head, said: "Stupid bitch."

CHAPTER 14

Friday afternoon, April 14th. The weather had turned warm the past few days, and the sun was out. Vince and Billy were sitting in a stolen Ford Taurus on a side street, next to Mickey's, a bar on Packer Ave., just a block from "the Linc," the new stadium where the Eagles play. Packer's a long, wide street, and from Delaware Avenue to Broad Street it's lined with food packing plants, the Turf Club, the parking lot for the Linc, and a Holiday Inn. There are also exits for I-76 and I-95, plus it's near the Walt Whitman Bridge, leading over to Jersey. Perfect for a quick getaway. This end of Packer, near Broad, was business and residential. There were some houses, an Italian restaurant, and the bar. Sitting there, watching the place, they had everything they needed: gloves, ski masks, and two Colt Python .357s—no serial numbers. Just waiting now for Mo to show up. For some reason, Johnny Stacks insisted he be there, said it was a three-man job. Vince didn't like it. He didn't trust that guinea fuck, and what the hell did Johnny Stacks care if Mo was there anyway, so long as he got his money? It was like he was trying to keep an eye on the two of them. Something about it stank.

Sitting behind the wheel, Vince looked over at Billy. "Relax."

"I'm okay."

"Yeah? Your face's jumpin' like crazy. Just take it easy."

"I sure could use a drink."

"Afterwards. Remember, this ain't no big deal. Like you said—it's easier'n most of 'em we done."

"I wasn't gonna say nothin', I know how you think it's stupid, but my horoscope today said—"

Vince cut him off: "C'mon, Billy, those things are a load a shit."

Billy sighed. "Okay, I won't say nothin'. . . ."

"I mean, think about it: How could the position of the planets when you're born have any effect on your life, what happens to you day to day?"

"But Vince, there's things scientists can't explain."

"Like what?"

"Like . . . I don't know. Like what happened to the dinosaurs, or why some people get cancer."

"So because scientists haven't figured out why people get cancer, you think we should believe, what?—Mars and Jupiter control our lives? That don't make too much god-damned sense, Billy."

"We just don't know everything, that's all. That's all I'm sayin'."

"Well, look, why planets? Why not rocks or telephone poles or, I don't know, butterflies?"

"What d'you mean?"

"What I mean is, you ain't got no reason to pick one of 'em over the other. If all you got to go on is, scientists don't know everything, you got just as much reason to think butterflies control your life as you do thinkin' the planets control it."

"C'mon, Vince, that's stupid—how could *butterflies* control your life?"

"They can't, Billy, that's what I'm tryin' to tell you—they can't and neither can the planets."

Billy frowned. "I don't know. Somehow the planets seem different."

"Yeah? Why?"

"I don't know. But astrologers got it all worked out. I mean, you should see these charts and tables and shit they got—books full of 'em."

"Yeah, and nobody's ever made a chart a somethin', didn't make no sense or was wrong?"

"Yeah . . . I guess so."

"Look, Billy, today?—let's keep an eye on Mo. I don't know why that fucker's gotta be in on this job, and I don't trust it."

Billy looked over at him. "Yeah, I thought about that, too. It's kinda weird, ain't it?"

"Yeah, and remember, don't say nothin' 'bout the broad or the other job. All right?"

"Yeah, sure. So we're gonna do this, then go grab her?"

"Yeah, after she gets off work. Then we can go have a drink someplace."

"You decided, you know, what you're gonna do with her?"

Vince said: "I got a coupla ideas. First things first, though. We don't need to worry 'bout that right now," and he pointed to a car coming down Packer Ave.

Both of them watched Lenny's copper-colored DeVille pull up to the corner. Mo got out of the passenger side carrying a black gym bag, and Lenny pulled away.

Vince looked over at Billy. "Remember—keep an eye on him."

Eva came by after she got off last night, and he made manicotti for her, they drank a lot of wine again, and then he fucked her. He really wanted to this time. She didn't have to seduce him, he went after her, and they made love half the night. Both so exhausted from all that screwing, they didn't get up until late in the morning. The time they spent together was all about eating and drinking and fuck-ing, nothing else. It was pure pleasure, like he didn't have to worry about feelings or entanglements or commit-ments, like there weren't any consequences—both of them knowing it wasn't anything permanent. And there was hardly any of that weird feeling anymore, that feeling that they were doing something wrong. Yesterday Morris was still brooding about Vicky, wondering whether he should call her—after what Enin said, that she was depressed, upset, bitchy. It was like he was paralyzed, not knowing what to do, and that really bugged him. But since Eva got here last night, he hadn't thought about her at all—well, not much anyway.

They were just finishing up brunch. Morris had wanted to make a quiche for her, but Eva wouldn't let him go to the market, said it was stupid going all that way when they had food in the house. She insisted they have the leftover manicotti—there was plenty of it left. It was what she wanted, so he heated it up.

Sitting there in his bathrobe, Eva pushed her plate away, took out a cigarette, gave one to Morris—he was smoking with her after every meal now—and lit them both. She said: "God, it's so nice out. Wish I didn't have to go to work."

"Yeah? What would you do if you didn't have to go in?"

She raised an eyebrow at him. "Hmmm. . . ."

"God!" he said. "You're insatiable!"

She laughed. "You complaining?"

"Not at all. It's just, you're gonna wear me out."

"Hey, I'm the one's gotta go to work. You can lay around all day."

"I'm gonna collapse, what I'm gonna do."

"Fine," she said, fake petulant, blowing out a cloud of smoke, "I'll take my clock elsewhere to be cleaned."

He grinned at her. "Now, let's not be hasty. . . ."

"Good," she said, "I don't know who'd feed me like this, anyway," sweeping her hand over the table, cigarette between her fingers.

"Oh, so you actually like it? Jesus, I was wondering if you were ever gonna say anything." He rolled his eyes.

She laughed. "You're so funny. I never met anybody so particular about food. Most of the guys I go out with're happy havin' McDonald's, and none of them's ever cooked for me before. I don't know anybody can cook like this. 'Course I like it. In fact," she said, stubbing out her cigarette on the plate, "I like all of it—*a lot*."

She slipped off her chair, took a step toward him, and scooted him out from the table, then knelt down in front of him, hands on his thighs. He was wearing only a T-shirt and a pair of boxer shorts, and he started getting excited immediately. She rubbed her hands up and down his thighs, watching the bulge in his shorts grow. "Mmmm. . . ." she said, looking at it, and she slipped the bathrobe back off her shoulders. She had nothing on underneath. She grabbed him through his shorts, and looked up into his eyes. "Don't look like you're too tired to me." He grinned at her, and she took it out, bent down, started licking it, then put it in her mouth. He grabbed her head, ran his hands through her black hair, caressed her cheeks.

As she was going down on him, he reached over, stuck his fingers in the tomato sauce on his plate, lifted her head, and spread it on his cock. She grinned. "Is this my dessert?" He nodded, and she started licking off the sauce, carefully, deliberately, with long strokes, moaning at the same time. He leaned his head back, shutting his eyes. It was pure, distilled pleasure, verging on pain. When he felt like he couldn't take it anymore, he grabbed her, lifted her up, and bent her face forward over the table, pushing aside the food and dishes. A hand on her back, holding her down, he entered her quickly, thrusting hard, the dishes and silverware rattling. Her moans turned into little cries. Morris kept thrusting, pounding her, the table shaking, food spilling off the plates. He felt her contracting around him, his head spinning, he started coming, and she screamed. A few more thrusts and they were both quiet, breathing hard, lying across the dining table, knees weak, sated.

★   ★   ★

The traffic was as clear as it was going to get. The three of them got out of the car, walked to the bar, wearing gloves, carrying the masks, pistols tucked in their belts. Mo had a sawed off double-barreled shotgun under a gray overcoat. Stepping up to the door, they pulled the black ski masks over their heads. Vince said: "We got the plan, right? You let me do the talkin'." He looked at Mo. "And no shooting, unless it's absolutely necessary—understand?" His face was covered now—all you could see were those dark, sleepy eyes and his thick lips. He nodded, slowly.

Vince and Billy took out their pistols, Mo dropped the overcoat, they pushed open the door. Vince called out: "Nobody move! This's a robbery!"

It took a second for their eyes to adjust to the darkness, coming in from the afternoon sun. There were four people: Three guys sitting at the bar and the bartender. Two of them at the bar were younger, in their 30s, and fat—guts bulging under dirty T-shirts. The third was old and grizzled, sloppy drunk, head down on the bar, looked like a wino. The bartender was in his mid-40s, receding dark brown hair, big pork chop sideburns, wearing a white shirt. They all had their hands up, except the wino.

They spread out, and Vince said: "You three, get over there," motioning toward the wall on the right. The two fat ones got up off their stools, hands up, walked over. "Now, sit down!" They sat, and Vince said: "You, too, Pops!" The wino was glassy-eyed, maybe too drunk to get what was going on. Billy went over, grabbed him by the collar, pulled him off the stool, dragged him over to the table, the wino mumbling something incoherent.

Vince yelled out: "All right, let's all be cool, and everything's gonna be okay!" He turned toward the bartender and recognized him. Shit! It was Charlie Sims. Vince knew him—they used to run together before he hooked up with Billy, pulled a few jobs together. Goddamn, he'd be sure to recognize Vince's voice. Well, fuck it, there wasn't anything to do about it now, and Charlie wouldn't rat him anyway. Right? They were tight in those days, no bad feelings. Charlie would keep his mouth shut. "Mr. Bartender, keep them hands up where I can see 'em!"

Mo went around, other side of the bar, found the .357 the owner kept there, stuck it in his belt. He led the bartender out from behind the bar with the shotgun.

Vince said: "Now you're gonna open the safe, motherfucker."

The bartender was scared. "But I ain't got—"

Vince cocked his pistol, pointed it at him. He could feel the sweat dripping down the inside of his mask. "Don't give me no shit—I know you got the combination. I also know you got the Friday paycheck money. I ain't the guy you wanna fuck with—believe me!"

The bartender said: "Vince? Vince—that you?" Mo stepped up, put the shotgun barrel against the guy's cheek. "All right!" he cried out. "Okay, I'll open the safe. Just don't hurt me. Vince? I don't wanna get shot. I'll open it, whatever you want, no problem!"

Vince said: "Just show us where the safe is."

Billy kept his gun on the customers. Vince and Mo followed the bartender down a short hallway to an office.

Inside, the guy flipped on a light switch. The dark green room was windowless, small and cluttered. A desk, two chairs, hat rack, papers all over the place, boxes stacked against the wall, and a floor safe. Mo pushed him with the shotgun barrel toward the safe. He got down on one knee, started spinning the dial. "I ain't gonna give you guys no problem—don't you worry 'bout that none," he said, nervously, his voice cracking. "Lotta fuckin' money in there—this's a good score for you guys, no shit."

Mo said: "Shut up and open it."

He made a few turns with the dial, they heard a click, and he pulled on the handle. It came open, and Mo grabbed the guy, pushed him up against the wall, held the shotgun on him. Vince bent down, pulled two bank bags out of the safe, looked inside.

Mo said: "Is there?"

"Yeah, it's here. He's right, looks like a good score."

Mo said: "Good," and he pulled the .357 out of his waistband and shot the bartender twice, the noise deafening in the little room. The guy was blown back against the wall and fell to the floor. Mo shot him again lying there, and laid the gun on the desk.

Ears ringing, Vince yelled: "What the fuck you do that for?!"

"He knew you."

Billy was yelling down the hall: "What's goin' on?! Vince?!"

Vince said: "Let's get the hell outta here."

They walked quickly down the hallway, the two fat guys were cowering in their seats, the old man passed out on the floor.

Out the door, stripping off the masks, guns tucked away. No cars coming, Vince threw the keys to Billy. "You're drivin'." They got into the Taurus, Billy started it, peeled out, made a right, down Packer Ave. toward Front Street.

Billy: "What happened?"

Vince pulled his Colt Python, spun around, pointed it right at Mo. "Why the fuck you shoot him?"

Mo, calm: "He knew you, could identify you."

"You shoulda let me worry 'bout that. I told you, god-damn it, no fuckin' shooting! Didn't I tell you?"

"It was necessary."

"The fuck it was!"

"Everybody know you tied to me and Johnny. You get caught, we get caught."

Billy: "Who was it?"

Vince: "Charlie Sims, guy I used to hang with—a good guy. Didn't fuckin' deserve to get shot like that."

Billy: "We never shot nobody before."

"I know. He dies, and it's the fuckin' gas chamber."

Mo: "Welcome to the big time."

"Yeah, you may think this's funny, motherfucker, but I don't. I oughtta fuckin' waste you right now. Leave you for the cops to find."

"Yeah, an' then Johnny find *you*."

Billy: "This's bad. Man, this is real bad."

They turned off Front Street, onto Oregon Ave. After the big UPS building, this side of Oregon's virtually deserted all the way to Delaware Avenue and the docks. When they got to Delaware, Vince said: "Pull over," still pointing the gun at Mo. Billy stopped the car. "Now, get out, motherfucker. I had all I can take a you today. Leave the shotgun and the money. Tell Johnny I'll get hold a him when I'm good and ready." Mo looked like he was going to say something, and Vince cocked the pistol. "You better not say nothin's gonna piss me off. I'll do you right now." Mo opened the door, got out, without saying anything, shut the door. Billy pulled away, leaving him standing there.

There were already four cruisers, two unmarked cars, CSU vehicles, and an ambulance at the scene when Dick Franks pulled up in front of Mickey's Bar. The Channel 6 and Channel 10 news vans were there, Channel 3 and Fox on their way, no doubt. Franks found out this morning he was back on the job—cleared of all suspicion in the Webber shooting, made out to be a hero in the media— God, he loved it. Nobody could fuckin' touch him—not the Commissioner, not I.A.B., nobody. Even got a few hours sleep last night, but he was still shaky, still needed some coke bad.

Slomann and Busch were handling the Mickey's Bar robbery/homicide. The L.T. told him to get down here, help out with the interviews. He got out of the Plymouth, made his way through the police line, into the bar. Inside, Dave Busch—a big black guy, mid-30s, thick moustache, looked like he could play for the Eagles—was talking to the customers, two fat South Philly looking types, and one old drunk. Busch put his hands on his hips, seeing Franks walk in, and his huge frame seemed to swell. "What you want here, Franks?" in a booming bass voice.

"Where's Slomann?"

"In back."

"That where the shooting took place?"

"Yeah—now, what you want here, Franks? Look like you slept in the gutter last night."

"Hartmann told me to come down, help out," and he flashed Busch that patented Dick Franks toothy grin. Busch just shook his head, frowning. Franks walked past him, down a short hallway to an office. Slomann was there, the M.E., and a CSU evidence tech, all three kneeling over a body on the floor, blood everywhere. There was a safe, opened. "What d'you say, Jimmy? Robbery/homicide— don't get much more exciting than that, huh?"

Slomann stood up, a couple inches shorter than Franks, but just as broad. An ex-college football star, he had pock marks on his face, a large bulbous nose, and thinning sandy brown hair. "What you want, Franks?"

"Who's the DB?"

"Charlie Sims—know him?"

Hell yeah, he knew him. Franks busted him a few years ago for armed robbery, but 'lost' some evidence for a cut, and Sims walked. It was a merry Christmas *that* year. "I heard of him," Franks said. "Hartmann said I should come down, give you boys a hand."

"Go help Dave with the interviews."

Franks said: "Right-O," giving him a little salute.

Back out to the bar. Busch was taking notes in a note-book, the customers just sitting there. A uniform was trying to get the old man to drink a cup of coffee. He kept pushing it away, the coffee spilling. Franks chuckled. Busch glanced over at him like he was pissed. Franks said: "What d'you want me to do, Dave?"

"Interview the old man."

Franks laughed. "This fuckin' drunk? I doubt he remembers his own goddamned name, much less what happened this afternoon."

"Yeah? Well ask him anyway."

The old man's head was down. Franks tapped him on the shoulder. "Hey, old timer, you hear me?"

He mumbled: "I hear you."

"Then look at me."

He raised his head, shaking, his eyes bloodshot. "What? What's this all about? Who are these people. . . ?"

"You see what happened here today?"

"I seen it! I heard it!" His head went back down.

Franks tapped him again. "What'd you see?" No answer. Louder: "What'd you see?"

He mumbled: "Men . . . and horses. Galloping, running crazy."

Franks sighed—the guy was ready for the psycho ward. "What men? You know any of 'em?"

The old guy lifted his head again, looking around like he was trying to focus. "Yeah . . . yeah. It's the man who said, the man who . . . seizes. . . ."

"What? Drink some a that coffee. You ain't makin' no sense." Franks pushed the cup toward him."

He looked down at the cup, then up at Franks, his eyes wide. "It's the man who knows, the one on the corner who don't need no introduction . . . got a wine bottle in his pants, a glass for a hand, map of the universe in his head, a tattoo of the queen around his ankle. . . ."

Franks said: "What the fuck?"

"—he says it was a present from insane gods, but I don't

believe him. In that condition, he'd say anything. . . ." and his head went back down.

Franks looked over at Busch. "I hope you got all that down—some important evidence there," and he walked over, leaned up against the bar. Felt like a drink, but he knew Busch would be pissed if he took anything.

Busch ignored him, turned back to the other two witnesses. "So you said they came in, and they was three of 'em?" The two fat guys nodded. "And they was wearin' ski masks, carryin' pistols."

The one in the orange T-shirt said: "No, only two of 'em had pistols. The other had a shotgun."

Busch said: "So the one of 'em only had a shotgun?"

The other guy, looked like a trucker, wearing a red ball cap and an unbuttoned flannel shirt, said: "No, I looked up and seen he had a pistol tucked in his belt."

Orange T-shirt said: "I didn't see no pistol."

The Trucker said: "Well, he had one, tucked in his belt."

Busch said: "Okay, so they came in, then what happened?"

Orange T-shirt: "The one of 'em said, 'this's a robbery,' then told us to get over to the table against the wall."

The Trucker: "'Cept Wally here," nodding toward the wino, "was too far gone to understand what was goin' on. So the one of 'em comes over, grabs him, drags him over there."

Busch: "The one that was talkin'?"

The Trucker: "No, another one, the shorter one."

Orange T-shirt: "Yeah, it was the shorter one."

Franks sighed. This was starting to get boring. He took out a penknife, started cleaning his nails. His hands were shaking too bad, kept jabbing himself. He put the knife away again.

Busch said: "Then what happened, after you were over here, the short one drags Wally over—then what?"

Orange T-shirt: "Then the one was talkin' says to Charlie: 'Now you're gonna open the safe.'"

The Trucker: "No, first he said, 'Be cool, and everything's gonna be all right,' then he said to Charlie: 'Now, open the safe.'"

Busch: "So what did Charlie do?"

The two of them looked at each other. The Trucker said: "Well, he kinda acted like he wasn't, you know, gonna cooperate."

Orange T-shirt: "Yeah, that's sorta how it seemed. But then the one talkin', he cocks that big pistol and tells Charlie. . . . What'd he say?"

The Trucker: "He said somethin' like, 'I know you can open the safe, so don't give me no shit.'"

Orange T-shirt: "Yeah, it was somethin' like that. And he said he knew about the paycheck money."

Busch: "Paycheck money?"

Orange T-shirt: "Yeah, Mickey keeps money on hand every other Friday to cash the guys' paychecks—you know, guys come in from the plants. I forgot to say that earlier."

Franks raised an eyebrow. "Lotta money?"

The Trucker: "Have to be—they's a lotta guys in here on Fridays, wouldn't you say?" looking over at the other man.

Orange T-shirt: "Yeah, Friday's always packed. They'd have to be a *lotta* money."

Busch took out his notebook, wrote something down. "All right, then what happened? Is that when Charlie seemed to recognize the one of 'em?"

Orange T-shirt: "Yeah, that's when Charlie called the one guy 'Vince.'"

Franks stood up straight. Holy shit: Charlie Sims used to run with Vince Kammer. Now, that's a hell of a coincidence—Vince just getting out. This was Vince's M.O., too—an out of the way bar, ski masks, everything except the third man and the shooting. He said: "Repeat that."

Orange T-shirt looked at him. "Yeah, he called the one who was talkin' 'Vince.'"

The Trucker: "Like he recognized his voice or some-thin'."

Busch looked over at Franks. "That mean somethin' to you?"

Franks: "No, nothin'. I just couldn't hear what he said, was all," and he laughed to himself. Goddamn, this was perfect, picture perfect. Vince's out, he's got those diamonds, and now a shitload of cash from a goddamned robbery/homicide. He was just asking to be leaned on. To Busch: "So, you got things covered here?"

Busch sarcastically: "I think we'll manage. What—you got someplace to be?"

"Yeah," said Franks, "I gotta see somebody," and he walked out.

Billy got in the passenger side. "Okay, she's coming." His face was dancing like crazy.

Vince said: "Good. So we follow her 'til she turns off Oregon—right? And then we look for a chance to grab her." They were sitting in the stolen Ford Taurus, in the parking lot of the diner. 8:15 P.M. It was dark now. "Try'n calm down, will ya? You're makin' me nervous." He handed him the pint bottle of Jim Beam, almost empty. Billy uncapped it, took a long drink, belched.

In a moment Jeanette Carpioli walked out of the diner, down the steps, across the parking lot. Vince started the car, gave her a few seconds head start, and pulled out of the lot, making a left onto Oregon. The street was busy on Friday night, lots of activity, cars and buses going in both directions.

He passed her, then pulled into a gas station to let her catch up. They watched her walk past, then make the right onto 5th Street by the bank. Vince pulled back out onto Oregon, made the right turn. 5th was jammed all the way to the stop sign at Shunk. Billy had his head out the window, keeping an eye on her. He brought his head inside, saying: "It's too busy. Vince? It's too busy!"

"Don't worry 'bout it—it'll be clearer on Shunk."

They made it to the stop sign, made the left onto Shunk Street. It was almost empty. Vince passed her. Excited, Billy said: "What you doin'?" turning around, looking at her. "You passed her. What you doin'?!"

Vince drove down to the corner of 7th Street, pulled over. "Now, get out. She comes along—you'll be waitin' for her. I'll drive around the block, be coming up from behind." Before Billy could object or ask another question, Vince said: "Go!" and Billy opened the door, climbed out.

Vince made the turn, raced down 7th Street, made the right at Porter, then came back up 6th. He made the right back onto Shunk, and crept along. She was halfway down the block now, between him and Billy.

A car came up behind him, lights in the rearview. He pulled over, let it pass. Now it was clear. He pulled the black ski mask down over his face—and hoped to God Billy remembered to put his on.

She was almost to 7th now. Billy was out of sight, around the corner. Vince pulled up to the corner, just as she got there. Billy jumped out, ski mask down, pistol drawn, pointed at her. She threw up her hands and screamed. Vince reached over the seat, opened the back door. "Get in!" he yelled.

Lights hit him from behind—somebody was coming.

"Get in, goddamn it, or you're dead!"

"Don't hurt me!"

Billy stepped forward, grabbed her, she screamed again, he started pushing her into the car. Vince checked the rearview—the car was coming, halfway down the block. He leaned back over the seat, grabbed her, started pulling her into the car. Billy was pushing her. She kept screaming.

A couple of kids turned the corner up on the next block, coming this way.

Vince: "Get in, goddamn it, right now, or you're dead!" pulling on her.

The car still coming, almost on top of them, lighting the whole scene with its headlights.

They got her in the car, Billy followed her in, slammed the door. She was crying: "What d'you want?!"

Vince threw it in gear, hit the gas, making the turn down 7th, made the right on Porter.

She was yelling, crying.

Vince: "Keep her quiet!"

Billy stuck the pistol in her face. "Shut up! Just shut up!"

Vince: "Keep your goddamned mouth shut, or he's going to fuckin' cap you right now—got it?!"

Jeanette was sobbing uncontrollably.

Billy said: "Shut up, will ya? *Please*, just shut up."

Vince said, quietly, to himself: "Everything's gonna be okay now. Everything's gonna be o-kay."

It was just after 9:00 P.M. when Turner and Wojcik made it to the scene: Race and Delaware, underneath the Ben Franklin Bridge. The site was swarming with uniforms and CSU personnel. Flood lights had been set up, illuminating the whole area. At the police line, Turner grabbed an officer he recognized, Frank Delgrazo. "Frank—where's Henry? He's in charge, right?"

Delgrazo nodded. "Yeah, he's over with the M.E. They just got done movin' the bodies," and he hooked a thumb over toward the river.

They ducked under the yellow police tape, made their way over to the center of activity. Ryan Henry, South Division homicide detective, was standing there, talking to a CSU evidence tech. Approaching, Turner said: "Ryan—Hartmann said you may've found our kids, Bucknor and Ohal."

"Yeah, maybe. Have a look." He nodded toward the two sheet-covered bodies.

Turner took a couple of photos out of his pocket. They knelt down by one of the bodies and pulled back the sheet. Wojcik said: "Looks like Ohal."

Turner nodded. "That's him. How 'bout that one?"

Wojcik pulled back the other sheet. "Bucknor?"

Glancing at the picture, Turner said: "Yeah, our boys, all right." They re-covered them, stood back up. He said to Henry: "Execution?"

"Yeah, one in the back of the head, each."

Turner and Wojcik looked at one another. Turner said to Henry: "Hartmann detached us to homicide, said to give you a hand, if these're our kids—and they are."

Henry: "Good—I can use the help. What d'you got so far?"

Turner: "On Monday we got the missing persons call, did some interviews. Haven't figured out the connection yet, but these two assaulted a girl—Anne-Marie *Decongelio*—'bout two weeks ago, fled the scene, were never apprehended. There's a third kid, involved some-how, in the hospital. Somebody really put the screws to him, and we think he gave up his friends—but he ain't talkin'."

Henry: "The girl's name's Decongelio?"

"Yeah."

"Why's that sound familiar?"

"Don't know. Weird thing was, family wouldn't talk to Special Victims. Girl gets assaulted, they don't wanna do nothin' 'bout it."

Looking back at the bodies, Wojcik said: "Looks like they handled it themselves."

Turner said: "We ain't certain 'bout that yet," wanting to be careful, thorough.

Henry called out: "Delgrazo!" and he motioned for the officer to come this way. Delgrazo walked over. Henry said to him: "Name 'Decongelio' mean anything to you? Anne-Marie Decongelio—juvie female?"

Delgrazo said: "Anne-Marie? Ain't that the daughter of Angela Decongelio? I think it is."

Turner: "Who's Angela Decongelio?"

Delgrazo: "Sister'a Johnny Staccardo."

Turner felt shivers go up his spine. "Johnny Staccardo? Little Johnny Stacks?"

Delgrazo: "Yeah."

Wojcik: "Johnny Stacks?—well, I'll be damned."

Henry: "I thought he was just into bookmaking, extortion. I didn't think he did shit like this," pointing toward the two bodies.

Turner: "First time for everything."

Wojcik: "You know them fuckin' guineas." Turner saw Delgrazo look over. He elbowed his partner. Wojcik caught the look, shrugged. "Sorry," he said.

CHAPTER 15

Saturday morning Franks was wired. No sleep again last night, and he'd smoked the last of the crack. Since the Mickey's robbery yesterday afternoon he'd been looking for Vince Kammer, searched everywhere, all his old haunts, asking everyone he could track down. It was like the fucker'd disappeared. No sign of his old partner, Billy Hope, either, which might mean he was in on Mickey's too. Franks was gonna try Sonny Jackson's again, see if Superfly had the inside dope. Sonny blew a little weed, but was never known to use serious drugs, so there probably wasn't any point to leaning on him for some coke. Franks pulled up in front of Sonny's apartment, 11th and Bainbridge, got out of the car, rang the bell. Coupla minutes the door opened, Sonny peeked his head around, sleepy-eyed. Franks pushed open the door, stepped inside, shut it behind him. The living room was bare, pale blue walls, old green carpeting, a sofa, chair and a TV, a box of Cap'n

Crunch sitting on the floor. Franks said: "Remember me, Sonny?"

Yawning: "Shit, yeah, Franks. You something of a Philly legend."

Franks smirked. "Where's Kammer?"

"Vince? Don't know, man. Ain't seen him since he got out."

"Where's Billy Hope?"

"Beats me. I ain't seen him for weeks. Fucker owes me money, too."

Franks nodded. "You wouldn't be blowin' smoke at me, would you, Sonny?"

"Nah, man. I ain't seen neither one of 'em."

Franks threw a quick jab into Sonny's gut, he doubled over, sucking wind. Franks grabbed his arm, twisted it behind his back, pushed him toward the kitchen. Up to the counter, Franks slammed Sonny's hand down, held it in place, pulled a heavy chopping knife out of a butcher block sitting there, pressed the blade against two fingers. "Now, motherfucker, where's Kammer!"

Sonny, gasping: "Swear, I don't know, Franks. I saw him last week, but he didn't tell me nothin'!"

Franks, pushing on the blade, breaking the skin, blood trickling. "Gonna be tough hotwirin' them cars, no fuckin' fingers! Where's Kammer?!"

Sonny, panicked: "Okay, Franks, okay! I think he at his brother's."

"You think?"

"He didn't say nothin'. That's just what I heard!"

"Who's his brother?"

"I don't know, man. He straight, not in the life!"

"Where's he live?"

"South Philly—I don't know where."

"You ain't shittin' me?"

"No, man, no!"

"You know what happens, I find out you're lyin'."

"I know, I know!"

Franks pressed harder, Sonny yelled. Franks: "Say it!"

Sonny, sweating: "I lyin', you take my fingers!"

"You believe it?"

"Fuck yeah, I believe it!"

Franks pulled back on the knife, let him go. "Good. Then we understand one another." Sonny cradled his cut fingers. Franks threw down the knife, walked out.

Morris slammed his fist down on the kitchen counter, shouting: "Goddamn it!" He was making *poussin à la confiture d'oingons*—baby chickens in an onion compote, a kind of sweet stew, and he couldn't get it to turn out right. It was so goddamned easy he could show a busboy how to make it, and it tasted like shit. How hard could it be? Butter, onions, sugar, and some dry red wine. It was the right consistency, like jam, but something was off. He thought: This isn't helping. Usually cooking helps you clear your head, think about things, you do some of your best, most level-headed thinking when you're cooking. But you're all over the place, your mind's still cluttered, you don't know what the hell you're doing. Why didn't Vince come home last night? I don't know. Yes you do, you know very goddamned well why he didn't come home. He's done something with that girl, the waitress. You tried Billy Hope's number earlier, and he wasn't there either. You called Ted Cosmatos's TV repair shop—Vince said the other day they had to stop by there and 'get things ready', right?, wasn't that what he said?—and all you got was a message saying the place was closed until the third week of April. Him and Billy did something with the girl, they grabbed her and took her to the repair shop. Gotta be. So what're you gonna do? Something happens to that girl, it'll be your fault. Yeah, why? 'Cause you knew he had something planned, and you didn't say anything, you didn't do anything. If she's dead, how're you gonna live with that? You know who you should talk to, don't you? Vicky. She always knows what to say. She's a smart girl, that one. And man, did you mess that whole thing up. You shoulda never banged Eva. C'mon, that's not true, there's nothing wrong with Eva. She's fun, the sex was dynamite. You just shoulda never yelled at Vicky, losing your cool like that. What the hell's wrong with you?

He tasted the compote again. It was too sweet, what it was. He walked over, threw the whole thing into the garbage, pan and all. Stood there a minute, fuming, started to punch the wall, then stopped himself. He reached into the trashcan, pulled out the pan, took it to the sink. Started running water into it.

The phone rang.

He shut off the water, went into the living room, answered it brusquely. "Yeah?"

"Morris?"

"Yeah."

"It's Eva."

"Oh. . . . How you doin'?"

"Okay. Listen—Jeanette didn't show up for work today—"

Well that's it. Vince's done it now. "Shit."

"They called her house, no answer. Called her mother's house, nobody knows where she is."

"Goddamn. Vince didn't come home last night."

"Oh, shit. . . ."

"Yeah."

"What d'you think happened?"

Morris said: "I'm not sure, but I got an idea where they might be."

"Yeah?"

"I heard Vince say something the other day about an old friend of his, guy who owns a TV repair shop."

She said: "Who is it?"

"His name's Ted Cosmatos—"

"*Cosmatos?*"

"Yeah, he's Greek—a friend of Vince's, and Vince said they had to stop by there and get some things ready, something like that. Only the place is closed. I called there today, and they're away on vacation a whole month."

"So what d'you think—they took her there?"

"I don't know, could be. Tell you what—I'm gonna find out. I'm goin' over there. Maybe if he's got her, you know, they kidnapped her or something, I can talk some sense into him, before they hurt her, get themselves into somethin' they can't get out of. If they're not there, then. . . ."

"Then what?"

"Then we gotta call the cops."

"Well, let me know if you find out anything, will ya?"

"'Course."

"Listen, call me before you call the cops, okay? Just in case she shows up or somethin'—all right?"

"Yeah, sure." The thought flashed through his mind that he'd like to see her again, that he wanted to ask her to come over. He thought: Let it go, let her go, just drop it, forget it, if you wanna have any chance of straightening things out with Vicky.

There was a knock at the door. He said: "Somebody's at the front door. I gotta get it."

"All right," she said. "And Morris?"

"Yeah."

"I really did like your food." There was something final in her voice.

"Thanks," he said, wondering a little at her tone, and hung up.

He walked through the living room, opened the door. A guy was standing there, looked like a cop, self-assured, smug look on his face, except that his eyes were bloodshot, and he looked like he'd been through the ringer. He was big, must have been six three or so, broad shoulders, thin blond hair, wearing a blue sports jacket, white shirt, blue and red striped tie, and khaki's. Morris said: "Yeah?"

The guy flashed him a stupid grin. "Hi-a. Vince Kammer here?"

Morris frowned. "Who wants to know?"

The guy pulled out a badge. "Detective Franks, Philadelphia P.D. How 'bout if I come in?"

Morris felt his heart skip a beat and stepped aside, opening the door wider. "Yeah, all right."

Franks came inside, closed the door behind him.

★   ★   ★

Lenny'd never seen Johnny this pissed before—pissed *and* worried. They were at Dominic's. Johnny kept walking around the dining room, rubbing his fat stomach, saying: "Anything happens to her, that's my ass!" his voice raspier than usual.

Mo was sitting at a table, calm as always, smoking cigarettes. Lenny kept following Johnny around, trying to calm the fat guinea down. He kept thinking there oughtta be some way to turn this to his advantage—you know, help Johnny out here, get himself back in the club, outta the doghouse.

Johnny said: "Goddamn, why didn't we have somebody watchin' her? We shouldn't a listened to that fuckin' broad—put a tail on her anyway. What the fuck we getting for the money we're payin' her, anyway? Ain't like she's been followin' the girl around, watchin' her any place but at work. And Mo—goddamn it, even though I said not to whack Vince, you was supposed to be watchin' him!"

Lenny grinned—it was the first time he'd heard Johnny give Mo any kinda shit at all. This was fucking great.

Mo didn't say anything, of course, the sleepy-eyed fucker, sittin' there, drinking his fucking espresso, like there was nothing going on.

Lenny said: "Calm down, Johnny. We'll find the fuckers. We'll get her back—they ain't got the balls, really do anything to her."

Johnny turned, looked at him. "That's Eddie the fuckin' Carp's daughter. I was supposed to be lookin' out for her.

Eddie's part a the family! Them was direct orders." He belched, rubbing his stomach.

Lenny said: "Jesus, Johnny, take a breath. Sit down—everything's gonna be okay. We'll find those fucks. They don't know we know they grabbed her, right? They don't even know we're supposed to be lookin' out for her. So they ain't gonna be lookin' out for us. Okay, so we ain't found 'em yet, but there's only so many places they can be, right?"

Johnny sat down, a table away from Mo—Lenny couldn't help but grin. "Goddamn, I hope you're right, Lenny." He took out a handkerchief, wiped his forehead.

"Sure, I'm right—you'll see. You said you gotta go talk to Joey later, right? Tell him what's goin' on?"

"Yeah—shit, I ain't lookin' forward to that."

"Okay, so tell him we're on it. All right? Calm yourself down, and we'll talk this thing over, work up a plan, get her back. We ain't got this whole thing wrapped up by the time you leave to go see Joey, I'm sure when you get back we'll work it out, find out where those fucks took her."

Johnny belched again. "We gotta think a somethin'."

"Yeah, sure we will. Look, they gotta contact us 'bout the robbery, right? Split up the money? They do, then we know where they are. Plus, I'm sure she's okay. Think about it—Vince and Billy? Man, they're thieves, but they ain't never killed no one. They ain't gonna do her. What'd Mo say 'bout Vince when he saw that bartender get whacked? Vince was all freaked out—right? He ain't got the balls for it. Ain't that right, Mo?"

Mo just sat there, silent. He took a drag on his cigarette, blew out the smoke, the piece-a-shit guinea fuck.

Lenny said: "Maybe get Sonny Jackson in here. He's gotta have some idea where they are. Gimme a coupla minutes alone with that big spook, I'll find out where they're at," and he chuckled. "So, calm yourself down—you know, maybe eat somethin', then we'll work out a plan."

Johnny let out a loud fart, then sighed. "No, I don't think I could eat nothin' right now."

"Well, don't worry 'bout Joey none. He's reasonable—right? They ain't gonna whack you for this."

Johnny looked up at him suddenly. "Jesus."

"You got nothin' to worry 'bout."

Johnny got up slowly. "I gotta use the can," and he went down the hallway, to the restrooms.

Lenny watched him disappear around the corner, then sat down at the table, across from Mo. Mo said, in his quiet way: "How you gonna find them, *stronzo*?"

Lenny shrugged. "I don't know. We'll figure somethin' out. Only so many places they could be—right?"

"You like to talk, but you don' never *say* nothing, you don' never *do* nothing. A man think about things, and he act. He don' keep talkin' all the time, like some woman."

The phone started ringing.

Lenny couldn't believe his fucking ears. "So what you sayin'—I ain't a real man?"

"If you are, you don' act like it."

There was a pause, Lenny staring across the table at him, seeing red, beyond pissed. He'd had all the ball busting he was gonna take from this fucking wop. Nobody talked to him like that—*nobody*. The phone kept ringing. Mo took a drag on his cigarette, said: "Make yourself useful, *stronzone*, go answer the phone."

Lenny felt his hand twitching, wanting to pull the Smith & Wesson. And he heard a clock all of a sudden start in his head. Tick, tick, tick. He could see the second hand moving. Tick, tick, tick. Another word, say another word, please, give me an excuse, and I'll shoot you through the eyes, Johnny or no Johnny. Give it to me! Tick, tick, tick.

He took his eyes off Mo, looked down at the table, grabbed his gun hand, held it back. Not now. It's not the time or the place. You'll get your chance—later.

He stood up slowly, walked over to the bar, answered the phone. Hello? Tick, tick, tick. The voice on the other end of the line gave him the answer.

He hung up, re-tucked his black shirt, straightened his black jacket, then walked back over to Mo, grinned at the guinea cock sucker. "Tell Johnny I'm goin' out for a little while," and he turned and walked out the door.

He'd only been here two minutes, but this cop sitting on the sofa in Morris's living room came across as a real asshole. He had a self-satisfied air and a constant smirk on his face, like he knew he was gonna get what he came here for. Morris was thinking: What's the deal with this guy? Acts like he's stoned. And what the hell does he want with Vince? Don't tell him anything about the girl, the waitress, before you get a chance to talk to Vince. Maybe you can still help him keep outta trouble. If he goes right back to prison, that'll finish him, no doubt about it.

Morris handed the cop a mug of coffee, and sat down on the easy chair, next to the sofa. He grabbed the pack of Marlboros, took out a cigarette, lit it. He glanced over, saw the cop's hand shaking. Franks sipped the coffee and set down the mug. "So you don't know where Kammer is?"

"No, he didn't come home last night, and he hasn't called."

Franks grinned. "Let's cut the shit, all right? Mr. Morris Aaron White. You got a juvenile record—sealed of course, and three arrests as an adult—one weapons charge, one disorderly conduct, one criminal possession of marijuana. Two charges dismissed, no big deal, coupla joints in your pocket, whatever, *but* you drew parole for the gun."

"That was a long time ago." He took a drag on the cigarette.

"Yeah, but you ain't exactly no virgin, now are you?"

Morris felt himself getting warm. "What's this about?"

"I think you know where your brother is. I think you know all about what he's been up to."

"Half brother—and you're wrong, I don't know what he's been doing. He only got out of Graterford last week, didn't have a place to stay, so I let him stay here 'til he gets settled. I've hardly seen him." Annoyed, he stubbed out the cigarette in the ashtray.

Franks sat forward and straightened his tie. "So you don't know nothin' 'bout his little adventure yesterday?"

Morris swallowed. Oh, shit, here it comes. "No."

"Your brother and a coupla buddies held up a bar down by the stadium, killed a guy in the process."

Eyes wide. "Jesus Christ!"

"Yeah, that's right. And it wouldn't take much to convince a DA you was involved in the whole thing."

"What're you talkin' about?!"

"Oh, conspiracy, concealing evidence, harboring a

fugitive. I could probably even swing it so's you were there."

"That's bullshit!" Morris jumped out of the chair, and the cop was up off the couch, slammed a fist into his stomach. Morris doubled over, the wind knocked out of him, and the cop stuck a gun in his face. "Sit your ass back down." Trying to catch his breath, Morris lowered himself back into the chair, his heart beating like crazy, wondering what the hell was the matter with this crazy son-of-a-bitch. "Now," said the cop, "you're gonna tell me everything you know."

Morris took a deep breath, the pain shooting through his gut. "I swear—I don't know anything."

The cop was still standing over him, that gun in his hand. His breath stank. "Let's start with who he's been hangin' out with."

Morris thought quickly. "Coupla guys came around one day. I never seen 'em before."

"They have names?"

"Uh . . . Lenny, I think, was one. The other one was. . . . I don't remember."

"What'd they look like?"

"One was average height, in his thirties, dressed in black—that was Lenny. The other was kinda fat, foreign, maybe Italian, dark hair, dark skin, heavy-looking eyes."

"Mo," said the cop. "Lenny and Mo?"

Morris said: "Yeah, that's right," hoping he wasn't getting Vince into any more trouble.

"What'd they want?"

"I don't know, but they took Vince with 'em."

"*Took* him?"

"Yeah, the one in black, Lenny, had a gun. They came in one day last week, woke Vince up, led him out the door."

Franks smirked. "Yeah, I can imagine what they wanted."

Morris looked at him. "What?"

"Same thing I want—them diamonds."

"Diamonds?"

"Don't fuckin' play coy with me. You know exactly what I'm talkin' 'bout. Them diamonds from Cohen Jewelers, place Vince robbed four years ago. *I* was the investigating officer, and them diamonds was never recovered. Word on the street was Johnny Stacks set up that robbery—Lenny and Mo work for Johnny. Inference to the best explanation: Vince has the diamonds, and Johnny wants his cut."

Morris thought about it a second. "He always said he never got those diamonds. He split. The police showed up before he could get them."

Franks grinned. "Yeah, and you and me know better, don't we? Vince held out on Little Johnny—big mistake. But good for me. Now listen careful: Here's the deal, all right? Vince hands them diamonds over to me, and I'll find somebody else to hang this Mickey's robbery/homicide on—fact, I got somebody already in mind, just perfect for the rap. Otherwise, Vince's goin' down, but big time, and you with him. The Governor'd just jump at the chance to sign a couple more death warrants—makes him look tough on crime."

Morris felt his chin drop, amazed. He couldn't believe the balls on this guy. "And what's to keep me from callin' the *real* cops, telling them about this conversation?" The asshole.

Franks laughed. "First, you wanna save your brother—don't you?" His voice dropped. "And if you so much as think of telling anyone," jamming the gun back in his stomach, "I'll cap you without even thinking about it." He leaned down close, breathing that shit breath into his face. "You believe me, don't you?"

Morris looked into his bloodshot gray eyes. "Yeah, I believe you."

Lenny pulled up outside the TV repair shop. Tick, tick, tick. Still pissed at what happened this afternoon. He didn't know exactly what he was going to do here, didn't have a plan. He just knew he was going to help out Johnny, whatever it took. Get their take from the robbery, let the girl loose, whatever. Only Vince and Billy'd better not give him any shit. He'd had all he was going to take today. Tick, tick, tick. Gina busting his balls this morning about not going to her mother's. Then Johnny sending him out for lunch, like he's some kinda goddamned errand boy. And Mo the guinea ball-buster saying he wasn't no real man. Tick, tick, tick. Jesus good God, enough is enough.

He reached over, opened the glove box, took out the snub-nose .38. Getting out of the Caddy, he tucked it in his belt.

There was a sign on the door saying the place was closed until the third week of April. Lenny peered through the steel grating covering the window, didn't see anybody.

He walked around to the back of the place, through a side alley.

After all, there's only so much a man can put up with—only so much he should *have* to put up with, right? What'd that fucker Mo say? A man don't sit around, talkin' about shit—he just does it. He got that right. Mo's a fucking greaseball asshole, but he knew what he was talking about when he said that.

Lenny turned the corner. Billy was standing there at the back door, balancing two carryout bags on his arm, trying to unlock the door. Lenny stood there and watched him fooling with the keys. Billy hadn't spotted him.

All of 'em—Gina, Mo, even Johnny—thought they could do or say whatever the fuck they wanted to him, order him around, insult him, and thought he wouldn't do nothing about it. Tick, tick, tick. Gina fucking coming on to Mo the other day, right in front of him—can you believe that bitch? And Mo saying that shit, he was gonna fuck her till it came out her mouth—what the fuck kinda guinea shit is that? And that nigger cutting him off in traffic the other day, and his Ma buying him blue socks, and fucking Christina laughing at him. Everybody fucking against him, everybody laughing, having fun with him. Tick, tick, tick. All of it just fucking adds up. He wasn't getting no respect, and it gets to a guy after a while, and he just has to say, 'Enough.' Enough, goddamn it, enough!

Billy got the door open. Lenny walked up behind him, followed him into the back room. Vince was sitting at a table, drinking a beer. The girl was laying on a sofa, maybe asleep. Billy set the carryout on the table. Vince looked this way, surprised. He said: "What're *you* doin' here?"

Tick, tick, tick. Lenny drew the .38 and shot him in the face, the report crazy loud in the small room. Vince was blown out of the chair, back against the wall. Billy turned, in shock. Lenny shot him in the stomach. Billy doubled over. Lenny shot him again, through the shoulder, then again in the groin. Billy collapsed onto the floor.

The girl was sitting up on the sofa now, hands covering her ears, shaking. "Who . . . who're you?!" she yelled.

Lenny looked over, could barely hear from the ringing in his ears. The clock had stopped ticking. "I'm Lenny," he said. "Lenny Deuces."

CHAPTER 16

Saturday afternoon: On the way to questioning Johnny Staccardo, a.k.a. Johnny Stacks, they stopped for burgers. Turner couldn't get his down, tossed it, just drank cold coffee, a little milk in it. Wojcik wolfed down two double cheeseburgers, fries *and* onion rings, then made his third trip to the can today, came back to the table belching Jack Daniels and Certs. They rolled.

Johnny Stacks ran his bookmaking and loan shark-ing out of a legit dago restaurant called Dominic's. So far Johnny'd managed to weasel out of every charge the Organized Crime Unit laid on him, every indictment the D.A. hit him with. Turner wanted this collar so bad he could taste it. He wanted to wrap up the Bucknor/ Ohal shooting without stepping on anybody's toes, maybe get a transfer into Homicide, permanently. He didn't want to say anything to Dwight, you know, hurt his feelings, and he didn't want Dwight fucking up this case. He loved the poor, broken-down fucker, but he was about ready to be sent out to pasture. Nick's career was just getting started.

They pulled up outside the restaurant in the unmarked Plymouth. Wojcik took a sip of coffee, said: "I hear Johnny Stacks is a big fat bastard, goes 'bout three hundred."

Turner looked over. "Yeah?"

"Yeah. You know how guineas love them cannolis and shit."

Turner, pissed: "Well, keep a lid on that shit when we're talkin' to him, will ya?"

Wojcik looked back, confused. "What'd I say?"

"Nothin'. It's just we don't wanna give this fucker anything. We need to keep him off balance, but we don't want him pissed off. 'Cause then he'll clam up, and we'd have to try'n get a warrant. It'd just complicate everything. Know what I mean?"

"Yeah, sure, Nicky. No problem." Wojcik paused, then said: "You want him, don't you?"

"If he drilled that kid? Capped Bucknor and Ohal? Yeah, I want him."

Wojcik grinned. "We gonna take him down, Nicky?"

Turner grinned back, letting go of the anger. "Like Easy Dora's pretty pink panties."

Wojcik slapped him on the back, laughing.

They got out of the car, walked into the restaurant.

Wojcik was right. Johnny Stacks wasn't so goddamned "little." A big, fat fucker—275, 300, easy—dressed in an expensive-looking blue silk suit. Him and another guy, looked Italian, heavy eyes, dark skin, alone in the restaurant. Seeing them come in, Fat Man said: "We ain't open."

Turner flashed his badge. In his hardass voice: "That's good, 'cause we ain't hungry. I'm Turner, this's Detective Wojcik." They walked over to the table. "You Johnny Staccardo?"

Fat Man looked at Sleepy Eyes, then back at Turner. "Yeah."

"We'd like to ask you some questions."

Staccardo belched. "Yeah, okay," his voice like gravel.

Turner looked at Sleepy Eyes. "Who're you?"

He took a drag on a cigarette, blew out the smoke. In a thick Italian accent: "Erasmo."

"Erasmo *what?*"

"Pacitti."

Wojcik snorted. Sleepy Eyes looked over at him. Nick ignored it. "You work here?"

Sleepy Eyes, slow, like he was cautious about everything: "Yeah."

"In what capacity?"

"*Capacity?*"

Wojcik: "What the fuck do you do?"

Sleepy Eyes: "Manager."

Wojcik: "*You're* the manager here."

"Tha's right."

Turner and Wojcik still standing, Turner said to Johnny Stacks: "Like to ask you about your niece."

Johnny Stacks, hinky nervous: "Yeah? Which one? I got a couple of 'em."

"Your sister Angela's daughter."

"She got two daughters."

"I think you know which one I mean."

"'Fraid I don't, officer." He belched again, rubbing his stomach.

"*Sergeant* and I think you do. Your niece was assaulted two weeks ago."

"You mean Anne-Marie."

Wojcik said: "That's the one."

Turner: "We got a record of a 911 call. The girl was sexually assaulted by two black juvenile males."

Johnny Stacks: "Yeah, my sister told me 'bout that."

Wojcik: "*Now* he remembers."

Johnny: "So what d'you wanna know?"

Turner: "A detective from Special Victims contacted the family, but they refused to talk to him, didn't want to file charges, said if the offenders were apprehended, they wouldn't prosecute."

"Yeah, so?"

Wojcik: "'*Yeah, so*'? That's all you got to say? Coupla niggers try to rape your niece, your sister don't wanna press charges, and all you say is 'yeah, so'?"

Johnny: "Hey, look, I got on 'em 'bout pressin' charges and shit, but you don't know how it is for a little fifteen-year-old broad like that. They're all sensitive and shit, you know, about their bodies. They didn't hurt her or nothin', not really, so her mother and my brother-in-law, they wanted to spare her any more, you know, further embarrassment." He belched again.

Turner walked around to the side of the table, leaned over one of the empty chairs. "Yeah, I can kinda see what you're sayin', but then I been thinkin', what if this wasn't random? What if these punks knew who she was, picked her out to fuck with her on purpose—see what I mean? Then if the parents don't do anything, don't file charges, get 'em brought in, then what's to stop 'em from doin' it again?"

Johnny: "Hey, I tried to tell 'em that. They didn't wanna hear it."

Turner sighed. "Only so much you can do, right? Bein' the uncle?"

Johnny flashed a nervous smile. "Yeah, sure."

Nick: "But then, you see, the story don't end there."

"No?"

"No. See the two kids who attacked your niece? Somebody clipped 'em."

"Yeah?"

"Yeah. Execution style."

Wojcik: "One in the back a the head, each."

Johnny raised an eyebrow. "No shit?"

Turner: "No shit."

Johnny: "Well, can't say I'm sorry to hear it." He lifted his leg, let out a loud fart. "Little fuckers deserved it."

Turner: "Yeah, well think about it. Coupla kids mess around with Johnny Stacks's niece, right? The family refuses to press charges, we can't figure out why. And then the two kids end up dead, whacked—*Italian* style. Little suspicious, ain't it?"

Johnny: "Hey, if they did shit like that, you know, fuck with little girls, who knows what else they was into—you know? They coulda been into all kinds a shit, drugs, whatever, right? You know how them niggers are. Mighta been all kinds a people wantin' to do 'em." He pulled out a handkerchief, wiped the sweat off his fat neck.

Turner smiled. "Yeah, well, you can see why we'd wanna come talk to you, right?"

Johnny: "Yeah, sure. I understand."

Turner looked over at the other one, Sleepy Eyes,

Erasmo. "Don't you ever say nothin'?" He drew on a cigarette, blew out the smoke, shrugged.

Turner looked over at Wojcik. Wojcik shrugged too. "Guess he ain't got nothin' to say."

Nick: "Yeah, maybe." Looking back at Johnny Stacks. "So, you clip them kids?"

Johnny, emphatic: "No! 'Course not. Jesus. I don't do that kinda shit. This's a legit business," sweeping his hand around the dining room. "Man, you fuckin' cops're all alike. You see an Italian, you think he must be mob. Jesus Christ, *vaffanculo!* Gimme a fuckin' break." He belched again.

Turner, standing back up straight again: "Yeah, maybe you're right. You know, you got some nasty-ass indigestion there. Oughtta have it looked at."

Staccardo: "Yeah, somethin' I ate, I guess."

Turner nodded at Wojcik. They walked toward the door. Nick looked back. "Hey, Johnny."

"Yeah?"

"You never asked how we knew them kids was the ones, assaulted your niece."

"Huh?"

"Yeah, they was never caught. Family didn't fill out a complaint. So how'd we know when we found them two bodies, they was the ones?"

Staccardo stared at him, belched loudly.

Turner laughed. "Thought so! See ya 'round, Johnny."

They walked out.

Lenny was strangely calm. I mean, he was excited and shit, but he wasn't nervous. Behind the wheel of his copper-colored DeVille, Eddie Carpioli's daughter in the seat next to him, a big bag of cash in the back seat, he felt good, really good. He didn't think about it, didn't plan it. He just knew what had to be done—it was the way Mo said, a man don't talk about it, he acts. And, man, did Lenny act. He clipped those two fuckers before they could say shit to him. You see Vince? He was all set to give Lenny some kinda shit again—like the other day in the car, making fun of him, saying he was using the wrong words and shit. Well, he didn't say nothin' today, didn't get two words out, Lenny drew that .38 snubby, capped him, shot him right in the face, then did Billy. It was perfect. He used the .38—like he was supposed to—didn't leave any prints anywhere. Nobody saw him go in or out. And, then—did you hear it? She asked him who he was. Fuck, it was like a goddamned movie, like somebody'd written the lines for her to say. Sitting there, bawling, crying and shit, hands over her ears, 'who are you?' God that was great. 'Lenny,' he told her, 'Lenny *Deuces*.' See, and this way it works out so much better, now she knows his name, she'll tell everyone how it went down. Wouldn't a worked anyway with those two niggers, since he'd a had to cap both of 'em, so it's just as well Mo did 'em. This way, he had a witness. He just wished Mo was there to watch the whole thing, the fuckin' guinea ball-buster. Lenny woulda capped him too, while he was at it. Watch Billy go down, then turn, put one right between that fucker's sleepy eyes—show him who's a *stromboli*. Anyway, Johnny's sure as shit gonna hear 'bout this—hopefully she'll tell him herself, so he won't have to. Sounds better coming from somebody else, so it don't sound like you're just bragging or whatever, right? Shit, she's sure to tell her old man, fuckin' Eddie the Carp, maybe even Joey. Christ, maybe Lenny can move up, get into Joey's crew. Whatever happens, ain't no way he's gonna do anymore goddamned gofering, going for lunch, picking shit up at the store. Them days are over.

He looked over at the girl. She was kinda fat, not too good looking. She still looked scared, like maybe she was in shock or something. Lenny said: "You okay?" She had her head leaning up against the car window, didn't say nothing. "Them guys hurt you?"

She turned her head this way. "No."

"That's good."

She ran her eyes over him, up and down, like she was checking out his black clothes. "Joey send you?"

"Yeah, well, sorta . . . I mean, not directly. I work for Johnny Stacks, he got the order, and I sorta carried it out."

He grinned at her, waiting for her to thank him, you know, blubber and shit about how he saved her life, how she owed him. Man, too bad she wasn't better looking, he'd let her show her gratitude another way. He laughed to himself, glanced back over at her. She had her head against the glass again. Didn't look like she was gonna say nothing, thank him or anything. Maybe she was in shock. Well, fuck it, long as she tells everybody what happened, seal his rep.

As he pulled up in front of Dominic's, he saw two guys come out, get in a silver Plymouth, drive away. Lenny frowned, wondering what that was about. He got out of the car, took the bag of money, led the girl up the sidewalk, inside.

Mo was standing at the bar, pouring shots of sambuca into cordial glasses. He dropped a couple of coffee beans into each one. Johnny was pacing back and forth. Lenny said: "What's goin' on?"

Johnny looked over, saw the girl. Lenny expected him to be happy, shake his hand, pat him on the back—somethin'. But that ain't what happened. He said: "What's this? What the fuck is this?" like he was in shock, too.

Lenny grinned. "I went and got her. Here's the money," offering up the bag.

Johnny put his hands on his fat hips. "Did you see them two just walked outta here?"

"Yeah. Who was they?"

"Who was they?" Johnny looked over at Mo, then back this way. "I'll tell you who they was—cops, fuckin' detectives, askin' all kinds a questions about them two niggers. So how's that gonna look, you come walkin' in the front door carryin' a bag a stolen fuckin' money?"

"I didn't know they was gonna be here."

Softening his voice, Johnny said to Jeanette: "You okay, sweetheart? Them fuckers hurt you?"

She walked over to the bar, took a stool. "I'm okay. Need a drink, though." Mo poured her a shot.

Johnny patted her on the back, said: "Don't worry, them fuckers'll get theirs."

Lenny chuckled. "Already got it."

Johnny looked this way. "What? What d'you mean? Where are they?"

Lenny folded his arms across his chest, waiting for the broad to spill it, tell his story. Standing at the bar, Mo drank the sambuca, poured another for himself and the broad. Seconds passed, she didn't say nothing. Goddamn it, he wanted *her* to tell it.

Johnny yelled: "What the fuck happened?! Where are they?"

Looking over at the girl, Lenny said: "You wanna tell him?" She had her back to him, didn't say anything.

Johnny yelled: "No, you tell me! Goddamn it, what happened?"

Lenny stopped smiling, getting a little nervous, wondering why the fat fucker was yelling like that. "I capped 'em, Johnny."

"You *what*?!"

"Yeah . . . I fuckin' capped 'em. Both of 'em."

Johnny threw up his hands. "Jesus fuckin' Christ! I got cops swarming all over me, and he fuckin' whacks two guys! Lenny, you fuckin' moron, that's the last goddamned thing I need! The cops are fuckin' watchin' me like a god-damned hawk. First them two niggers, then the robbery, now this!"

Lenny didn't get why the fat fuckin' guinea was so bent outta shape. "Jesus, Johnny, I thought you'd be happy. You were catchin' shit from Joey about the broad, so I went'n got her."

"Yeah, I wanted her back. That didn't mean you had to fuckin' whack 'em!"

Lenny said: "Plus I thought you wanted the money back," holding up the bag.

"Aw, Jesus, Lenny, use your goddamned head! That money's the only thing connectin' us to the bar robbery! The cops figure out Vince and Billy done that robbery, then find us with that money, they're gonna know, one, we did the robbery, and, two, we did Vince and Billy! It woulda been better, you just fuckin' left it with their dead bodies."

Lenny frowned, not quite sure what the fuck he was talking about. "You want, I could go back, leave it with 'em."

Johnny threw up his hands again. "Jesus Christ! No, I don't want you to go back. Fuckin' think about what you're sayin'. Cops're probably already there, and if they ain't, goin' back would only double the chance a you gettin' caught!"

Standing at the bar, Mo shook his head, drank another sambuca.

Lenny was tired of this back and forth shit. First he wanted the girl back, now he's pissed 'cause Lenny done it. First he wanted his cut of the money, now he don't. What the fuck? Lenny said: "So, what you want me to do?"

Johnny belched, loud. "What I want you to do? I want you to keep your fuckin' prick in your pants. No more shooting. You hear me?" He looked back and forth between Lenny and Mo. "Both a you'se. No more fuckin' shootin'. Got it?"

Lenny said: "Yeah, sure, Johnny, whatever you want," and he dropped the money on the table and walked out.

Morris stood at the window watching the rogue cop drive away, thinking: Goddamn, the shit's piling up fast. Vince's swimming in it, and now you're being dragged in too. Jesus Christ, a week out of Graterford and look at the mess he's got himself into. You told him first thing not to get involved with those bookmakers, and what does he do? Straight away he's doing business with them again. And this cop—could you believe him? Pulling that Neanderthal bullshit, those strong arm tactics, threats of violence and prosecution. No doubt he could do it, plant evidence, dig up a witness, whatever he had to do. And with those old arrests, that could mean real trouble. But, Jesus, that was ages ago—12, 13 years. Yeah, right, no judge is gonna give a shit about that—those were serious offenses, *adult* offenses. If the cop pulls it off, you could do some hard jail time. What you need to do first thing is talk to Vince, find out what's going on, if he hurt that woman, if he really did that robbery, whether or not he's got those diamonds. Find out how deep the shit is. Whether there's any getting out of it.

Morris grabbed his jacket, ran out the door, jumped in the Nova, tore off down the street.

The TV repair shop wasn't far—Christian, just on the other side of Broad. Twenty minutes and Morris pulled up in front of the place. Killed the motor, looked up, and his heart jumped—there was a cop car sitting there.

Out of the Nova, through the alley, around back. The door was open, a cop coming out. "What's going on?"

The cop put up his hands to stop him. "Nothing to see."

"What's going on? Where's Vince?!"

The cop put down his hands, frowning. "You know somebody here?"

"Why?! What's happened?" Peeking around him, through the doorway, he saw the blood on the floor. "Jesus! What happened?" Pushed up to the door, the cop held him back.

"You can't go in there. It's a crime scene."

He saw Billy lying there in a pool of blood, near the door. And across the room another body behind an overturned table, Vince's boots. "Vince! Jesus! What happened?! Is he dead? Is he dead?!"

The cop: "Yeah, he's dead. They're both dead."

CHAPTER 17

Mo said: "Them cops ain't connected us to the robbery."

Johnny looked over. "Yeah? You don't think so?"

"Yeah. That one, he was bein' cute—you see that? Thinks he's real smart. Talking to you about your niece and them two kids, then waiting 'til he was leaving to ask you how they knew they was the right ones. Typical fucking *sbirro*. All the same."

"You don't think they knew we did the robbery?"

Mo pulled out a cigarette, put it in his mouth. "No. If he did, they would say something, try an' trip you up somehow. Don' worry 'bout it." Flicked the lighter, lit the cigarette.

"Yeah, maybe you're right. And there's no way they can trace them two dead niggers back to us—right?"

"No, unless the *stronzo* fuck up somehow, tell somebody."

Johnny ran his hands through his black hair.

"Yeah—Lenny. Couldn't fuckin' believe that shit. He goes out and clips Vince and Billy. I didn't think he had it in him."

"Me either, but now too bad he did. He sloppy, not careful 'bout nothing. No telling if he did it right or not."

Johnny nodded. "We gotta take care a that situation." He belched.

Mo leaned forward. "Now you talking sense. You let me handle it."

"Yeah, but you know, with all this heat, there can't be no trace, nothin'. He disappears, he's gotta be gone for good."

"'Course. You let me take care of it. Then you ain't got nothin' to worry 'bout."

Johnny reached over, grabbed the pack of Camels, took a cigarette, lit it. "Let me tell you somethin' else—now, with Vince and Billy outta the way? Ain't nothin' standin' between us and them diamonds. No fifty percent shit. All of it's ours now. Seventy-five grand minimum. If the situation starts lookin' bad, you know, Lenny fucks up or whatever, the heat really comin' down on us, we could use that money. That, with what I got put away, plus the dough from the robbery, we could skip town pretty easy."

"Visit the old country, huh?"

Johnny nodded. "Yeah."

"How you expect to find them diamonds, though? Lenny said they wasn't there at the TV shop."

"They gotta be *some*where. Tell you what—check where Vince was livin'."

"His brother's?"

Johnny drew on the cigarette, blew out the smoke. "Yeah, check at his brother's."

"If his brother knows them diamonds are there, he might not wanna give 'em up."

Johnny looked over at him. "So be persuasive."

Morris set a carton of Marlboros and a fifth of Jack Daniels on the counter, pulled out his wallet while the girl rang it up. It was Sunday morning, so because of the blue laws in Pennsylvania he had to come to New Jersey to get the booze. He was up all night staring at the walls after what he saw yesterday, and now he just felt like a drink. The image of the bloody back room at the TV repair shop was burned into his mind. He couldn't let it go. After he talked to the cops and left the scene, he drove to the northeast and told his mother. All she said was, served him right. Morris knew eventually it'd get to her, tear her up, she'd grieve in time. But right now she was numb, just like he was. It still felt unreal, like the whole thing was just a story or a movie, the kind of thing that happens to somebody else, not you. It was different from when his old man died of cancer a few years ago. Then he had time to get used to the idea, watched him waste away in that hospital bed, getting thinner and weaker, in the end just hoping for relief, just waiting for him to kick off. But Vince getting murdered—it was too sudden. Your mind can't get around it right away, your emotions are all . . . well, it's just impossible to say exactly, to put it into words.

He took the cigarettes and booze, left the store, got into the car. His head buzzed a little from lack of sleep, and his eyes were red. He put on his black sunglasses, then cracked the label on the Jack, took a long drink, wincing at the burn, burped. He started the car, headed back to Philly.

He'd had a lot of time to think about this, Vince going back to work for those gangsters, getting killed, and the more he thought about it, the more the whole thing pissed him off. As the hours passed last night, a wave of anger swelled up inside him. He was pissed about that cop pushing him around, threatening him. He was pissed at Vince for getting involved in all that shit, the robbery, the kidnapping. And most of all he was pissed at whoever shot him. Vince was kind of a hardass, but he wasn't such a bad guy, and he didn't deserve that. And some time around dawn Morris made a resolution. He promised himself he'd find out who killed him and why. He already knew parts of the story, what Vince was involved in, but he wanted to know all of it. Whatever the reason, somebody was going to pay for it.

He couldn't find a space on his block, so he parked around the corner, took his whiskey and cigarettes, walked to his house. He fumbled with the keys, got the door unlocked, and a shadow fell over him. He turned to see Lenny and Mo standing there, Lenny with a stupid grin on his face, flashing those silver teeth. Morris looked back and forth, one to the other, and he felt like he wanted to fuck with them bad, beat the shit out of them. If he only had his piece.

Lenny said: "We need to talk," and pulled an automatic pistol discreetly out of a shoulder holster, held it down against his leg. They both moved up the stoop, backing Morris inside the house. Lenny closed the door behind them. "We heard 'bout Vince gettin' whacked. That was a real bitch. Thing was, though, he had somethin' a ours, and we need to look through his stuff, see if it's here."

Morris looked down at the gun. "I don't guess I have a choice."

Lenny: "No, 'fraid you don't."

Mo said: "You watch him, I'll go look in Vince's room," and he went upstairs like he owned the goddamned place.

Morris held up the bottle of whiskey. "Mind if I fix myself a drink?"

Lenny said: "Knock yourself out."

He went into the kitchen, got a glass, poured some Jack, dropped an ice cube in it. He told himself to play it cool here. There's no telling how involved these bastards are, and no telling what they're capable of. He took a deep calming breath and walked back out to the living room. Lenny was looking through his cookbooks on the bookshelf, the pistol still in his hand. Morris took out a cigarette, lit it. "So you guys work for Johnny Stacks, that right?"

Lenny, absent-mindedly: "Yeah, that's right."

"I told Vince not to get involved with you guys when he got outta the joint. But I guess he didn't listen." Lenny chuckled, glanced over. Morris said: "You get involved with gangsters, doing gangster shit, no telling what might happen."

Lenny was almost beaming, the fucker, like he was proud of it. "You got that right."

Morris took a sip of Jack, it didn't burn this time, and his stomach was starting to warm. He said: "What if what you're looking for isn't here?"

Lenny said: "Guess we'll see, won't we?"

Overhead, they could hear Mo walking around, the

floorboards creaking. Morris reached over, knocked the ash off his cigarette. "You know Vince didn't come back here after the robbery on Friday."

Lenny was paging through a book on pastries. "Yeah, so?"

"So, if you want that money from the robbery, it wouldn't be here."

Lenny smirked. "No, I know that money ain't here." He held up a picture of a tart. "You make these?"

"Probably could. I don't really do desserts, but it's probably not too hard."

"It looks good. How 'bout a blintz? You ever make a blintz?" Morris shook his head. "My granny used to make these really nice blintzes. Man, were they fuckin' good."

Morris took another drag on the cigarette. "You know one thing bothers me—I've been thinking about it all night, and I still can't figure it out."

"Yeah, what?" He went back to flipping through the pages.

"It's that robbery money—"

"Yeah, well, I told you that ain't what we're lookin' for."

"Yeah, you said that. But that's not what bothers me. See, I was there at the Cosmatos place yesterday. I saw Vince and Billy—their bodies." He saw Lenny raise an eyebrow and smirk. The piece of shit. "And thing is, that money from the robbery wasn't there, I didn't see it anywhere, and the cops didn't say anything about it."

Lenny frowned. "Yeah, so?"

"Well, that's what's bothering me—where'd the money go? See, if Vince and Billy did that robbery, then shouldn't they have had the money? Shouldn't it've been there?"

Lenny closed the book. "What're you gettin' at?"

"Well, what I'm thinking is, maybe Vince and Billy *did* have the money, and whoever killed them took it. Maybe that's even why they were killed—to get that lousy money. See what I mean? Find the money, you find the killer. And the way I figure it, there's a lot of assholes out there who'd do that, kill a guy for that much money."

Lenny put the book back on the shelf. "Go on."

Morris reached over, knocked the ash off his cigarette. He knew the whiskey had gone to his head a little, he had the beginning of that nice warm glow, and he told himself: Be careful here. Be very careful. Watch the gun. "You said a minute ago you knew the money wasn't here."

Lenny, slow: "Yeah?"

"So, how'd you know that?"

Lenny raised the gun, aiming it this way. "You talk an awful fuckin' lot, Mr. Cook."

Morris stubbed out his cigarette. "I'm a chef." He took another drink of whiskey, staring at Lenny.

Lenny, still aiming the gun: "Whatever. You just better watch what you say."

Mo called down from the upstairs: "Lenny?"

Lenny walked slowly over to the stairs, eyeing Morris. "Yeah?"

"There's a box up here, metal box. It's locked. . . ."

Lenny turned to look up the stairs, the gun was pointed down.

"See if he has the key. . . ."

Morris took a quick step and smashed him on the side of the head with the highball glass, the thing shattered, the booze splashing everywhere. Lenny fell onto the stairs, dropping the pistol. Morris ran for the door, got it open, outside, down the street, didn't look back. He rounded the corner, jumped into the Nova, fired it up, burned rubber getting out of there.

Morris's hand was cut from the broken glass. He was dripping blood, wiping it on his jeans and on a map of Delaware he kept in his car. He drove around the neighborhood for an hour, keeping an eye out for the copper-colored DeVille, trying to figure out what to do. He was sure now that Lenny and Mo had something to do with killing Vince, probably did it themselves. He'd hit a nerve asking Lenny about the robbery money, and that meant he was right: Whoever killed him took that money. But what was bothering him now was how they found Vince. Vince was too smart to get caught with his guard down, and he wouldn't have trusted these guys. Hell, they came and took him out of the house at gunpoint last week. There's no way, *no way*, he would tell them where he was going to be taking the waitress, no way he'd even take her someplace obvious, someplace they knew about. So how'd they figure it out? How'd they get to him?

When he finally drove back to his house, the Cadillac wasn't there anymore. He parked, glanced up and down the street, and went inside. The place had been turned upside down, everything gone through, the furniture torn up. His beautiful gold inlay dinnerware was smashed into pieces on the floor. He stepped over it, went upstairs, into his bedroom. Took a chair over to the closet, stood on it, opened a panel in the ceiling. He reached in, took out his gun, his .38 Special.

He tucked it in his belt, went back downstairs, grabbed the bottle of Jack Daniels, and walked out the door.

He sat in the Nova across the street from Vicky's apartment all evening, waiting for her to get home, smoking cigarettes and drinking whiskey. The .38 was on the seat next to him, and every once in a while he'd reach over and touch it or pick it up and look at it. It felt good to be holding it again, it almost felt good to need it again the way he did. Maybe that sounds kind of messed up, but the fear and the rush of adrenaline revitalized him, it was like it cleaned him out, made him whole again. Or that's what it felt like anyway.

A little after ten Vicky pulled up in her black BMW. Morris checked both ways down the street, then got out and followed her up to her apartment building. Hearing his footsteps, she turned, frightened, and screamed. "Oh, my God, Morris, you scared me!" Then noticing his cut hand, dried blood on his clothes, his haggard face, she said: "What happened?"

He was having a hard time catching his breath, seeing her again. After all he'd been through the past couple of days, he felt like he was going to burst into tears, but he told himself not to. "Hi, Vick," he said.

"What happened to you?" she repeated.

"I'll tell you about it." He looked up and down the street again. "Can I come in?" Tears started welling up in her eyes. He said: "Please don't cry. Can we go inside?" She nodded, then turned and opened the door, and they went in.

Inside she made him sit down, then got a tweezers and

a moist towel for his hand, and she picked out the shards of glass and cleaned his wounds. He felt almost faint sitting there with her touching him, holding his hand like that. He'd almost forgotten how pretty she was, how much he liked her and wanted her. Neither one of them said anything for a few minutes. She wouldn't make eye contact with him, cleaning his hand, then bandaging it. When it was done, she looked up at him, started to say something and burst into tears. He grabbed her, pulled her close, feeling her sobbing. In a few minutes she calmed down, then pulled back to look at him, and their lips met. They kissed passionately sitting there on the sofa, and then she took him by the hand and led him to her bedroom.

CHAPTER 18

It was Monday, noon, at the Melrose Diner. Turner hadn't touched the corned beef sandwich. He pushed it aside. Felt the coffee cup—still too warm. Took another ice cube from his water glass, dropped it in.

Mouth full of French fries, Wojcik said: "You watch the Sixers game?"

"Nah, who'd they play?"

"Pistons."

"Right, now I remember. Won, didn't they?"

"One hundred, ninety-four."

"They playin' tonight?"

"Yeah, Pacers. Then they're at Chicago tomorrow."

Turner said: "They're doin' all right."

"What's a matter, Nicky? You ain't hungry?"

"Nah. Lately, I don't know. I ain't got much of an appetite."

"You ain't gonna eat that?" nodding at the corned beef.

Turner grinned. "You can have it."

Wojcik reached over, took the plate. "So, what'd Henry say this morning?" Stuffed half the sandwich in his mouth.

"He said they're keepin' up the surveillance on the restaurant. Anything happens, anything looks suspicious, they'll call us."

Wojcik snorted, chewing. "What the fuck's gonna happen now? Them two kids is already dead."

"Yeah, I know. I said we should go back, talk to Johnny Stacks again. He said give it a coupla days. Maybe by then ballistics'll come up with some kinda match on them two slugs."

"Fat chance. Some piece prob'ly stolen three years ago in Jersey? Lotta fuckin' good that's gonna do us."

Turner took a sip of coffee, winced. "I know, I know. That's what I told him. He wants us to go back, re-interview the family, friends. Also see if we can get the girl to talk, Anne-Marie."

Wojcik laughed, food spray hit the table. "Sure, her uncle whacks two kids that was tryin' to rape her, and she's gonna tell the nice policeman all about it. Jesus." Another bite, he finished the sandwich, pushed the plate forward, and burped. "Man, that was good." Started sliding out of the booth. "Be back in a minute—gotta take a shit."

Nick said: "Hey, partner?"

Wojcik paused, sitting on the edge of the seat. "Yeah?"

"Take it easy on the sauce, will ya?"

Wojcik flushed a little, then said quietly: "Yeah, sure, Nicky," stood up, walked to the bathroom.

Turner sighed, wishing he hadn't said anything.

★   ★   ★

It was the next morning, lying there in Vicky's bed, when it came to him. The way to do it, the perfect way to fuck with them. It had to be something indirect, something subtle they wouldn't suspect, something well thought out. The key to it all was the cop, Franks. That guy was out of his mind, and what was he after more than anything else? The diamonds, the ones Vince never even stole, that he never had. Who cares why, all that mattered was it was pretty goddamned clear Franks would do *anything* to get them. So what if he thought the gangsters had them? What if he was convinced that the gangsters had what he wanted, what he was prepared to lie, to plant evidence, probably kill, to get? It was fucking perfect. It's the way to get back at the son-of-a-bitch who had the balls to push you around like that, strong-arm you, and it's a way to get back at the gangsters who killed Vince. Fucking perfect. Whatever happened, if the cop killed them, put them away, if they killed him and got caught, it'd be what they deserved, all of them. Justice, man, the justice of the streets—which is the only kind they understand. But how to do it? How do you convince him that Lenny or Mo or Johnny Stacks has the diamonds? Christ, that's the easy part. You tell him Vince had the diamonds when he was killed. I mean, you figured out that the gangsters killed Vince, surely Franks will know that, or it won't be hard to convince him of it, and then you tell him that Vince had those stolen diamonds with him, and—here's the important part, of course—they weren't there afterwards. You were there, the cops searched the place, he could even look it up on the police report: no diamonds. So, whoever killed Vince took the stones. Had to be. God, it was perfect. He leaves you alone, they get what's coming to them, and that's that. And look at it this way, if it falls through, if it doesn't go down the way you thought it would, you can always just tell the cops what you know, and they'll nail the gangsters for killing Vince and get Franks for all the illegal shit he's involved in. Perfect.

Vicky said: "What're you grinning about?" The morning sun was creeping through the blinds now.

"Nothing. I just feel good's all."

"How's your hand?"

He raised it, turned it around, looked at it. Some blood had seeped through the bandage, but it felt okay. "Fine. Doesn't hurt anymore." He drew her closer to him, holding her tight.

She reached up, ran her hand over his chin, said: "Your beard's prickly."

"Sorry, I'll shave today."

"Good," she said, then added, "your eyes look tired. Did you get any sleep?"

"A little." There was a pause, and he sighed. "Look, Vick. . . ."

"Yeah?" She glanced up at him.

"About what happened, what I said the other night. . . ."

"No, you don't have to explain or say anything."

"It's just that. . . ."

"Just be quiet. You don't have to say anything. It's forgotten, okay?"

"So you still. . . ."

"Huh?"

"Never mind."

She was running her hand through the hair on his chest, scratching him lightly with her fingernails, and said: "You're in some kind of trouble, aren't you?"

He squeezed her. "No, not really. Nothing I can't handle."

"You . . . you want to tell me about it?"

"Not right now," he said. "Later . . . sometime I'll tell you the whole story, the whole thing."

He felt her lips pressing against his chest, and then she said quietly: "Maybe you should go to the police."

"No," he said flatly, "I can't do that. They can't help me. This's something I gotta take care of myself. . . . Hey, you're shaking."

"Because I'm worried about you. I don't want anything to happen to you."

A warm, tingly feeling flooded through him, hearing her say that. "Yeah?"

"Yes, I care about you too much."

"Nothing's gonna happen. Trust me. You gotta trust me."

He heard her sigh. She said: "Okay. I won't say anything else."

He squeezed her again and bent down and kissed her on the top of the head.

After they got up, and Vicky said a worried goodbye and left for work, Morris got out the phonebook, flipped through the city blue pages. He didn't know exactly where to find Franks, so he called the closest precinct house and asked. The desk sergeant told him the South Division detectives were all stationed at 24th and Wolf. He found the number, called and asked for Detective Franks. It seemed like he was holding forever, but Franks finally came on the line. Morris said: "I need to talk to you, Franks."

"Yeah? You got somethin' for me?" his voice sounded even more edgy than the other day.

"No, I don't have them, but I know where they are, how you can get them."

"That so?"

"Yeah. Here's the deal—"

"No," Franks interrupted him. "Not over the phone. Meet me."

Morris hesitated. He told himself: Be careful, this guy's dangerous. "Okay, someplace public, though."

Franks snorted a laugh like Morris had said something funny. "Broad Street Diner in half an hour."

Morris glanced over at his .38 sitting on the coffee table. He nodded to himself. "All right, half an hour," and they hung up.

Lenny and Mo were in the Cadillac, on their way back to Vince's brother's house, see if they could find the guy, the cook. Lenny had to get stitches in the side of his head where the fucker blindsided him like that. They told Johnny the story. The guy seemed to know about the robbery, knew Vince was involved. They didn't find the diamonds when they tossed his place. Johnny was shitting bricks about the whole thing, said find out for sure what he knows. Find out what it'll take to keep him quiet—buy him off if you have to. Lenny just wanted to clip the fucker. He reached up, felt the stitches and the knot on his head. It was weird, Mo didn't say jack shit about it, didn't bust his balls at all about the cook getting away like that, how he got over on Lenny. I mean, normally he'd give him that fucking guinea look, say something about it, call him one a them guinea names. This time he didn't say nothing. Lenny looked over at him, watched him staring out the window. Lenny cleared his throat. Nothing. The guinea ball-buster didn't look over, didn't move, just kept staring out at the road. He said: "What if he ain't there?"

"What?"

"Vince's brother—what if he ain't there, ain't at home?"

He looked over finally. "We find out where he is."

"Yeah? How the fuck we gonna do that? We don't know nothin' 'bout him."

"We search his place again, find out where he works."

"I heard Vince say he's a cook."

"Okay, we find out where, what restaurant." There was a pause. Mo took out a cigarette, lit it. "By the way, Johnny give us something else to do."

Lenny glanced over at him. "Yeah?"

"Yeah. You know that empty store, belong to his sister's husband?"

"The one on Seventh? That neighborhood with all the gooks?"

"Yeah, tha's the one."

"What about it?"

Mo took a drag on the cigarette. "Johnny say some kids been in there, maybe dealing outta the basement. Said we should check it out. Run 'em outta there."

Lenny nodded. "Yeah, we can do that." He reached up, fingered the stitches again. Something about all this didn't sound right. Johnny didn't get along with his brother-in-law. What the fuck did he care, there's gooks in the empty store, dealing or not? He looked back over at Mo, telling himself to keep an eye on this guinea fuck. Don't let him catch you with your guard down.

He pulled down Hoffman Street, pulled up in front of Vince's brother's house. They got out of the car, went inside.

Morris pulled off Broad Street and parked on Ellsworth, around the corner from the Broad Street Diner. Walking across the parking lot he could feel the .38 tucked in his belt, pressing against his spine. He stepped between two cars and a door opened, and there was Franks with a grin on his face and a pistol in his hand. "Get in the fuckin' car."

Morris felt his throat catch. Goddamn it! He didn't want to be alone with this fucking maniac. "No, we do this inside," he said, his voice trembling slightly.

"I don't like to repeat myself, so pay attention. If you don't do exactly as I say, and I don't get exactly what I want, somethin' bad's gonna happen to your little friend, *Ms.* Ward."

"You fuck!" and Morris lurched forward.

Franks raised the gun, Morris stopped short, staring down the barrel. Franks said: "Now, get in the fuckin' car."

Morris walked around and climbed in the passenger side, Franks got in behind the wheel. He was jittery, looked like he was on something, his eyes dilated and bloodshot, dark circles under them. Morris took a deep breath, trying to control his rage, wanting to pound this fucker's head in, and said: "Just know—you lay one hand on Vicky, and I'll kill you."

Franks smirked. "She is a sweet piece, ain't she?"

Morris dug his fingernails into the vinyl seats. "Look at me, Franks, I'm not joking. You touch her, I'll fucking kill you."

"All right, all right," said Franks, "we understand one another. Now let's hear it."

"I know where the diamonds are, or at least who has them."

Franks was still holding the gun on him. "Why you tellin' me this now?"

Morris thought quickly. "Because I believed your threat. I don't wanna get nailed for the Mickey's robbery. And because Lenny and Mo are after me. I figured we'd make a deal: You get what you want and then get them off my back."

He frowned. "What do they want with you?"

"They came back to the house, and I let it slip that the money from the robbery wasn't there."

"So they put two and two together, figured out you knew Vince did the robbery. Vince works for them, so they realized you know they were in on the robbery too." Franks nodded, like he believed the story.

"Yeah, so when I realized I said too much, I bashed one of 'em on the head and split."

"Lenny?" Morris nodded. Franks laughed. "I can see it. He's some idiot, that one."

"Yeah, well, he's an idiot with a gun. I think he killed Vince."

"Nah, ain't got it in him. If it was either one of 'em, it was Mo. Only thing is, I don't know why Johnny'd order 'em to whack Vince. Don't make any sense."

"I'll tell you why: Vince and Billy kidnapped Jeanette Carpioli."

His eyes got wide. "Eddie the Carp's daughter?" Morris nodded. Franks whistled. "Why?"

"Eddie messed with Vince big time."

"At Graterford—sure." Franks's hand was shaking, he shifted the gun to the other one. "So where's the diamonds?"

"Vince had them with him at the repair shop."

"No shit?"

"Yeah. And they weren't there afterwards, so whoever killed him and Billy took the diamonds."

Franks nodded, thinking about it, then looked over sharply. "How'd you know Vince had 'em with him?"

Morris felt beads of sweat rolling down his sides. The pistol was digging into his back. He shifted in the seat. "He carried them with him wherever he went, in this little pouch."

"Sounds like Vince." He started up the car.

"So?"

Franks looked over at him. "We're gonna take a little ride."

Jesus! That's not how the plan's supposed to go! "Where?"

"Let's you and me go have a talk with Johnny Stacks."

"What the hell do you need me for?!"

Franks grinned. "You don't think I'm just gonna take your word for all this? We go talk to Johnny, and if you're on the up and up, I'll cut you loose."

"The guy wants to kill me!"

"Nah, he ain't gonna kill you. Too much heat on him already. Besides, I'll take your deal and tell him to leave you alone once we get it all straightened out. If he thinks you ain't gonna rat him, he'll call off the dogs." He put the car in gear. "But if I find out you're lyin', you're gonna be sorry you ever laid eyes on me."

Morris, looking out the window, trying to figure out what to do: "I'm already sorry."

Franks laughed, head back. They pulled out of the lot.

There was no sign of the cook. They looked through his stuff again, found an address book and some canceled paychecks. Looked like he worked at a joint called Le Tour something or other. They'd check it out later. Right now they were on their way to the empty store, see if there really were kids dealing out of the basement.

Lenny still didn't like it. Something about it gave him the creeps. The guinea ball-buster was just too quiet. I mean, he was *always* quiet. He didn't say jack unless there was some kinda opportunity to give Lenny some shit. But today was different. It was a different kind of quiet. Like he was watching Lenny, keeping an eye on things. Lenny said: "Why's Johnny want us to check out this place?"

Mo said: "Told you, he thinks there's kids been in it." He took out a cigarette from the pack of Camels, lit it.

"Yeah? He don't even get along with his brother-in-law." Nothing, silence. The fucker didn't say a word. "And why didn't *he* just check it out—the brother-in-law?"

"Don't ask me."

"Yeah, well, I'm askin'. Johnny gave you the orders. Nobody tells me shit anymore."

"We just follow orders, we don't ask questions."

See? Ordinarily, he'd a called Lenny one of them names, *testa di casa*, or whatever, he'd tell him he didn't need to know, something like that. Today, nothing. *We just follow orders*. Since when did this fucking wop ever *just* follow orders? He's always trying to tell Johnny how to run the business—God knows why Johnny listens to the fucker, he don't even speak plain English. 'Course Johnny's a wop too. Fucking guineas, always sticking together. No, something was different. Something was up.

Lenny reached over and felt the Smith &Wesson in his shoulder holster. He told himself to watch his back. Don't let this fucker get behind you. No telling what he's up to. He looked over at Mo. "Use the ashtray, will ya? I vacuumed the car this morning."

They pulled up in front of the empty store, 7th and Tasker. The street was fucking disgusting, dirty and grimy, trash all over the place. It was gook central, coupla slopes wandering around, talking gibberish, gook writing in the storefronts across the street. Lenny looked over. One place was called OK Cleaners. You imagine? Not Excellent Cleaners or even Good Cleaners. No, this place was just *okay*. Lenny shook his head, getting out of the car.

They walked over to the store, Decongelio Deli. Mo dug through his pocket for the keys. Lenny stood by, watching the greaseball open the door, feeling nervous, feeling his heart beating. Mo held the door open, let Lenny go in first, holding the door. *See?!* The fucker woulda never did that before! Something was definitely up. Lenny stepped to the side, his back against the wall. He could feel himself sweating, his black shirt sticking to him.

Mo came in, flipped the light switch, but the electricity was off. There was still plenty of light out here in front, the afternoon sun coming through the windows. He turned around, closed and locked the door, then said: "We gotta check out the basement."

Lenny nodded. "That's where the kids been doin' their dealing?"

"Yeah." Mo walked around the front counter, looked back. "You coming?"

Lenny pushed away from the wall, followed him. They went through a door behind the counter into an office. Place was empty except for a filing cabinet, an empty schnapps bottle, and a broken chair. It was darker in here, less sunlight. There was another door opposite where they came in. Mo walked over and opened it. "This's it, the basement."

Still standing in the doorway, Lenny nodded. "Yeah? Dark?"

"Yeah, kinda." Mo hesitating there at the top of the stairs.

Lenny felt his throat catch, his mouth was dry, his heart pounding. "So what you wanna do?"

Mo shrugged. "Go down, check it out." Lenny just stood there. Mo: "Well?"

"Well what?"

"You coming?"

Lenny took a few steps across the room. Mo pushed the door all the way open, walked down a couple of stairs. Lenny followed him, watching the fucker's back, his arms, his hands. He couldn't see his hands, couldn't see what they were doing. What was he doing with his hands?! Two more steps, the wooden stairs creaking. The basement quiet, dark. It smelled musty, damp. Lenny's heart ready to explode, he couldn't catch his breath, couldn't breathe, like he'd been punched in the stomach. Another step. He could see the basement now, eyes adjusted to the dim light. Glanced around: There's nothing down here, no reason to be here, no kids been down here. That was bullshit. Looked at Mo again—still couldn't see his hands, what was he doing with his hands? Goddamn it! Lenny slowly pulled out the Smith & Wesson, not making any sound, clicked off the safety, pointed it right at the back of Mo's head. Two more stairs and they were in the basement. Lenny cocked the pistol. Mo heard it, froze, turned his head slightly to the left, looking back. Lenny said: "What's 'three' in Italian?"

Mo frowned. "Three?"

"Yeah? What's 'three' in Italian?"

Mo said: "*Tre*."

Lenny repeated: "*Tre*," and shot him in the back of the head.

CHAPTER 19

The plan had backfired, and Morris was in deep shit. There was no way—*no way*—this cop was just going to talk to Johnny Staccardo and then let him loose. For one thing, Johnny didn't even have the diamonds, of course, and when they got around to asking Morris where they really were, he sure as hell wasn't going to be able to tell them—and for another thing, Morris just knew too much about this drugged-out cop and all his illegal shit. And, hell, if the cop didn't want Morris out of the way, the gangster would. Morris knew way too much about him too: His involvement in the Packer Avenue robbery and in the murder of Vince and Billy. Morris knew he was swimming in it this time. He felt the .38 tucked in his belt, pressing against his back, glad he had it, but also worried: Christ, it'd been years since he'd even looked at the thing, much less used it.

They pulled up in front of some South Philly restaurant. Franks shut off the engine, looked over. His eyes looked wild and unfocused. "You sure there's nothin' else you wanna tell me before we talk to Johnny?"

Morris swallowed hard. "No, nothing."

Franks nodded. They got out of the car, Franks came around and jammed his gun in Morris's side. They crossed the street and went into the restaurant. Walking into the place, right away Morris saw the girl, Jeanette, the waitress from the diner, sitting at a table with a big fat guy with greasy hair. There was another woman opposite the fat guy, with her back to Morris. They were finishing eating, the three of them, looked like spaghetti and marinara, drinking red wine. The fat guy looked up, frowned, then cracked a grin. "Well, if it ain't Dick Franks, one a Philly's finest."

Still standing in the doorway, Franks said: "Hi-a, Johnny. Thought we'd pay you a little visit."

Johnny wiped his fat face with a red table napkin. "Brought a friend with ya."

Franks said: "Morris White."

Johnny said: "Never had the pleasure . . . oh, wait a minute—White? You're Vince's brother, ain't you?"

Morris was checking out the scene, wondering how to position himself: "Yeah."

Johnny, fake sincere: "My condolences about your brother." He pointed toward the girl. "This here's Jeanette, Eddie the Carp's daughter."

Morris glanced over at her.

"And I think you know this one." Johnny nodded toward the other woman.

She turned her head.

It was Eva.

Morris felt his jaw drop.

What the. . . ? What the hell was she doing there?

Then it hit him: It was her! She's the one who fingered Vince—*that's* how they found him. On the phone the other day, Morris told her where Vince was hiding. He told her it was a TV repair shop, owned by a friend of Vince's. And what did she say? She asked who it was! And, Jesus fucking Christ, Morris told her! Vince was too smart to get caught like that. It was Eva who gave him up! Morris told himself: You sold Vince out. You told her where he was, and she told *them*! He's dead because of you!

Morris tried to steady himself. His knees felt like they were going to buckle.

Eva drank the rest of the wine in her glass, set it down. "I was just leavin', anyway," she said and scooted back from the table, stood up.

Johnny shrugged, reached inside his coat, took out an envelope, handed it to her.

She turned and walked across the room, past Morris, without making eye contact, without even looking at him, went out the door, closed it behind her.

Morris tasted the bile in his mouth, his head light. He told himself to keep it together, told himself he can't fall apart now.

Franks: "Well, ain't this cozy now, just the four of us? We got the introductions outta the way, so let's cut the horseshit. We're here to talk business."

Jeanette sat there quietly, pushing food around on her plate. Johnny stood, walked over to the bar, took out a bottle of sambuca. He said: "Sure, Franks. What's on your mind?" and he belched.

"You know what's on my mind: diamonds."

Morris saw the edges of Johnny's mouth curl around, standing there pouring the sambuca. "Wanna drink?"

"No, thanks."

Johnny, acting casual: "What diamonds might you be referring to?" He walked back to the table, set down one of the glasses in front of the girl.

Franks grinned and shifted his body, so the gun was pointed away from Morris now. "You know goddamned well what diamonds. The ones from Cohen Jewelers. Two hundred and fifty grand worth. Though I have my suspicion they was over-insured."

Johnny took a sip. "I'll say. Try a hundred grand."

Franks whistled. "Jesus, quite a payday for old Marty. Too bad he didn't live to enjoy it."

Johnny walked back to the bar, took a stool. It creaked under his weight. "Yeah, too bad. So what kinda business you wanna talk?"

Franks took a few steps into the dining room, pulling Morris along by the arm. "Here's my proposition. You hand them diamonds over to me, and I'll find somebody to hang that Mickey's job on. You keep the cash."

Johnny snorted: "Ha!"

"You don't like it?"

"No, I don't like it."

"Why the hell not? You're gettin' a fuckin' bargain: one robbery/homicide for free. I find somebody to hang it on, the heat disappears. Your boys really botched that job, by the way. Not your style at all."

Johnny took another sip of his drink. "Yeah, well, even if I had something to do with Mickey's—which I ain't sayin' I did, by the way—you're still barkin' up the wrong tree here. I ain't got them diamonds."

Franks: "C'mon, Johnny, don't shit a shitter. Vince had them diamonds at the TV repair shop, and your boys whacked Vince—don't try'n deny it."

From across the room they saw Johnny turn white. "What? Vince had the stones with him?"

Franks, angry now: "You didn't know that?" He turned to look at Morris.

Morris, calm, regaining his balance: "Vince carried 'em with him wherever he went."

Johnny ran his hands through his black hair. "He had the diamonds there, with him, when he got whacked?"

Morris: "Yeah, and they weren't there afterwards, so whoever the fucker was, shot him, took those stones."

Franks took another step toward the bar. "Johnny— what're you sayin', goddamn it?"

Johnny: "I'm tellin' you, I ain't got them diamonds."

The front door banged open, they all turned to look. Lenny was standing there, framed in the doorway by the afternoon sun, gun in his hand. Jeanette gasped. He had a crazed look on his face. He took a step inside, let the door close behind him, locked it. "Johnny, what'd you tell Mo? What orders you give him?"

Johnny'd gone a shade paler white. "Where's . . . where the hell's Mo?"

"What'd you tell him?" The gun half pointed toward Johnny at the bar.

Johnny: "I didn't tell him nothing!"

Franks, his pistol still pointed down, toward the floor: "What's going on?"

Lenny swung around, pointing the gun this way, like he just realized Franks and Morris were there.

Johnny: "Nothin'. Nothin's goin' on. I didn't tell Mo nothing. What the hell's wrong with you? Where is he? Goddamn it, Lenny, where the fuck is he?"

Lenny pointed the gun back at Johnny. "*Tre.*"

Johnny: "What?"

Lenny: "*Tre.* What's 'four' in Italian?"

Johnny, sweating, nervous, keeping an eye on Lenny: "You wanna know the truth, Franks? It was Lenny, whacked Vince."

Franks: "No shit?"

Johnny: "Ain't that right, Lenny?"

Lenny was looking right at Johnny, like he didn't even know Franks had a gun in his hand. Out of the corner of his eye, Morris could see Franks tensing up, shifting his feet, getting ready to shoot. He glanced side to side, looking for something to duck behind when the guns started going off. He wondered how fast he could get his own pistol out. He was sweating so badly it was starting to slip down inside his belt.

Lenny said: "What's 'four' in Italian?"

Johnny: "Ain't that true? Didn't you whack Vince and Billy?"

Lenny, glancing back at Franks. "Yeah, one and two. I whacked 'em. And then I capped Mo."

Johnny: "What?!"

"You better fuckin' believe it. I capped him, shot him in the fuckin' head. *Tre.* Ain't no greaseball gonna get over on me, put one the back a my ear. And now I'm gonna fucking waste *you*!"

Johnny, ready to shit himself: "Franks wants them diamonds, Lenny. The ones Vince had on him when you whacked him."

Lenny frowning: "There wasn't no diamonds."

Franks: "Bullshit! Vince had a pouch fulla diamonds on him when you clipped him. Now, where are they?"

Lenny, looking back and forth between Johnny and Franks. "I'm tellin' you, I didn't see no diamonds." He thought for a second, then said, angry: "Don't fuckin' try'n trick me!" still pointing the gun at Johnny. "You told Mo to clip me, and now I'm gonna fuckin' do you! Now tell me, goddamn it: What's 'four' in Italian?"

Franks said: "*Quattro*," raised his piece and fired. Jeanette screamed. Lenny spun around, fell back over a table and onto the floor. Happened so fast, Morris didn't even have a chance to move.

Franks walked over toward him, pistol still in his hand, kicked away Lenny's gun. Lenny wasn't moving, a pool of blood forming underneath him. Franks: "You know what? I believe him. I don't think he knew Vince had them diamonds."

Johnny: "Well, I sure as hell ain't got 'em."

They both turned and looked at Morris. Telling himself to keep calm, he said: "Hey, don't fucking look at me. Vince carried the diamonds with him everywhere, wouldn't let them out of his sight."

Franks, sounding paranoid, his brain drug-addled: "Yeah, you keep sayin' that. How do I know you ain't lyin'?"

Just keep calm. Divert his attention. Morris said: "Well, Lenny wasn't the only one who left the repair shop alive."

Franks: "What're you talking about?"

Morris pointed at Jeanette: "She was there. Ask her."

Johnny: "Leave her outta this!"

Franks: "What?"

Morris: "I told you, Vince and Billy grabbed her, kidnapped her. She was there with them. She walked outta there with Lenny."

Franks walked over to the table, grabbed Jeanette, put the gun in her face. "What about it?"

Jeanette was cowering in her seat, tears streaming down her cheeks. Johnny was up off his stool, a gun in his hand, pointing it at Franks. "Leave her alone, Franks!"

Franks looked up, saw the gun, aimed back at Johnny. Morris saw his chance, drew his .38. Johnny to the left, 15 feet, Franks to the right, eight feet. *Pick a target!* He aimed at Johnny. They both saw the piece, Johnny started swinging his gun back and forth, Franks to Morris.

They could hear police sirens now, in the distance. Franks laughed: "Somebody heard the shot."

Little Johnny was pissing himself, trying to cover both of them. Morris knew *somebody* was gonna get shot. He glanced over: The table Lenny fell over was on its side. It could provide cover. But he knew if he moved, somebody'd fire. He watched Johnny's gun, back and forth, one to the other, Morris to Franks. *Time it so he's pointed at Franks.* Back and forth, back and forth, Morris jumped, Franks swung this way, shot, part of the table splintered. Jeanette screamed. Johnny shot, Franks was blown back. Johnny aimed this way, fired, the wood splintered again.

Morris was up over the table: He fired, hit Johnny in the stomach. Johnny staggered, trying to aim back. Morris fired again, Johnny dropped his piece, fell against the bar, then to the ground. Jeanette kept screaming, hands over her ears.

The front door burst open, cops came in, guns drawn. Uniforms and detectives in body armor, aiming at Morris. Turner yelled: "Drop it!" Morris tossed the gun. "Get your hands up, now!" He put them up.

Cops swarming the place now, grabbed Morris, pinned him to the ground, gun to his head, hands behind his back, handcuffed him.

CHAPTER 20

The interview room was small and bare, just a table and chairs. The walls were dark green, a one-way mirror set in the middle of one of them, somebody watching from the other side. The fluorescent lights hummed loudly against the ceiling. Morris had been in here for three or four hours now, being grilled by two detectives, Nick Turner and Ryan Henry. They let him have a pack of Marlboros; he was lighting one off the other. He'd waived his right to a lawyer, told them he didn't do anything wrong, didn't have anything to hide, and he'd gone over the whole story several times now, everything he could remember, holding nothing back. The only thing that might get him in trouble was the gun. He'd had it since he was a kid, bought it off a friend, and for all he knew it might've been stolen. Plus he'd shot that kid in North Philadelphia with it when he was in college. As for the rest, he wasn't worried. Well, not too worried. He shot Johnny Staccardo, but that was in self-defense. Detective Henry was sitting with him at the table. Detective Turner was standing and kept asking him about two black kids he never heard of. "So you didn't know anything about Johnny's niece or Tyrone Bucknor or Todd Ohal."

"No, like I said, I don't know 'em, never even heard of 'em."

"Wayne Reese?"

"No, him either."

"Lenny never said anything, Mo never said anything?"

Morris rubbed his tired eyes. "No. Look, I didn't know those guys, Lenny and Mo. Wasn't like I hung out with 'em. They came by the house twice. I was with them maybe half an hour altogether."

Henry: "But they were trying to kill you?"

"Yeah, I think so."

Turner: "Because of the stolen diamonds?"

"No, really because I knew they were involved in that robbery."

"The Mickey's robbery."

"Right."

Henry: "Tell us again about Detective Franks, how you met him."

Morris took a drag on his cigarette, stubbed it out. "I only met him the other day, coupla days ago, Saturday I guess. He came by the house looking for Vince." He took out another cigarette, the pack was almost empty, lit it.

Henry: "But Vince wasn't there."

"Right. So he starts telling me he wants the diamonds. Says if he gets the diamonds, he'll find someone to hang the Mickey's robbery on, and if he doesn't get them, he'll find a way to incriminate me for the robbery."

Turner: "But you didn't have anything to do with that?"

"No! Christ no, that was the first I'd even heard of it."

"But Vince did have something to do with it?"

"I don't know. I guess so, everybody seems to think he did."

"And he kidnapped the girl, Jeanette Carpioli?"

"Yeah, at least I think he did. That seemed to be his plan, anyway."

Henry: "Him and Billy Hope?"

"Right."

"So after they robbed Mickey's and kidnapped the girl, they hid out at Cosmatos's TV Repair?"

"Right."

"But Lenny found them there, shot them, took the money."

"Yes."

"And how did you know that, again?"

"That's what Johnny Staccardo said when Lenny came into the restaurant. He said Lenny killed Vince."

Turner, flipping through a yellow legal pad: "And Lenny admitted that was true?"

"Yes. He said he shot them, and then he shot Mo."

The door opened, somebody motioned for Turner and Henry. They stepped out into the hallway a moment. Morris took another drag on the cigarette, killing it, stubbed it out. One left. He put it in his mouth, lit it. He felt grimy, sweaty sitting here. Needed to get some sleep and then a shower and shave. He had a huge nicotine buzz on top of his exhaustion.

The two detectives came back in the room. Both of them sat down at the table this time. Henry: "Franks is still in surgery. Both Lenny and Johnny Stacks were DOA. You could be looking at a murder rap here."

"I'm telling you, it was self-defense!"

"He was shooting at you?"

"Yes!"

"So Johnny shot Franks, and then shot at you?"

"Right. Only Franks shot at me first. I saw the table lying there, overturned. I knew it would be something to hide behind, so I jumped for it."

"Then Franks fired?"

"Yes."

"How many times?"

"Once I think. Yeah, just once."

"And then Johnny shot him."

"Right. Franks shot at me, Johnny shot him. Then Johnny shot at me, and I fired back."

Turner: "Tell us again why you shot him twice."

"I hit him once, and he was aiming back at me. He was going to shoot at me again, so I fired a second time."

Henry: "And why didn't you just come to the police in the first place, instead of getting into all this?"

Morris hesitated. "I don't know. I just wanted to get Franks off my back, and I didn't know who to trust. You know, if he's crooked, how do I know if I report him to some other cop, it won't just go right back to him, piss him off even more?"

"So you called him?"

"Yeah."

"And how were you gonna get him off your back?"

Morris sighed. "Well, I figured if he thought, you know, if he was convinced that Johnny Staccardo had those diamonds, he'd lay off me."

"So you set up a meeting?"

"Right. I didn't want to. I wanted to say this stuff to him over the phone, but he insisted that we meet."

"Only it didn't work out like you thought, because he took you to the restaurant by force?"

"Yes, he put a gun on me, asked me some questions, then we drove to the restaurant."

"And he made other threats?"

"Yeah. He said if he didn't get what he wanted Vicky was going to have an accident—that's the way he put it."

Henry checked his notes. "That's Victoria Ward?"

"Yes."

"And she's your girlfriend?"

Morris felt himself grinning, he couldn't help it. "Yeah."

Turner: "And once more, where'd you get the .38?"

"Like I said, I've had it since I was a kid. I bought it from a friend of mine when I was, like, fifteen."

"That would have been, what, twenty years ago?"

"Right."

"Who was the friend, and where'd he get it?"

Morris looked at Turner. "I don't remember." It was the first lie he'd told them.

Turner and Henry looked back and forth at one another. Henry said: "All right. Here's the deal: It looks like you been playin' it straight with us. The girl corroborates your story, how things went down at the restaurant. So does CSU. You probably won't be charged with anything in the shooting, but the D.A. might want to hit you with a weapons charge, since the .38 was unregistered." They stood up. Henry went to the door, opened it. A uniformed officer came in, led Morris out of the room, back to the holding cells.

Henry walked out and Wojcik came in. Turner looked up at him. "Well?"

Wojcik: "Wayne Reese spilled. When I told him Johnny Stacks, Lenny, and Mo was all dead, he gave it all up. It was Lenny and Mo who drilled him, and it was about Johnny's niece, just like we thought. Said they blindfolded him, took him some place, worked him over, blindfolded him again, took him out, dumped him down near the Linc. He gave them Bucknor and Ohal."

Turner's eyes lit up. "Fantastic! Good work, partner."

Wojcik tried to suppress a grin. "Hey, Nicky?"

"Yeah?"

"Can we get somethin' to eat now? I'm starving."

"Sure, partner." He stood up and grinned. "I'm kinda hungry myself."

CHAPTER 21

Whan Morris was released from jail the next day, Tuesday, he drove to the diner. Before he went home and showered, before he saw Vicky, he had to face Eva. He wanted to look into her eyes, see what was there, and tell her again that he knew she killed Vince, watch her face when he said it. He didn't know exactly what he was going to do, how he was going to react to seeing her. Maybe it depended on what she did or said, the way she looked at him. Maybe she'd know what to say.

As he walked into the place and spotted her standing next to the counter, regret hit him: regret for all the stupid things he'd done, fighting with Vicky, selling out Vince when all he wanted to do was help him, sleeping with Eva. He wondered how he'd ever let it all get so screwed up and why things couldn't have been simpler.

He walked across the dining room toward her. She saw him coming, put her hands on her hips. He stepped up to her and saw that there was no expression on her face, in her eyes, no defiance, no remorse, no hatred, no lust. Nothing. The seconds ticked away. Finally, looking right at him, she shrugged nonchalantly, as if nothing had happened, nothing had passed between them, as if there was nothing to be said, nothing to be done.

He drew back and punched her in the mouth. She fell backwards, overturning a chair, hitting the floor, tip change scattering. A woman screamed, everybody looked this way. Morris turned around and walked back out.

CHAPTER 22

Saturday afternoon Morris was sitting on a park bench in Rittenhouse Square, drinking coffee out of a paper cup. A beautiful spring day, it was warm, the sun shining, lots of people out walking dogs, rollerblading, lying in the grass. Two squirrels chased each other around the trunk of a tree, until one decided to dip into a garbage can for a snack. A crowd of pigeons descended on a hot dog bun somebody'd dropped. Morris felt good sitting here, at peace with himself and the world for a change.

Vince was buried the day before. The morgue released his body on Wednesday, they had the viewing Thursday and the funeral Friday. His mother refused to go. He tried to talk her into it, but she wouldn't budge. She'd feel bad about it eventually, but that was something she was going to have to deal with.

He closed his eyes and laid his head back for a moment, listening to the sounds of the people, the dogs, the kids. The sunlight coming through the treetops warmed his face and forced swirling color images through his eyelids. He started dozing off when he felt someone sit down on the bench next to him. "Hi."

He opened his eyes. Vicky was sitting there, smiling at him. He felt warm and good, looking at her. "Hi."

"Been here long?"

"Half an hour."

She leaned over and kissed him. "How're you feeling?"

"I feel great."

"Me, too," she said, looking around. "What a beautiful day."

"Um-hmm."

"What do you want to do for dinner?"

He sighed. "I don't want to think about it right now."

She moved in closer, and he put his arm around her. She said: "How about pie and ice cream?"

"For dinner?"

She grinned. "When I was little, I used to think the best thing in the world would be to have pie and ice cream for dinner every night. Now I'm an adult, I could have it if I wanted, but of course I don't want to anymore."

"Funny isn't it?"

"What?"

"Well, when your wants and desires are simple, you're easily satisfied. But in that case you wouldn't be experiencing the full range of everything there is to try, everything the world has to offer."

"You mean if all I wanted was pie and ice cream, I'd be easily satisfied, but I'd be missing out on so much, that. . . ."

"That you wouldn't be any better off. In fact you'd be worse off."

"So it's better to have more complex and sophisticated desires, even though, what? It's harder to satisfy them."

"Yeah, I think so."

"But in that case you're likely to be more unsatisfied because your desires are harder to fulfill."

"Yeah, I know. There's a saying: 'It's better to be an unsatisfied Socrates than a satisfied pig,' and the more like Socrates you are, I guess, the more unsatisfied you're bound to be. Kind of sad, isn't it?"

They both sighed. There was a long pause, the two of them sitting there quiet, hands entwined. She said: "What are you going to do about a job?"

"Oh, I don't know. Maybe I'll open a food truck." She laughed. "I'm serious. It'd be the first French haute cuisine food truck, probably ever. Can you imagine? I'll serve *coq au vin* in a cup, little individual patés, and *poulet aux citrons confits* on a hoagie roll." They both started laughing hard.

In a moment, they calmed down, and she said: "I almost forgot. Something came for you at the restaurant. A package."

She took it out of her purse, handed it to him. It was from some law firm in town. He tore off the wrapper. There was a small box and a note. "This guy was Vince's lawyer."

"What's it say?"

"Something about him being instructed to send this to me, if anything should happen to Vince. Says he has no knowledge of the contents." Morris opened the box.

Tissue paper inside, pulled it out. There were five large diamonds underneath. He gasped.

She said: "What is it? Morris? What is it?"

He looked up at her. "It's our restaurant."

. . . acknowledgements . . .

First, I want to thank Tom Fassbender and Jim Pascoe
for their enthusiastic response to and support of my
work. I'm incredibly proud to be a part of the UglyTown
family of authors. Thanks also go to Sergeant Matt Veasey
and Detective John Hopkins, for their invaluable information on the inner workings of the Philadelphia P.D.

Last, I am particularly grateful to my friends and family,
who have been unwaveringly supportive and helpful,
especially Bill Irwin, Pepper Landis, Amy McArdle,
John and Linda Pappas, Read Schuchardt, Aeon Skoble,
and the beloved ladies of the Denver Circle:
Betty Brightwell, Mary Marson, Phyllis Otte, Isel
Rupple, Betty Steele, and Marge Wagner.

DARK AS NIGHT